Love Finds You

in

Bethlehem

NEW
HAMPSHIRE

Love Finds You in *Bethlehem*

NEW HAMPSHIRE

BY LAURALEE BLISS

summerside
PRESS

Love Finds You in Bethlehem, New Hampshire
© 2009 by Lauralee Bliss

ISBN 978-1-61664-327-0

All scripture quotations are taken from the King James Version of the Bible.

The town depicted in this book is a real place, but all characters are fictional. Any resemblances to actual people or events are purely coincidental.

Cover and Interior Design by Müllerhaus Publishing Group, www.mullerhaus.net

Published by Summerside Press, Inc., 11024 Quebec Circle, Bloomington, Minnesota 55438

Fall in love with Summerside.

Printed in the USA.

Dedication

....

To Cecile "Ceil" Steiner, a blessed woman and prayer warrior of the Lord, longtime friend, and a New England lady with style.

Acknowledgments

With thanks to Paul of the Bethlehem Historical Society for his guided tour and stories of Bethlehem's fascinating history. To my editor, Rachel, who took a chance on my story even in its infancy. To Carrie and Robin, for your valuable insight into the mind of my manuscript. To my father-in-law, Ken Bliss, who let us borrow his wonderful car to make the journey north. And to my husband, Steve, who traveled the snowy roads with me to discover this quaint town at Christmastime.

FOR ALL ITS POMP AND CIRCUMSTANCE LATER ON, THE REGION THAT
would eventually become known as Bethlehem, overlooking the Franconia
and Presidential ranges of the wildly beautiful White Mountains of New
Hampshire, held little appeal for settlers. By 1787, things began to change.
A few families—the Browns, the Warrens, and the Turners, became the first to
take up the mantle and settle an unpredictable region beset by harsh winters.
The families turned to the surrounding woods for their livelihood, finding
wealth in the trees that provided lumber, and from that moment, Bethlehem
was born. More people began to arrive and a town charter was established
(which some claimed occurred on December 25), further substantiating the
name of Bethlehem. After the Civil War, when visitors sought a respite from
city life, guest houses and hotels began making their appearances in town.
The visitors claimed that Bethlehem's place on a hill overlooking the
mountain ranges provided for healthy air. Others sought its beauty and simple
living. Late in the nineteenth century, the annual Coaching Parade, which
showcased coaches arrayed in ribbons and other decorations, brought even
more visitors to the town. Thus was born the vacationer's paradise to revive
the soul and spirit and provide enjoyment to all who came.

Lauralee Bliss

Chapter One

....

1890, the height of the Gilded Age

"I don't know if I can make it!" cried a young voice.

The paintbrush shook in his hand, creating a zigzag of azure across the canvas. Tom Haskins tried to set the brush on the easel, but it fell to the ground, coloring the blades of grass a murky blue. Nearby, a young couple stumbled out of the woods. The man supported a finely dressed lady who limped along, wincing in pain.

"What happened?" Tom called, hurrying over to assist them.

"It was silly of me," the young woman moaned. "You know the many rocks here. I was looking at a flower and didn't see where I was going. I tripped."

"My wife hurt her ankle," the man continued. "I don't think it's broken. It's all right, my love," he now said to her in a soothing voice. "We'll take you right away to the doctor and have it examined. I'm sure in a day or two you'll be fine."

"Oh, I hope so. I'd hate to ruin our holiday over such a foolish thing as this. You deserve it after all the hard work you put into the company."

"Never fear, my dear," he soothed her. To Tom he said, "My carriage is there," and pointed to the coach Tom had seen when he arrived at this fine wooded setting not far from the town of Bethlehem.

Tom supported the woman on one side while the husband assisted on the other, escorting her to the awaiting coach, where the driver had opened the door and stood ready to give further aid. Tom watched as the husband helped his wife inside and carefully cradled her injured leg with a pillow. The man then stooped to give her a kiss of comfort.

"All is well," he said once more as he straightened, glancing at Tom. "Thank you for your help, Mr.…."

"Tom Haskins." He shook the hand the man offered him.

"Edward Newkirk…and my wife, Margaret." The man squinted. "I noticed that you're an artist. I saw the landscape on your easel when we came out of the woods. Did you know that, Margaret? He's painting the splendid White Mountain scenery."

"How nice. But I do need to go, Edward. My ankle hurts dreadfully."

"Yes, of course." Edward looked to Tom once more. "I would like to talk about your work sometime. We're staying at the Sinclair Hotel. Would you do us the honor of joining us for dinner? Perhaps tomorrow night when my wife is feeling better?"

"Yes, please do," Margaret added. "We would very much like to hear about your paintings."

"Well, thank you. I would be honored."

Edward nodded. "Tomorrow, then."

Tom watched the coach drive away, his thoughts all abuzz. And not just about the dinner invitation, for which he was eager to attend. Or the painting, as he returned to his work site wondering what he might find. It was the image of the couple that remained branded in his mind…the way they interacted with each other; cared for each other; and showed tender, godly mercy and love in the midst of trials.

He sat before his easel and found that the painting had not been ruined as he'd feared. He'd hoped, after all, to create the perfect sky to mirror the perfect day in late July. Now it was only slightly altered, just like his thoughts. He dabbed a darker blue to create a larger sky to complete the picture and then leaned back slightly on the stool to marvel at the final product. Many would think him prideful in the way he appreciated his work. It was not pride, though, but rather disbelief that *his* hand could create such realistic landscapes. He was no special man in particular. He'd received no serious art lessons, save for the one man who held to the talents inherent in the Hudson River School and who taught him a little about becoming a landscape artist. The rest had been a gift bestowed by God.

To Tom's studious gaze, when he beheld the scenery and the people he wanted to capture within a painting, his mind separated the scene into a myriad of colors. From the strokes of brushes in different sizes, dipped into the appropriate color and painted onto the canvas, the image was born. Perhaps he was like the famous Italian sculptor, Michelangelo, who believed that his work existed within the very fabric of the stone, only to be released under the chisel's blade. Likewise, Tom chipped away at the white of a linen canvas with his brush, allowing the picture to come forth. He captured whatever images existed around him in the place he called home, the White Mountains of New Hampshire.

But now he wanted to dedicate a new painting to the couple he'd seen today, of helping one another and living out the bond of matrimonial love. Love. How far removed that seemed in his life. Tom packed his art supplies into a horse-drawn cart while allowing the warm breezes of summer to dry the new color he'd added. He liked it best when he found his attention drawn into his work. Now thoughtful contemplation took over as he reflected on the couple in his memory. The loving care of the man for his wife. The way they interacted in thoughtful words and glances. The ability to share life, no matter what it presented.

Tom dismantled the easel. At age thirty and still unmarried, love had seemed to pass him by. It hadn't been his fault entirely. Only two years ago he had been at home caring for his ailing father. When Father passed away, Tom found himself consumed by his work. There had been brief attention paid by several ladies, but none had drawn him. He'd convinced himself that God would rather he paint than marry.

Tom climbed into the seat and flicked the reins to begin the bumpy ride back to town. He'd accomplished much in his life, he reasoned. A prosperous business as an artist…a nice home with all the furnishings one needed for comfort…. But now he began to consider what he lacked. The companionship of marriage, where two people shared in life's trouble and happiness. A sweet voice exclaiming over him or his work. A soft hand to take his elbow and walk the dusty street. One to share in this work and whatever else the Lord would have them do. To make a fine home and raise a family. To live in love forever—like the husband and wife he'd just met. Despite the accomplishment of his paintings, he yearned for that important piece of life that still eluded him.

Tom arrived in Bethlehem in time to see his good friend Lawrence Boshen strolling along the wooden walkway on Main Street. To Tom's chagrin, Lawrence's newlywed wife, Loretta, walked beside him, her hand nestled in the crook of his elbow. Tom had attended their lavish wedding just last year at the Maplewood Hotel.

After the wedding, Lawrence asked if Tom would be next. A year later, he was no closer to any such covenant.

Lawrence waved to Tom. "Have you completed another masterpiece?" he called out.

"Better than before." Tom brought the cart to a halt before them, eager to show his friend what he'd accomplished. "What do you think?"

"Excellent! Perfection. Be sure you have some paintings for the Coaching Parade. It's coming up in a few weeks, and I know you will sell plenty."

Tom thanked him for the reminder and for his encouragement. He tipped his hat to Loretta and watched them stroll away, giggling to each other. He returned the painting to the cart, but instead of expectation, he sensed loneliness. He looked at the other couples passing by. They stared into each other's eyes, to places often kept buried, as if attempting to uncover the inner soul of their lifetime companion. He felt God whispering to his own secret place of want, nourishing the seeds of hope for a future covenant. He felt confident that God would direct his steps, as He directed his paintings. Tom must be faithful in planting and watering and allow the Creator to cause the growth. And that flower of a woman to call his own would surpass anything his feeble mind could ever imagine.

Tom arrived at the two-story framed house with the black shutters and large front porch, a home that was now his after his father's death. Before he took ill, Father's life was spent in the upkeep of the fine home with many rooms. Father often housed guests and made a bit of money at it in the peak of the fall and summer seasons. Even though Tom knew the house was far too large for a single man like him, one day he hoped to hear the sounds of life again, of feet padding the hall and warm voices filling the spacious rooms. Entering the home, the only sounds greeting him today were the rhythmic ticking of the clock in the parlor, the clank of the oak door that shut firmly behind him, and his heart seemingly beating in his ears.

Tom had just removed his coat when a knock came on the door. He never thought such a sound would prove delightful. Perhaps an older gentleman would be there, with his eldest daughter on his arm, waiting to be introduced.

He shook his head to compose himself, and it was good that he did. He opened the door to reveal a distinguished gentleman in a dark suit, with graying hair and a mustache. Tom stepped back. "M–Mr. Astor!"

"Thomas, my good man." His mustache twitched. He waited a moment. "Do you plan to invite me in?"

"Yes, of course. Excuse me, sir. Please come in." Tom stepped aside.

The man nodded and walked in, surveying the interior. Tom had all he could do to look and act dignified. He immediately smoothed down his hair and checked that the cuffs of his sleeves were buttoned. James Astor of New York City, a relative of the wealthy Astor family, was a prosperous businessman and frequent visitor to Bethlehem. Mr. Astor often bought whatever Tom painted. In fact, Tom had received a letter from him not long ago detailing the man's plans for a lengthy stay in Bethlehem and his hopes that Tom would have more paintings for his choosing.

Now Tom silently thanked himself for having painted a new scene today. "Sir, I have a new painting that I'd like you to see." He hurried to fetch the work he'd done that day—the balsam fir and hardwoods of New Hampshire. "Isn't it fine? See the texture of the woods? It nearly looks alive, almost as if you could smell the balsam."

Mr. Astor chuckled. "You never cease to be amazed by your work, eh? And so you should." His mustache twitched in amusement as he gazed at length at the landscape. "Very good."

"I'm sorry I appear vain. I was only anxious to have you see it when you came to town. And then I was thinking of another scene I would like to paint, one from a new destination. I have not yet painted the view from the summit of Bethlehem's own mountain, Mount Agassiz. Would that interest you?"

"Perhaps." Mr. Astor looked around before settling into a chair.

"Can I bring you some tea, sir?"

"Scotch would do, Thomas. But you're not a drinking man, am I right?"

"No, sir. But I do have lemonade."

Mr. Astor nodded and relaxed in the chair.

Tom left to fetch the man a drink. He hands trembled slightly as he poured the beverage. He prayed he didn't look as nervous as he felt. He must remain confident.

Mr. Astor took a long drink and leaned back in the chair. "Ah, excellent. So what else do you have for me?"

Tom went at once to gather his remaining works. Ducks on a still pond. The sun setting beyond a row of distant mountains that comprised the Presidential range. A couple enjoying a picnic. Mr. Astor examined each one. His face remained impassive, much to Tom's anxious heart. "Thomas, I must tell you, I think of you as a protégé in many ways. Not that I am an artist by any means, as you are well aware. I'm a businessman, as are all in my family. I have a desire to see you succeed in this business."

"Thank you, sir. I appreciate all you've done for me and your interest in my work."

"It's not my interest alone, young man; many of my associates are intrigued by your work, as well. In fact, several have decided to spend their holidays here in New Hampshire, all because of the fine landscapes you paint."

Tom sat straighter, feeling the strength of confidence surging in him. "Thank you, sir."

"I want to see you rise to the pinnacle of your talent. To see you go to new places."

"Well, as I mentioned, I believe a walk to the summit of a mountain with my paints and brushes would be a fine illustration," he mused. "Mount Agassiz is the logical choice."

Mr. Astor looked around the drawing room. "Such a large house for one man. Have you considered adding to your life's pursuits by finding a wife?"

A tickle gripped Tom's throat, and he fought to silence a cough. "Sir?" he managed to say.

"My darling wife died not too long ago, and I'm seeing more and more how her influence affected my work. Now that she is gone, there is a certain emptiness I can't describe."

"I'm sorry, sir."

"Thank you. But I've come to discover how much marriage is a necessity. If you marry, you will see your work grow beyond your expectations. A woman makes a man complete in his business. Your creativity will expand. The colors and textures of your work will take on new vitality. Two are better than one."

"I'm certain of that, sir. In fact, I met a couple today while I was painting. She had hurt her foot, and it was interesting to see how they interacted. I'm trying to study people more, sir, to help better my work. To bring more humanity into the landscapes."

He nodded. "A relationship in your life will add that dimension you seek. You would do well to heed your observation in the matter. In fact, I would introduce you to some ladies, only the ones I know here are visitors. And I do not personally know those who reside in this town."

"Bethlehem is small. We're here mainly to serve the needs of the guests who come to visit."

Mr. Astor nodded. "But it is not the only town in this region. Thomas, you must think on this as a step in your career that you cannot pass up any longer. Your work will improve. Then I can show you off to more of my clients. Good things await you—perhaps even a Currier and Ives print of one of your paintings. Would you like that?"

Tom caught his breath. "Yes, sir. That would be excellent!"

Mr. Astor stood to his feet. "I must be going. I'm meeting a friend for tea at the Maplewood Hotel."

"Sir? Did you…did you prefer any of the paintings?"

He shook his head. "Not at this time. I hope that when next we meet you will have a better selection. And more of that humanity, as well. Good day, Thomas."

"Good day, sir." The door shut heavily before him and, with it, the command that remained. *Find a wife, Tom, and you will have buyers and perhaps even a new outlet for your work.* He wanted to resist Mr. Astor's suggestion, yet he couldn't afford to offend his mentor and the primary buyer of his work. The future of his work rested on this. And then there was his lonely heart to consider. His age. And Lawrence pestering him about it. He'd prayed earlier that the Lord would show him his path.

Find a wife. That seemed to be the call on his life this day. Yet how exactly was he to accomplish it?

* * * *

"Thank you for inviting me to dinner." Tom admitted he was quite hungry for a good meal. He never ate well as a bachelor, and this invitation was a blessing.

Margaret and Edward Newkirk looked composed and elegant before him—her in an agreeable evening gown and Edward in his fine black suit. They made a radiant couple. For a time they exchanged pleasantries about their holiday in Bethlehem and how they loved the scenery.

"I'm glad you're feeling better, madam," Tom said after they placed their orders.

"Oh yes, my ankle is much better. Thank you for all your help."

Edward leaned over the table. "We wanted you here, Mr. Haskins, for two reasons actually. To thank you for your assistance yesterday and to ask about your work. Margaret and I couldn't help but notice one of your paintings in the hall of the hotel. Fine work."

Tom knew the painting he meant, one he liked very much, of the grand spectacle of the Presidential range. The mountains of Washington, Jefferson, and Madison, among others. An awesome display to behold and to paint.

"Do you paint much?" Edward asked. "Your style seems familiar."

"Yes. My landscape work is in the style of the Hudson River artists."

"Ah, that explains it. Quite an elite group. Now that you mention it, I can see the similarities. I'm a great admirer of Thomas Cole myself. I have several of his paintings of the Catskill region of New York State. That's why I asked the hotel proprietor if I might be able to buy your painting. I was willing to pay quite a bit. I wanted it for my collection."

"But they refused," Margaret continued. "They are fond of it as well. You're quite the artist here in this town, Mr. Haskins." She and Edward looked at each other and smiled.

Tom could see the communication at work between them, not in their words but in their silent looks of affection. "Thank you. I have others who like my work, too—a Mr. James Astor from New York City."

Edward's eyebrow rose. "Really. Impressive. We're also from New York. The Astors are a prominent and wealthy family."

"He has great plans for me. Only..." Tom hesitated. The couple looked at him with such compassion, he couldn't help but blurt out, "He is encouraging me to marry, of all things. He believes it will help my work and my life. In fact, he nearly demanded it." Tom chuckled but at the same time felt warmth enter his face. Suddenly he felt foolish for having said it.

The waitress arrived with their dinners. Edward offered a simple prayer and began to eat.

"Marriage is indeed an excellent thing," Edward went on. "He who finds an excellent wife does well for himself. The Bible even says so."

"Dear me, I cannot believe a fine and handsome man like you isn't married," Margaret added. "Why, a woman would be blessed to be your wife."

Tom hoped so. But he also hoped he might be a blessing to his intended, as this man was to his wife.

"Oh, you must tell Mr. Haskins how we met, Edward," Margaret urged. "It's such a wonderful story."

Edward laid down his fork. "Well, if you can believe it, Margaret came to me through an advertisement I placed in a newspaper."

"You placed an ad?" Tom said in astonishment.

"Yes, for a bride. I know it seems rather old-fashioned these days. But I thought I would see what happened. I did not live in the city at the time, just a small farming community in upstate New York. Perhaps like you, there weren't many eligible women around. Remember, men long ago used to place ads for wives to settle Oregon. There are still ads like that in papers in states like Kansas and Nebraska."

"But I don't live in the West."

"It doesn't matter. She will go to wherever you live. It happened that Margaret came from the city. And I had planned to move there anyway to begin a business. In your case, who would refuse to come to a place like this, surrounded by these grand mountains? And meet a talented man like yourself?"

"Look what happened to me." Margaret sighed in content. "It turned into the greatest blessing of our lives. Edward and I are perfect for each other. It's as if God Himself directed the result of the ad. The heavenly Matchmaker at work!"

Tom watched as they grasped hands and stared into each other's eyes.

"It's been three years now, and we couldn't be happier." Edward took up Margaret's hand in his. "Perhaps you should consider placing an ad, Tom. What harm could it do? I can help you, if you wish. I know the prominent papers of New York City. This ad could lead you to a bright and prosperous future, as it did for us."

"Place an ad in the paper," Tom repeated, as if trying to convince himself of such a thing. *Try to win love by some advertisement.* He looked at the smiling couple before him. Happy. Fulfilled. Blessed by God. A bright and prosperous future, Edward had said, the kind Tom needed and Mr. Astor requested. He could just picture the look on Mr. Astor's face when he came next and Tom was there with a bride on his arm. The man would buy all his paintings and ask for more. And Mr. Astor would tell him of the interest to create a Currier and Ives print of his work. Tom would be happy, too, sharing in the blessing with his wife. She would love his fine home, furnishings, and everything else he would provide for her. But most of all, they would enjoy being in love.

"We can write it together," Edward encouraged, "and I'll see that it gets placed in the paper. I know you'll receive many replies. To come from the city to a place like this will be the answer for some woman in need, and it will be completion for you."

And also fulfill the inquiry from all who have been wondering about this plan for my life, he thought. Like Mr. Astor. Lawrence Boshen. His own heart. Tom nodded to the delight of his hosts and thanked them for the suggestion. He agreed to blindly venture into the unknown. To take a leap off the cliff of faith. And where he would land, he had no idea.

Chapter Two

Sara McGee cradled the loaf of bread in her arm as if it were a priceless object worthy of serving to a king. She vowed to think of this meal like a banquet, even if the main course was bread. The loaf had been given to her by Mrs. Whitaker, like so many other meals the older woman provided. And each time Sara received one of the loving gifts, she would race to the small dark room in the corner of the basement to enjoy every tasty morsel.

Wiping damp strings of hair out of her eyes, Sara hastened to the place she called home—the basement of a furniture store in the center of New York City. The day had been hot, as was typical of summer living in the city. Sara slipped around the side of the building where a small window swung free, allowing her access to the dingy basement. By now the people of the establishment had already left for the day. No one knew she lived here, not even Mrs. Whitaker. She feared telling anyone, for they might alert the owners of the building and she could once more find herself homeless on the street.

The bread smelled so good that she nearly broke off a piece to eat. Instead she felt the urge to hurry. She worked quickly to bring each of her legs through the narrow opening, touching her feet to the stack of boxes that acted as a ladder. Climbing down, one by one, Sara reached the safety of the floor below only to feel something small and furry scurry past her leg. Startled, Sara bit her lip at the last moment to keep from screaming. In the window's dim light, she discovered that a rat had come to see if she might share her dinner.

"Not tonight. This bread is for the Lord and me. He is my guest."

She stumbled along, pausing every so often to make sure the owners had not ventured downstairs and put some surprise barrier in her way. She walked carefully, counting the usual twenty-eight steps until she reached her "home," a back room in the far corner. Inside the room on the left, beneath a small table, rested a piece of flint and a candle. In no time, a soft glow greeted her. Quickly she shut the door so no light would bleed out of the room and through the basement window, alerting others on the street to her presence.

Sara looked now at the bread. What a great bounty it was. She closed her eyes and thanked the Lord for it, as well as for Mrs. Whitaker. Without her, she surely would have starved after her mother died. Sara tore off a chunk of the bread and began to eat. As she ate, she fumbled for a few photos lying near the table. They were the only reminders of her mother, who had been taken from Sara when she was still young and pretty. Sara treasured them like the finest gold. Wealthy women might have their jewels, but Sara had her pictures.

She kissed the face of her mother, propped the small picture against the wall, and began telling her of the day she had on the streets of New York. She told her how she'd found some fish heads at the market and fed them to a few stray cats that lived nearby. A mother gave her a nickel for helping with her children. And Mrs. Whitaker gave her yet another nickel for rearranging the baking supplies in the storage room.

Sara put down her bread and reached into the pocket of her

dress to pull out the money. She felt rich indeed and wondered what she might buy with the two nickels. *Lord, please show me what I should do. Buy more food, perhaps? Or an old dress that someone is willing to sell?* Sara closed her hand around the money then went back to eating. She would save the rest of the bread for her breakfast and perhaps a noonday meal if she had enough. Maybe she would buy some cheese to go along with it. Oh, to have a hunk of hard yellow cheese—the thought of the tangy flavor sent the juices swirling inside her mouth. It would be a heavenly banquet, better than tonight's.

Sara picked up a photo that showed her mother holding a cup of tea. The same porcelain cup stood on the stand. It was Sara's most treasured possession. The photos were important, but Mama used that cup each day to drink her tea. It meant more to Sara than anything else. Somehow the teacup kept her connected with her mother in heaven. As long as she had the cup, Mama felt close by.

With growing weariness, Sara straightened the few blankets on the floor that would become her makeshift bed. The candlelight flickered as she worked. She could not think about what tomorrow might bring. She only thought about yesterday, a year ago actually, when her mother was still alive and they had a nice room—small but cozy. At that time Mama worked as a seamstress. Sara wished she could have found work at the same establishment after Mama died, but they had refused to hire her. She was forced instead to look for odd jobs given out of the merciful hearts of those who felt inclined to help some poor woman of the streets. And she lived here in this small room, unnoticed by the occupants who owned the building... at least for now.

She could still hear Mama's voice, full of faith and purpose. "You're not poor as long as our heavenly Father is with you, Sara. He'll supply all your needs according to His great riches. And He cares about you, even more than I do, and I love you very much."

Sara smiled in remembrance. Most would think she had nothing left in her life. But at that moment she had everything. The friendship of Mrs. Whitaker. Beautiful memories. Peace in her heart. And the comfort of God shielding her mind, body, and spirit. She lay down on the dirty blankets. It was enough.

* * * *

"Sara McGee! At last I found you!"

Sara whirled at the sound of the frantic voice. She had been walking the streets, as she did every day, looking for a job to do while thinking of the coins jingling in her pocket and the cheese she would buy at the market. Now she saw the large figure of Mrs. Whitaker hurrying toward her. Sara stopped in her tracks, concerned that something might be wrong.

Mrs. Whitaker was panting heavily, beads of perspiration gathering on her brow from the warmth of the day. Suddenly she thrust something into Sara's hand. "This is for you."

Sara wondered why she, of all people, would be receiving a personal letter. No one knew her, save Mrs. Whitaker. "What is this? How did you get it?"

A broad smile filled the older woman's face. "It's a surprise. Come back with me to the bakery, and we will read it there."

Sara shrugged and walked along obediently. "I made ten cents yesterday, Mrs. Whitaker, did I tell you?"

"Very nice, very nice," she responded absently. Sara sensed that something was on the woman's mind. She couldn't begin to imagine what, except for the letter in her hand. "What is this, anyway?" She waved the envelope before the woman, hoping for a clue to its contents.

"You'll see, you'll see. Oh, I do pray it's a good letter." Arriving at the bakery, she pushed Sara towards the back room. "I must take care of the customers first. Read the letter yourself; it will be good practice. I'll come as soon as I can."

Sara did as she was told, for she would never deny the kind Mrs. Whitaker anything. She was like a mother to Sara in many ways, caring for her needs as best she could. She once said Sara would have lived in her home if not for her cantankerous husband. He would have nothing to do with "some foundling," as he called Sara, even though she was eighteen. But Mrs. Whitaker helped Sara in other ways, providing the daily bread and friendship that meant more to her than anything.

Sara found a place to sit on a crate inside the storeroom. The flour dust tickled her nostrils, making her sneeze. She scrutinized the envelope and tried to read the postmark.

"New Hamp–sher," she read. *I know no one in New Hampshire. At least I don't think I do.* But her name was clearly printed on the outside envelope: SARA ELISABETH MCGEE. *Elisabeth* had been her mother's name. Maybe a long lost relative of Mama's had finally contacted her. One who had money. Maybe she was now an heiress.

She undid the envelope with trembling fingers, trying hard not to tear it.

"Haven't you read the letter yet?" Mrs. Whitaker asked, her bulky form filling the doorway. "Goodness' sakes, child, what's taking you so long?"

"I—I hope I can read it."

Mrs. Whitaker shook her head. "Just give me a few more minutes and I'll come back and read it to you. You should have accepted my suggestion for more lessons. I had a customer who was willing to teach you." At that moment a customer bellowed for assistance inside the bakery, and Mrs. Whitaker disappeared once more.

Sara unfolded the letter to find paper currency inside. Her heart leaped. She then looked at the scrawls written on the linen paper. She brought the paper to her nose, wondering if she could inhale the fragrance of this place called New Hampshire and the person who had sent her the money. It did not smell like New York, with its cinder smoke and dust filling the air. Nor did it smell like fresh baked bread or fish at the market. She could make out nothing at all.

Sara examined the signature and recognized the letters: T–H–O–M–A–S. "Th...th," she began to sound out. "Th–om Az." She looked up, pleased with herself. "It's from a Th–om Az," she told Mrs. Whitaker when the woman returned. "And he sent me money!"

"Whatever do you mean?" The woman took the letter out of her hand. "Sara, honey, the man's name is Thomas. Mr. Thomas Haskins of Bethlehem, New Hampshire."

"Bethlehem! He lives in the place where Jesus was born?" Excitement bubbled up at the mere possibility.

"It's the name of a town in the state of New Hampshire. Let me read it." She cleared her throat. " 'Dear Miss McGee...' "

"That's me!" Sara exclaimed. "That means the money is for me!"

"Let's see what it says. 'I am responding to the letter you sent to me with regards to the ad placed in the newspaper.' "

Sara stared blankly. "Ad? What ad?"

Mrs. Whitaker waved her hand. "Never mind, never mind. Just listen now." She peered at the letter and continued. " 'I would very much like to make your acquaintance. Your letter indeed charmed me, and I do believe it would be good and proper for us to meet as soon as it is convenient. Please be so kind as to respond if you are interested and let me know your arrival date. I thought early October would do well and also give time to make arrangements. I have enclosed the money for your train fare. Thank you, and may God bless your journey. With fondest regards I am yours truly, Thomas E. Haskins, Bethlehem, New Hampshire.' "

Sara sat still, trying to make sense out of it. "What does this mean, Mrs. Whitaker? Why is a Mr. Haskins sending me money for a train? How do I know him? Why does he want me to visit? Is he a relative of Mama's?"

Mrs. Whitaker leapt to her feet and began to sway as if music were being played by some trumpeter. "It worked! Oh, bless my soul, it worked, dear Lord! And my husband said nothing would amount to what I do in life. But I have opened the door to a new life for you. I couldn't give you a home with me, but I could find a home for you elsewhere."

Sara stared, unblinking, wondering if Mrs. Whitaker was suffering some mental illness. "I—I don't understand...."

"I'll tell you. I saw an ad in the paper about two weeks ago. A man from New Hampshire was asking for a young woman to share a life by the mountains. When I saw it, I immediately thought of you."

Sara continued to look on in disbelief, even as her eyes began to hurt from staring so long.

"So I wrote him and told him all about you. And now he wants to see you! Isn't that wonderful?"

"He wants to see me? *Me?*" Sara looked down at her tattered dress and holey stockings. "He can't possibly want to see me. What did you tell him about me?"

"That you have beautiful brown hair and blue eyes. That you know how to sew. That you care about children and feed abandoned cats. That you will do anything you set your mind to and do it well. And that you love our heavenly Father."

Sara could not argue with the description, though she was uncertain her hair looked beautiful, being a snarled mass likened to a bird's nest perched on a lamppost. "I don't know about this."

"I do know. This is the answer for your life, Sara. It's a chance for a new beginning, a better life—a life away from the city and in the country with a wealthy man."

"He—he's wealthy?"

"I'm sure he is. I don't know for certain, but you can tell he is a learned man. And learned men make money. He's an artist by trade."

"An artist," she repeated. She used to look at the fine paintings displayed in a store not far from Mrs. Whitaker's bakery. If Mr. Haskins painted like that, he must be an interesting man, with a mind and hands that could create wondrous images. "But I can't visit a man I know nothing about. I'd be too frightened." Tears suddenly sprang into her eyes. "I would have to leave you." She thought of the little home she'd made for herself in the dark basement. It was hardly suitable, but at least it was familiar. "I'll be leaving the city where Mama and I lived all our lives."

"Your mama is in heaven, Sara. She would be glad you have this opportunity for a new life. And you can write to me. I'm sure a learned man like Mr. Haskins will teach you how to read better as well as write."

"I still don't understand why he wants me to come. What can I do there? Care for his home? His children? Is he married?"

Mrs. Whitaker laughed heartily and ventured forward to embrace Sara. "That's the whole reason for the ad. He's looking for a wife. I thought I told you."

Sara's mouth fell open. "A wife? You mean me? No!"

Mrs. Whitaker stepped back, the merriment disappearing from her plump face. "What do you mean?"

"He—he can't marry me."

"Why can't he?"

Sara shook her head. "Look at me, Mrs. Whitaker!"

"I am looking at you. And I see someone beautiful—a young woman that God created in His image. Caring, merciful, with talents all her own. Why shouldn't the good Lord arrange for you to be happy? To live the rest of your days in a beautiful place in New Hampshire as a man's wife?"

The word *marriage* rang in her mind like a tolling bell. "But have you told him who I am?"

"Just as I said. And every word is true."

"Did you also tell him I'm poor? That I own nothing to my name but a teacup and some pictures?"

"Why should he know all that? He is not marrying your possessions—just you." Mrs. Whitaker took the money and held it before her eyes. "At least you need to find out, Sara Elisabeth. Find out if this is the Lord's will for your life. Find out if He has called you to marriage with this man, to a better life than the streets of New York City. Is that so awful to consider? Will you throw away this wonderful opportunity because you doubt who you are?"

Sara stared at the money resting in her hand. What an opportunity it was, indeed. If only she looked as radiant on the outside as she sometimes felt on the inside. Slowly her fingers curled around the money. She brought it to her heart and nodded.

"Good! I'll write Mr. Haskins this very evening. We will buy your train ticket and have you there by October."

Just a few weeks… My life will change forever. How would she ever be able to say good-bye to the city and embrace a stranger's life by the mountains? *God will help me. If what Mrs. Whitaker says is true and this is God's will, then He will provide the way. Somehow.*

Sara returned that night to her home in the basement. But this was no ordinary night, thinking about what tomorrow would bring on the streets of New York City. Nor did she think about her next meal. In fact, she'd forgotten to buy the cheese she'd planned for this evening. She couldn't eat anyway. She only felt numb inside. Her mind was a jumble of thoughts about this man named Thomas Haskins, this artist in New Hampshire, and what would happen when she stepped off the train in a town called Bethlehem. But she had no choice. She'd given Mrs. Whitaker the money to buy the ticket. It was done.

"Oh, dear Lord, what am I doing?" Sara mourned aloud. She took up the picture of her mother. "Do you see what's happened, Mama? Some stranger in New Hamp–sher wants me to be his wife, a man I don't even know. Can this happen to someone like me? Or will it be the worst decision of my life?" She shook her head, trying to quell the doubts. "Make me strong, Lord, strong enough to do Your will in this. Help me be ready in mind, spirit"—she glanced down at herself—"and body as well. Oh, dear Lord, I'm so afraid."

Chapter Three

....

He'd done it. Tom contemplated his deed inside the sitting room of his stately home.

He had written the ad and, with trepidation, sent it along with Edward and Margaret. They were happy for him, confident it would lead to success. Tom needed success in both life and love. Just the other day, he'd met up with Lawrence near the mercantile as Lawrence and his wife, Loretta, were shopping for a new hat for her to wear to the Coaching Parade.

"You need a wife to spend money on, Tom," Lawrence had mused.

Tom whirled in a start, wondering if somehow his friend had been made privy to what he'd done, submitting an ad for a bride. Tom nearly mentioned it but did not. Now was not the time or the place. Especially if things didn't work out as planned.

"When are you going to make room in that busy life of yours for a wife?"

Tom's gaze darted to Loretta, who acknowledged him with rosy cheeks and a bright smile. "He has time, dear husband."

"No, he doesn't. He's forgetting about time. The years are slipping away. I see you're already getting a bit gray around the temples, Tom." Lawrence chuckled, even as Tom smoothed down his hair. "Better find a wife quick before you start bending like a cane."

Again Tom nearly told him he was attempting to do just that.

"Oh, Lawrence," chided his wife, "he will have someone well-seasoned and full of wisdom. Not to mention a house full of paintings. Now we should go before you say anything else foolish. Please excuse him, Tom."

"Another reason to find an excellent wife—to stop one from making a fool of himself," Lawrence added with a grin, patting his wife's hand.

Tom watched them stroll away. He'd seen the telltale signs of the years catching up to him in the mirror one day. And he refused to hold the title of long-standing bachelor of Bethlehem. That was why he'd taken the advice of Edward and Margaret Newkirk and placed the ad.

It soon proved fruitful. In a matter of a few weeks he'd received a reply from a woman named Sara McGee. He felt an initial joy at such a quick answer, but since then, Tom had found his creativity stifled like fire silenced by a bucket of water. Wasn't a wife supposed to help with his artistic endeavors and open new doors? Instead he sat by a view and did nothing. All the waiting and wondering was cluttering his mind. Wondering if he had made the right decision to place an ad. Wondering if he had done the right thing in answering the first letter that arrived. But this Sara seemed perfect. Accomplished. Loved life and children. Worked hard. And possessed an adventuresome spirit to leave everything she knew to come here.

He stirred in his chair, brushing his face with his hand as if to clear the cobwebs he felt. He'd trusted God with everything else; surely he could trust Him with this one rather important detail of life. And yet he fretted. He must turn away from an anxious spirit and embrace peace.

Tom now took up the paper lying on a stand—a notice for the upcoming Coaching Parade held annually in Bethlehem. The parade was gaining respect in New England, as various carriages and coaches, bedecked in splendid array, competed for prizes. Each year Tom stood by his display of paintings and sold them to the throng of visitors who came to Bethlehem to watch the parade. He would be glad for the festivity this year. It was something to occupy his mind rather than waiting to see what kind of woman arrived from the big city.

Again he wiped his face. It felt warm to the touch. He dismissed his apprehension for now and moved to look over his selection of paintings. Tom examined an older painting he'd done last year, one of a man and woman enjoying a picnic on a bright autumn day. The woman carried a parasol to protect her features from the harsh sunlight, and the man wore his Sunday best. The steep mountains of Franconia Notch framed the background. It was the perfect portrait of humanity he'd talked about with Mr. Astor. His thoughts centered on that picnic, and suddenly he imagined himself in the scene with the woman from New York. He was in his suit, she in a lovely gown. The parasol protected her from the sun. Her lily white hands were covered by gloves, and a large hat decorated her head. He thought of them sharing their daily bread while talking about their lives. And then would follow a kiss, so natural and wonderful in God's perfect setting.

His heart quickened when he realized how desperately he wanted companionship, to live the very scene he painted. Could such things happen by way of a simple ad placed in a city paper? Though the letter he received encouraged him, he still knew so little about Sara McGee. To pledge his life and love based on a few sentences scratched out on paper hardly seemed the right thing to do.

*But look at Edward and Margaret. God blessed them. Why can't I
receive it, too? I need to be confident of it. Walk by faith. Allow the Lord
to lead my actions and my heart as He did with them.*

At least he had the parade to occupy him, rather than these
questions. He would enjoy the many tourists and the people of
Bethlehem on this special occasion and sell whatever pieces he could.
And he would wait for the next letter detailing Sara McGee's arrival
and giving more clues about her.

* * * *

The day of the Coaching Parade in Bethlehem dawned sunny with a
clear blue sky, despite the rain that had fallen overnight. Tom had
awakened to see splatters of raindrops on the windowpanes and hoped
it would not dampen the day's festivities. But, like many storms in this
place, it came and went, and so too would the storms of life. He felt
relieved in the morning to see sunlight gleaming through the house as
he packed up his paintings. *Thank you, Lord, that You remain on the
throne. Help me take this day by day and leave the rest in Your care. Amen.*

A knock came on the door. He fumbled to open it, with paintings
tucked under each arm. Lawrence greeted him with a smile. "This is
your day, my friend. Have I a surprise for you!"

"You're just in time." Tom handed him several paintings. "Take
these, will you?"

"Yes, you're in luck, my friend," Lawrence continued. "Remember
our talk not long ago about how you need help in certain areas of
your life? I, as your best friend, have taken matters into my hands. I've
come up with the very solution to your problem."

Tom barely heard the words and, instead, mused over what he needed for the day. *Paintings. Wooden display stands. I should bring my easel and paints, also.*

"Are you listening to me?"

"Oh, what problem is that in particular?"

"Your bachelor status, of course. We talked it over, Loretta and I. And we have the very solution. Loretta's cousin has just arrived from Boston—Miss Annabelle Loving. You would make the perfect couple. The talk of the town."

Tom froze. With his thoughts centered on the parade, this news was akin to dunking him in a horse trough. "I don't understand."

Lawrence laughed. "You will. Come. Let's set up your booth, and I'll tell you all about her."

"Lawrence…" Tom paused to retrieve his hat and one last painting that was leaning against the wall. "That's kind of you, but I have other matters to tend to right now. We'll need to make several trips from the house to carry the wooden stands and my paints, as I've decided to set up my easel."

"You always have matters on your mind, except what's important. That's why I took it upon myself to help you in your time of need. And you, my good man, need to find a wife. So says scripture."

Tom wanted to tell him that he had already solved the problem by way of the ad but dismissed it as they walked out the front door into a cloud of excitement. Crowds were gathering along the street, anticipating the parade. And from where he stood, Tom could see a variety of booths set up along the walkway, from food booths serving cakes and pies to other artists such as weavers and sculptors and authors selling books. He found a place among the hustle and bustle

41

to set up business and asked Lawrence to retrieve the wooden stands.

"She's beautiful," Lawrence stated once he returned. "Annabelle, that is. I know you will like her."

Together they erected the wooden stands to display Tom's paintings for curious browsers. "Where do you want this one?" Lawrence held up the painting of the young couple picnicking.

"Here is fine," Tom said absently, trying to focus his attention on his display. He wished the man would not waste time with his matchmaking. He wanted the man's help in organizing the sale. "Don't worry me, Lawrence. It has been dealt with."

"Yes, it has, and..." Just then a band struck up a merry tune. "I love a good parade. When Annabelle comes, I will gladly watch over your booth while you two attend the parade and get to know each other. I hear the carriages this year are extraordinary."

Tom halted. "What?"

"Haven't you heard a word I've said? Annabelle Loving, Loretta's cousin from Boston—she's here. And she'd like to meet you. I told her all about your work, and she's fascinated. She was also quite taken with the paintings we have displayed in our home, like the one you did of the Old Man."

Tom cherished that scene, too—the man's face outlined in rocks and poised at the pinnacle of a mountain in Franconia Notch. Tom found the natural stone image a true wonder. Many artists sought to create it on canvas, and many buyers desired to have the scene displayed in their homes. "I should paint the Old Man again sometime," he mused. "It would sell quickly."

"Annabelle would buy it for certain," Lawrence said. He left for a few moments and came back with a small wooden folding chair and

Tom's painting supplies. "I must leave you now, my friend. I will see you shortly."

Tom thanked him for his help and wished him a good day. He studied the canvas before him, grateful that he had already begun a penciled outline of a new creation—the sunshine he so admired that morning. He mixed yellow and orange paint onto the palette. It would do better for sales, he reasoned, to show his talent to the roving masses. He looked at the sketch on the canvas and the colors on the palette. *Yes, a day of sun, of God's glory, will do well.* He took up the brush and painted long streaks of gold and orange.

"What will that be?" a young voice inquired.

Tom glanced behind him and saw a boy standing there, licking a peppermint candy stick. "The sun, for now."

"I want to paint. Can I paint something?"

Tom hesitated. "You're welcome to paint a few streaks of yellow on the canvas, if you wish."

The youngster yelped with glee and laid his candy stick on the ground, unconcerned about the dirt and the bugs rapidly covering it. He took the paintbrush Tom gave him and, as carefully as he could, painted several stripes of color across the canvas. He then handed the brush back to Tom.

"Very nice, young man. You should do more painting."

"Thank you." The boy picked up his candy stick and flicked off specks of dirt and crawling bugs before popping it back into his mouth. "I'll tell Pop about you. He wants a painting for our house." The boy took off, calling for his father.

Tom focused on the painting, amazed by the careful attention the boy had shown. The young lad had treated the opportunity quite seriously, reminding Tom of his interest in paints at that age. He did pictures in many mediums back then, using brushes, sticks, sponges, even his fingers. His parents were none too pleased, either, that his fingers were always stained the colors of the rainbow. But to Tom, it was glorious fun.

True to his word, the boy returned, pointing out to his father what he had done on the canvas. The father smiled, thanked Tom for sharing his talent with his son, and bought one of the larger paintings in his stock. Tom glowed. *This is going to be a fine day,* he decided, barely able to contain his excitement. He readied the brush to paint more splashes of sunshine to match his mood.

"So this is the famous painter my cousin's husband speaks so highly of." A feathery voice greeted him. He glanced up to find a figure dressed in pure white and wearing a large hat decorated with blue ribbons. Tom caught his breath. She looked like an angel. He immediately laid down his brush and stood to his feet. "Hello, Miss…"

"Annabelle Loving," she said, extending her gloved hand for him to shake. "And you must be Mr. Haskins. I am Loretta Boshen's cousin from Boston."

"Yes, yes indeed, Miss Loving. I'm Thomas Haskins, a resident of this town."

Annabelle chuckled before turning to view each of the paintings on display. She paused before the one of the couple sharing the picnic lunch. "Why, she looks like me," Annabelle said with a laugh. "She's wearing the same dress! Have you been painting my portrait when I'm not looking, Mr. Haskins?" She laughed once more.

It was all Tom could do to stand still. He felt hot all over. "It was quite some time ago when I painted it…," he began.

"Goodness, can't you tell when I'm teasing?" She patted his hand. "I've never been to Bethlehem, you see, so it can't possibly be me. Unless you saw me in a dream." She stood tall, with her head tilted to the sky. The sun cast fiery rays on her pale complexion, igniting her hazel eyes so that they appeared like fine emeralds. "It is beautiful here. I think I would like to stay for a long time."

"Yes, Bethlehem is a fine place. Plenty to see and do. That's why we have visitors here most times of the year and why we have so many hotels, as well."

She lowered her gaze to meet his. "I would love to have an escort show me everything about Bethlehem. And you seem the perfect gentleman for such a job. I would like us to get together soon, I think. In a day or two, perhaps?"

"I…," he began and hesitated. "Of course. It would be my pleasure."

She smiled, nodded her head, and began to move off down the street. "Oh, and Mr. Haskins," she added, turning back. "Please put aside the painting of the picnic. I would like to buy it. Lawrence will come by later to pay you and pick it up."

"Yes, yes indeed. Thank you, Miss Loving. Good day." He watched her walk down the street, her white dress like a beacon of heavenly light that mesmerized him. Only when he sat back down in the chair and stared at the canvas of yellow and gold did he consider what had transpired. *Why all this attention now?*

He sighed in frustration. God's blessings indeed came in abundance, but now he sensed his quandary. He knew nothing about Miss Loving, yet he had agreed to go on an outing. He knew nothing about Sara McGee, yet he had invited her to come to

Bethlehem as a potential bride. What was he doing? His actions of late even made him dizzy. Were they only the responses of a desperate man?

* * * *

By late afternoon, Tom couldn't wait to gather his supplies and return home to peace and a quiet house. The parade, with all its fancy coaches decorated in ribbons, flowers, and banners, had long since passed. The visitors had begun to disperse to their respective hotels and guesthouses. Tom began taking down his easel, and as he did, he looked at the painting that had begun so cheerfully with the colors of yellow and gold. Now he wanted to add a stark contrast to it… like blue. Life was full of contrast, after all. Bright and dull. Light and dark. Answers and questions.

"So, I hear you were introduced to Annabelle." Lawrence had returned, appearing fresh and lively as if the day had just begun. Tom, on the other hand, felt just the opposite—weary and confused. "Here's the money Annabelle promised you. And she said you would be going on an outing soon. Great news, my friend."

"She mentioned it, but we have not yet arranged anything specific." He knew his stiff voice didn't sound confident or jovial, but he couldn't help how he felt.

Lawrence gave him a strange look. "She's perfect, isn't she? Intelligent, poised, artistic in her own way… Do you know she's also a concert pianist?"

"She is a very pleasant woman, and yes, very beautiful, but I don't know if…"

"How can you know anything right now? You've only just met. Go on a few outings. Get to know each other. I'm sure you will find her enchanting."

"I believe she will do her best to enchant me."

Lawrence frowned. "So you're already intent on putting up a wall? I don't understand."

Tom blew out a sigh. "I should have told you this earlier, Lawrence. Someone is coming here to meet me. I was encouraged by a couple to place an ad for a bride in a city paper, and a woman has responded."

Lawrence stared, his mouth gaping and his eyes wide. "You placed an ad for a bride?"

"Many men have done it—like those settling out West who advertised for wives who wanted to make new lives. And yes, a woman answered my ad. I should be receiving her letter any day now, telling me her travel plans. I already sent the money for her train fare."

"I see." Lawrence swiped the painting that Annabelle had purchased. "I wish you had told me about this earlier, Tom. I might have spared Loretta's cousin embarrassment."

Tom sensed animosity rising as he looked at his friend. "I should have said something to you. I was thinking about the parade today, and..." He paused. "Look, I don't know what will happen with this. I only invited her here so we'd have a chance to meet and find out if marriage is suitable for us. It's a time for us to get to know each other...just as Annabelle suggested the two of us do. There is no commitment."

"Then if there's no commitment, you can certainly enjoy Annabelle's companionship for an outing, can't you?"

Tom hesitated. "I'm not sure. I did agree to one, but..."

"Good. Glad you did." Lawrence tucked the painting under his arm and issued a swift farewell.

Tom wiped his hand across his face, sensing more than ever the dark tones of black and blue rather than the gold and yellow he'd painted. He rather felt like he had painted himself into a corner, inviting two women into his life like this. *What should I do now?* Even then, his conscience answered him: Keep to his commitments and pray that God would show him what to do.

Chapter Four

The following morning, Tom yearned for solitude after all the festivities. The events had wearied him both emotionally and spiritually, and it didn't help that sleep evaded him. He'd risen from his bed in the middle of the night to study the letter that described Sara Elisabeth McGee of New York City. Then his thoughts drifted to the alluring Miss Annabelle Loving, imagining her gloved hands holding one of his portraits and a coy smile on her face. He thought about that face and considered what shades of paint he would need to create the subtle tones, the rosy hue of her cheeks, the sparkle of green to her eyes. Then his hand tightened around the letter from Sara, who would soon tell him her arrival day. Two women plagued his mind and left him restless.

A knock came on the door with a sound more like thunder to his ears. Who would be calling this early? When he opened the door, Lawrence stood there wearing a broad smile. He waved the morning edition of the *White Mountain Echo* like a banner before Tom's eyes. "It's a sign, I tell you. And you can say nothing against it."

"Sign?" he repeated. The only sign he was having right now was the beginnings of a massive headache.

"Come and see what I mean, Tom. It's right here in bold print, for all of Bethlehem to take notice."

Tom took the paper and scanned the front page. There were drawings of the decorated coaches on display in the parade along with various descriptions. And then a caption met his stunned gaze:

Area Painter Captures a Buyer and a Heart. The article went on to describe his work and how the wealthy socialite Annabelle Loving had enjoyed buying a painting. "What is this?"

"It's your answer," Lawrence said with a joyful lilt to his voice.

"Who would write such a thing?" Tom supposed it would have been easy for a reporter to view them from a side street and take note of their conversation. Maybe Annabelle had been coaxed into giving a tasty tidbit for printing in the newspaper. Or maybe she sought out the reporter herself, looking for publicity.

"See how it advertises your work, by showing that you've captured the admiration of a fine lady visiting the area? My dear man, you will have customers knocking down your door for the next week. You'd better arrange your paintings and be ready to make a good deal of money. Fame and fortune is calling."

If fame and fortune provided the peace he sought, Tom would gladly sell every painting he had. But he saw no such thing coming from an article like this. Only further questions and confusion.

Lawrence made his way to the couch in the parlor, where he promptly sat down. He took off his hat and waved it in the air. "If I were you, I'd tell this other woman, the one who answered your ad, that you're seeing someone else right now. Wire a telegram at once. She can come another time—although I doubt there will be a need."

"Lawrence, we've already discussed this…."

"And you're a fool, Tom. Here you have the attention of a fine and attractive woman. You have the admiration of all of Bethlehem for your work. Now you want to close the door on this opportunity."

"I only want to know what's best for my future and the future of whoever it is I marry. I don't want to make a mistake."

"Your future…," he mocked with a laugh.

"Yes, my future. Even Mr. Astor said it was a necessary step in my life. And he knows business."

"Marriage is business?"

"Marriage is a partnership, isn't it? Helping one another. Loretta helps you in your business…."

Lawrence opened his mouth to respond, paused, and then asked instead, "Why are you so compelled to accept whichever woman answers some newspaper ad?"

"I'm not accepting her. I'm meeting her. I have no reason not to see this opportunity through. Besides, I only just met Annabelle. She may find she had no interest in me or I in her. How then can I close the door on this?"

Lawrence began to fidget with his hat, and the man's face reddened.

"Please don't misunderstand me, Lawrence. I'm sure Miss Loving is a fine woman. But I know nothing about her. We only just met."

"So you intend to woo two women at the same time."

Now Tom began feeling warm. "I did agree to be Miss Loving's escort. I did not agree to become her match for life. And until God seeds the word in my heart, I will continue seeking and asking. But I can't go back on my word to this woman from New York. She is expecting to come, and I won't disappoint her."

"But you can't lead Annabelle on either, you know. That would disappoint her, too."

"I…" Tom paused. "Would you care for some tea and biscuits?" he asked, hoping to change the subject. Anything to rid him of this perplexing discussion.

Lawrence relaxed and put his hat beside him on the sofa and agreed. At least Tom had managed to douse the flame of questioning. But how many in this circle would he either end up disappointing or making glad? Lawrence. Annabelle. Sara McGee. Himself. *God, why can't things be simple? I was a simple artist painting simple scenery. Now my heart's canvas is smeared with confusion. Reds. Blacks. Or rather black and blue, like welts on the flesh.* How he had the urge to paint what was in his heart right now. He would submit to that urge as soon as he fed Lawrence and bid him good day. This would not be a painting that depicted the natural landscape either, but a painting of his soul at this moment in time.

"You haven't answered my question about seeing two women at once," Lawrence continued when Tom arrived with tea accompanied by a plate of biscuits with honey and jam in small glass bowls.

"Lawrence, let me see where this leads. You should be grateful at least that I have a couple of ladies to consider. Only a short time ago you were mourning my bachelorhood. Perhaps God is showing that this lies in His hands and is not something of our own making." Tom flavored his tea with milk and sugar. "I wouldn't want it any other way. Not about something this important. I have to be certain."

"Tom, by the time you make up your mind, it will be too late. And the only thing you will be married to is your dried-out palette." He stood to his feet. "I'm sorry; I have to fit a customer with a suit. I will leave you the paper, and maybe you will reconsider."

Tom looked at the cup of tea on the table near where Lawrence had occupied the couch. Marriage was too important to treat so frivolously. But he saw no harm, either, in seeing each woman for who she was and recognizing her heart. Or in following his own heart in the matter, unmoved by the will of his friend.

He drank his tea. Perhaps another impartial voice was needed in this situation, one who could help him in this decision. Someone he trusted and who looked out for his welfare when he was younger. He strode to his desk where the writing implements awaited. In no time he had written a letter pleading for help. If he knew the receiver well, she would have no qualms in giving him her opinion and lending a sisterly hand.

> *My dear Claire,*
>
> *I hope this letter finds you well. The summer here in Bethlehem has been busy and, as usual, I missed seeing you at the Coaching Parade again this year. I hope you will soon make plans to visit, as I know how much you enjoy the fall colors.*
>
> *And with that I make a humble request. Your younger brother seeks an older and wiser sister's advice concerning marriage. Yes, I have two prospects, if you can believe such a thing possible....*

He went on to describe both Annabelle and Sara, though he had little to offer Claire. But surely it was enough to pique her interest. Perhaps she would even jump on the next train when she received the letter. Claire had never lacked for wanting to be involved in his life. And, like Lawrence, she often asked in her letters when he planned to settle down.

Tom sealed the envelope and put it out for the letter carrier. On the street, the workers were busy cleaning up after the weekend of merriment. Many of the guests remained in Bethlehem and would likely stay for the upcoming fall season, having found a place of refuge and quiet beauty here in the town nestled beside the grandeur of the White Mountains. He decided on a brief walk, allowing the sights of it all to refresh him.

"Why, you're the painter!" exclaimed a young couple on the street. The gentleman waved the newspaper before him. "You are, aren't you?"

"Yes, I am. I specialize in landscapes."

In a matter of moments, he had a buyer who was eager to come by the house later in the afternoon to see his paintings. Perhaps there was something to be said after all in having an article written about him and Annabelle Loving.

Mr. Davis, another friend, now came up. "How wonderful to see that you may have found yourself a lady friend, Tom. Both the wife and I were worried about you. Say hello to her for me."

Tom bowed slightly and thanked him. A few minutes later he received yet another cheerful greeting and exclamation over the article. Overnight he'd become famous all over Bethlehem, and it wasn't even because of his paintings, which he'd thought might one day make him famous. Rather, it was because of an article about a woman admiring his work.

Tom suddenly encountered the letter carrier, who greeted him. "Mr. Haskins, I was just on my way to your home. I have a letter for you right here."

"Well, I'll take it now, but stop by my house anyway. I have a letter going to my sister." The carrier nodded, and Tom continued down the street only to stop short when he saw the return address. *New York City.*

He barely heard the words of Mr. Cousins, the butcher, hailing him from the doorway of his shop and telling him how he had struck gold by discovering such a fine lady. Tom only stared at the envelope. He nearly ripped it open in the middle of the boardwalk but thought better of it. Instead, he tucked it away in his pocket to read in the solitude of his home. He didn't wish for any other curiosity seekers. This was for his eyes to read and for God's spirit to guide him.

Tom arrived home and settled into a wicker chair on the front porch. His fingers trembled as he undid the envelope. It was as if he were already a nervous groom. He looked over the elegant handwriting, the same handwriting as the previous letter. He checked the signature. It was signed "Mrs. Whitaker."

Who is Mrs. Whitaker? He settled himself to read the contents.

Dear Mr. Haskins,

I pray this letter finds you well. I am writing this on behalf of my dear friend, Sara McGee, who is looking forward to meeting you. She thanks you for the generous money and the train fare, which has been received. She asked me to tell you that she plans to arrive on Monday, October 6.

I know you will be pleased to have Sara as your wife. I've known her since she was little, and I can say many times what a sweet and caring young woman she is. Just the other day she found a lost child on the street and took him in until his mother was found. This caring heart will surely endear you to her. Sara has been through many difficulties, but it has not dulled her spirit or her love for the Lord. She is beautiful on the inside as well as the outside, and you will be pleased indeed that you have chosen her as your bride.

The note fluttered with the breeze until a sudden burst of wind tore it from Tom's grasp. Startled, he flew out of the chair and nearly tumbled down the porch steps in his effort to retrieve it. He had until the sixth of October to get ready for her—just a few short weeks. His heart began to pound, glad he had time to put his home in order to prepare for her arrival. He was glad, too, that he'd sent the letter to Claire in the hopes she might offer her assistance. There was time for her to come, as well, and help set up house for his new guest.

Rereading the letter, he now couldn't wait to meet Sara McGee in person. What a kind and devoted friend this Mrs. Whitaker was to speak on Sara's behalf and vouch for her character. Sara's love of life and others impressed him. And she loved the Lord like he did. Each sentence moved him, and he wondered if this could be the answer to his longing. The words described a woman that might indeed capture his heart, if she hadn't already. All good and godly signs that sent his hope soaring.

Tom entered his home, no longer feeling like a painting of confusion in swirls of black, blue, or red. He sensed the colors of joy instead. Sunshine yellow. Aquamarine. Gold. The hues of a coming autumn when Sara would arrive at the Bethlehem depot. And he would be there with plenty of room in his heart to receive her.

* * * *

Tom began mixing paints for his next project—a simple one, really. He sat on the front porch with the easel in place, ready to capture Main Street of Bethlehem on the verge of autumn. Next year he vowed to paint the Coaching Parade and some of the splendid coaches on display. He mixed shades of light orange and yellow to create the effect of a few trees already in autumn array. He was sure to sell this work as soon as it was completed. In recent days he found his stock rapidly depleted since the news article had come out in the *White Mountain Echo*. He liked the business, but it also made him nervous to have only a few paintings in stock. He wanted to be ready for any eager buyer who crossed his path.

He picked up the brush and dipped it into the paint, creating careful and precise splotches to resemble leaves on the white canvas.

"And what are you painting today?" asked a high feminine voice.

The brush trembled, creating a sudden smear of color. *Not again!* He remembered the episode at Franconia Notch with the injured couple. He looked around the canvas to see a delicate face staring into his, only darkened by the shadow of a parasol.

"Miss Loving," he blurted, looking to find a resting place for his dripping brush. "What a surprise."

A smile encompassed her face. She wore a dress of a woven checked pattern in moss green that matched her eyes, with puffed sleeves, a tightly fitting bodice, and a gathered skirt. Her hand held a large wicker basket. "I hope you didn't forget your invitation, Mr. Haskins. You promised to show me the sights of your quaint town here. I thought a picnic would be nice, too." She gestured to the basket.

Tom looked at Annabelle, the basket, and then his painting.

"But I suppose you're too busy for a visit."

"No, no, not at all." He had promised to be her escort, after all, even if painting beckoned to him at this moment. He must remain a man of his word. Besides, Annabelle had taken the time to prepare a lunch and primp for the outing. He could do no less than go. In fact, he felt honored that she thought enough of him to prepare a picnic.

"If you would first allow me to pack this up…" He carried the easel inside the house, nearly tripping over his feet.

When he returned to the porch and began to pack up his art supplies, she said, "Oh, I love the painting I bought from you the day of the parade. I plan to hang it in my room when I return home." She hesitated for a moment. "Do you think I look like the woman in your painting?"

He peered at her to see again her bright smile. Perhaps one day he would try his hand at painting a portrait, even if portrait painting was not his strength. "There are many similarities. You would make a nice portrait just by yourself."

She smiled coyly. "How sweet of you. If I weren't leaving so soon, I would ask you to paint it, Mr. Haskins."

She was leaving? Then why was she interested in this meeting? Why did Lawrence insist they see each other? He cleared his throat. "You're leaving so soon?"

"Unless you can offer me a reason to stay… This is a beautiful place, but I had hoped for other things."

Tom wondered what but kept his questions at bay. "I suppose it might be better for you. I'm sure you wouldn't like the winters. A good deal of snow and cold winds for months."

"Boston has winter weather also. Lawrence says he has the most beautiful sled. He said we could take it anytime we wish. That is…if you would like me to stay longer, Mr. Haskins."

Tom frowned and moved the rest of his supplies inside, unsure of how to answer her—especially with the note from Mrs. Whitaker still fresh on his mind. "Let's take a stroll down the street," he suggested, avoiding her question. He straightened his jacket and offered his arm, which she took. With his other hand he reached out and took her basket.

Along the way, Tom pointed out the many shops and fine hotels that had been a part of Bethlehem for a number of years. They arrived at the train depot where soon he would meet the woman who had responded to his ad, though he said nothing of this to Annabelle. They turned and walked back down Main Street and to the Maplewood Hotel with its vast acreage and numerous outbuildings. The hotel itself was an immense structure of stone, with fancy appointments and rich rooms—a grand gathering place for the rich and the favorite hotel of Mr. Astor. Tom always marveled at the architecture and immense size, likening it to some European castle.

They came to the edge of town, where a range of mountains framed the horizon. Annabelle withdrew from his grasp and headed for a patch of grass to spread out the picnic she had brought. "This is a pretty place." She gazed at the scenery and sighed. "I don't think I will leave quite as soon as I thought, Mr. Haskins. Boston, after all, has no such scenery…though I do love to look at the water. I often go to watch the boats coming in and out of Boston Harbor."

"I've never seen the ocean," he confessed, wondering what it would be like to paint such a scene, with the waves caressing the shore, a boat coming to port, and the flight of seagulls in mid-air.

"Then you must come and visit me when I return to Boston. Or we can make the trip together. My family would love to meet you."

She wanted him to go to Boston and meet her family? The swiftness of all this took him by surprise. Tom instead tried to turn his attention to the fine meal of fried chicken, biscuits, and applesauce. He allowed his appetite to rule him after offering a quick prayer and began to eat.

While he ate, Annabelle chattered about her life in Boston and how her parents wanted her to attend the fine conservatory there. "I do love playing the piano, but there are so many more important things to learn."

"An artist should never waste his or her talent," he said. "Maybe you should think about school. Becoming a skilled musician is a worthy pursuit."

"Oh, what an encouragement you are to me, Thomas. I hope you don't mind me calling you that. 'Mr. Haskins' seems so formal, whereas 'Thomas' is such a fine, strong name. And we know each other after all, don't we?"

He looked up from his lunch to find her staring at him with another smile poised on her lips. The image of her face appeared to draw closer to his the longer he stared, until they seemed but inches apart.

"An artist should use their gifts for God…," he began again, finding it difficult to speak.

"Maybe that's why I like it here. I feel like I belong. Bethlehem is such an artistic place, with the pretty village and grand mountains. It celebrates creativity with the Coaching Parade every summer. And of course there's you, a fine painter who captures it all on canvas. I adore that."

Unexpected warmth flooded him when her lips pressed against his. He nearly fell back, startled by the contact. "Miss Loving…," he faltered.

"Oh, it was nothing, Thomas. Merely a thank-you for your encouraging heart." She began packing up the lunch. "I know you have to return to your work. I've taken up a great deal of your time. Thank you for a wonderful afternoon."

Tom was speechless. As they walked back toward town, she talked of his giving heart and her desire to remain another month or two at least. All Tom could think was that her stay would then carry into the very time of Sara McGee's arrival to Bethlehem.

"But if I do stay, I won't be able to attend the observatory this semester," she added.

"You should not give up schooling, Miss Loving."

"Call me Annabelle, please. We're both ready."

"Ready?" His voice ended with a high squeak.

"For first names."

"Yes, yes, of course." Their arrival back to his front porch came none too soon.

"Well, I'll consider what you said, Thomas. Though I do think I might stay here longer. I'm starting to fall in love." She offered another good-bye before turning to leave.

Tom had all he could do to stumble through the door and into a chair. Sitting on the table beside his chair was the letter from Mrs. Whitaker.

How can you lead on two women like this? He remembered the voice of Lawrence, rebuking him. *You're a cad,* Tom told himself. Then he remembered the kiss. He had kissed a woman, and another woman was coming here to be his supposed bride! *What am I doing, Lord?* He traced the words of the letter once more. *I only have a few weeks left to put my heart in the right place. But where should it be?*

Chapter Five

....

Sara sensed a sadness as she gathered up her meager belongings and put them into a shabby carpetbag. It seemed hard to believe that in less than a week she would be leaving the city for a new and strange place. Mrs. Whitaker had all but demanded that she give up her life of roaming the streets, as she put it, and stay with them until the time came for her departure to her new home in New Hampshire. The thought of living with the woman in her fine home should have excited Sara, yet she felt anxious instead. Change could be good for a soul but also frightening. Everything she knew was about to take a drastic turn into the unknown. She wondered what would happen.

It took little time to pack up the photographs, her mother's teacup, a ratty shawl, and her paper-thin coat. Before she left the basement, she sat on the wooden chair to consider her life. How often she sat in this same chair and pondered her future. Now she was about to embark on a new journey. In a few short days she would be on her way by train to Bethlehem. At least the name of the town gave her hope, even if the thoughts of a strange man greeting her at a depot filled her with trepidation.

"What a wonderful adventure it will be for you," Mrs. Whitaker had told her just yesterday. She'd also announced to Sara her going-away gift: a suitable dress for the journey. How thankful Sara was for the older lady's provision. It brought tears to her eyes the way Mrs. Whitaker cared for her, much like a mother in many respects. But she had to wonder if she trusted Mrs. Whitaker's decision to force this man, Thomas Haskins, upon her. And to say she should become his bride, no less! He was a strange man living in a strange place. And she really wouldn't know what kind of man he was until it was too late.

Sara decided to have Mrs. Whitaker reread the letter that arrived the other day. She wished she had learned to read instead, so Mrs. Whitaker wouldn't have to do it. But she did recall some of Mr. Haskins's past letters. His anxiousness to meet her. His descriptions of Bethlehem by the grand White Mountains. His love of painting. And the most recent letter that talked about a big parade. Sara wondered what a parade in Bethlehem looked like. She had seen parades here in the city, of course. People dressed in fancy outfits, waving at the crowds lining the streets. Buggies and wagons that were decorated with ribbons and flowers.

Sara had insisted that she help craft the last letter to Mr. Haskins, which he would receive before her arrival. Sara dictated the words while Mrs. Whitaker wrote it out in her fancy handwriting. When she found her mind blank, Mrs. Whitaker encouraged her with new ideas. In the letter, Sara described more about herself, her hopes for the future, and how she came to know the Lord of heaven and earth. "He will want to know all these things," Mrs. Whitaker stated. "You want to assure him of your Christian faith, as that is something his ad requested."

"So he is a Christian gentleman?"

"Of course he is. I know his letters haven't said as much, but he would not ask for a Christian wife if he wasn't one himself."

Sara hoped she was right. How often she thought about the night she gave her life to the Lord, shortly after Mama's death. On the day when Mama lay at death's door, Sara remembered Mama's weak voice calling for her. Mama's cold hand reached out to touch Sara's.

"You must know how much God loves you, Sara," she said weakly. "He wants you to know Him and to live your life for Him."

Sara wasn't certain what Mama was talking about. Who was this God that supposedly loved her, despite her hard life and a mother ready to die? Why would Mama want her to know Him? Mama's cold hand continued to grip hers with surprising strength. "Let Him into your heart, dear Sara, and don't ever let go. He will lead you and guide you for His name's sake."

That night Mama slipped away to heaven. Though her passing was filled with sorrow, Sara realized there was also joy. Mama's face looked so serene. She no longer writhed in pain. Even a small smile sat on her still, blue lips. She had entered through heaven's gate to eternity.

Sara considered the ideas Mama had spoken of so ardently. She sought out Mrs. Whitaker so she could learn about God. From the woman's tender words and readings from the Bible, Sara's spirit sprang to life. She asked the Lord of heaven and earth to dwell in her heart, and He'd been with her ever since. Caring for her. Whispering to her in the night shadows. Giving her comfort and a place of refuge. And now providing a guiding light to this new journey laid out before her.

Sara gripped the handle of the carpetbag while surveying the dim surroundings. Little remained of the makeshift home but a few sticks of furniture, a candle, and the dust. "Good-bye, dear room," she said softly. "You've been a fine place for me. Now I'm going elsewhere, to a new place I know nothing about." She heaved a sigh and tried to contain the anxiousness welling up within her.

Slowly she made her way to the basement window, where she would climb out for the last time. No longer would she feel like some rodent scrambling in and out of the narrow window. As Mrs. Whitaker put it, the time had come for her to act like a young lady and not some ragamuffin of the street. And for the next few days, Mrs. Whitaker would give her lessons on such things. "Time to bid your old life farewell, young lady," the woman had said with a wink. "You must embrace the new things God has for your life."

Sara arrived at the bakery to find Mrs. Whitaker serving a customer. She waited patiently outside, staring at the stone buildings. She watched the people walking along the street, the young men and women pushing their carts, looking to sell their wares to roving customers. Women grasped children's hands as they hurried to do their shopping. Men in tall hats and suits talked with each other or walked with their gazes focused ahead, intent on their business. Wagons, carriages, and carts moved along, stirring up clouds of dust. These were the sights and sounds of a busy city she would not likely see in some far-off village nestled beside the mountains.

Sara gripped the handle of the carpetbag. What would it be like to see mountains instead of buildings? She had never seen mountains except in pictures. They appeared tall and commanding, reaching toward heaven. Some were dusted with snow. What an awesome sight it must be.

Sara nearly bumped into the customer leaving the shop. She curtsied and begged her pardon then noticed Mrs. Whitaker waving her inside. "Have you your things?"

"There's not much," she confessed, holding up the carpetbag. "It's mostly empty."

"I often wondered where you stayed, but you never told me." She led the way into the house behind the bakery and stopped beside a closet that had been converted into a tiny room for Sara.

"You would have disapproved, Mrs. Whitaker. No one knew where I stayed. Not even the owners of the building." She hesitated. "I did wonder if I should have told them I was there. I was trespassing, after all…."

"Tsk, tsk. At least you're out of that place and no longer living a life of secret. I told Mr. Whitaker that I'm taking you in for a few days, but you must take care to keep out of sight in the evening. You know he has a bad temper."

"I will. I'm used to being very quiet at night." She often wondered why Mr. Whitaker didn't possess the charitable heart of his wife. What was it about people that moved some to pity for those less fortunate and others to look on them with stony indifference? It was like the contrast of day to night…or maybe the light of God shining in one compared to another that lacked it.

Mrs. Whitaker soon appeared with a dress, and her face lit up with a grin. "Here's the present I promised you."

Sara fingered the material of a soft blue that looked much better than what she was wearing. "It's very pretty."

"I kept it from when I was young. I know it's not the style of the day, without the puffed sleeves and straight skirt, but it will wear well until Mr. Haskins buys you new dresses. And he will, I'm sure."

"I hope so." Sara tried to contain her rising doubt. What would he say when he saw her? Would he be like Mr. Whitaker and take one look at her, pronounce her a foundling, and send her on her way? She dismissed the thought and went to try on the dress. The cuffs reached to her knuckles, and the hemline dragged on the ground.

"Oh, dear. I guess we are two different sizes. I haven't much time to take it in, either." Mrs. Whitaker fingered her chin. "No matter. I'll hem it, at least, so you won't step on it. It will have to do."

"It's better than anything else I have. Thank you."

"It's just enough so you can be properly introduced. A man should not be looking on the outside anyway but on the inside. And I daresay that Mr. Haskins has already fallen in love with you."

Sara stared at her, aghast, at the meaning of such words. "How can you say that?"

Mrs. Whitaker helped her draw the dress up and over her head. Sara quickly donned her tainted gray dress over her cotton slip and drawers.

"Don't you remember the letter he wrote back?"

"I was hoping you would read it to me again." Sara couldn't help the smile that escaped.

"How I wish I had the time to tutor you in reading and writing. But we will have to let Mr. Haskins do that as well." Mrs. Whitaker went to fetch the latest letter while Sara sat, waiting expectantly on the small cot that had been made up for her. Mrs. Whitaker returned and promptly began to read.

Dear Mrs. Whitaker and Sara,

Thank you very much for your recent letter. I was happy indeed to hear more of Sara and her kind heart. How we need such people to bring joy into the lives of those who have none. And I must say I'm eager to meet her and share that joy. You have written wise words when you say that beauty is found inside. That is the beauty I cherish, too, and hope to share. Please don't think anything of Sara's circumstances, for they

mean little in the picture of life. We will have much to do and
share when we meet. I look forward to it.

"Don't you see? It's a letter of love, for certain, and by one who looks at the heart."

Sara could hardly keep from climbing to her feet and doing a little dance around the room. "It's wonderful." She looked at her own disheveled dress. To know the man's gaze would not be on her tattered garment but on her heart sent songs of thanksgiving rising up within her. "Please, may I hold onto the letter?"

Mrs. Whitaker obliged. "I'll get the dress ready so you can wear it on the train. There are only a few days left."

Sara didn't want to think of losing Mrs. Whitaker, another one dear to her heart. It would be like the horrific pain of losing Mama all over again. No, she must think of the bright future before her, lest the tears blind her and she be too sad to even step onto the train. She would think of the blessings that lay ahead, a bright new land, a gentleman to woo her, and a new destiny to grab hold of and never let go.

* * * *

The day had finally come. Sara tried to hold tight to those blessings waiting for her, even as she winked back the tears. Mrs. Whitaker stood on the platform, dabbing her eyes every so often with a handkerchief. Soon the train would pull out of Grand Central Depot, and Sara would be on her way to the town of Bethlehem. The name of the Savior's birthplace. The mere thought brought calm to the emotional tide surging within.

The whistle sounded. Sara pressed her face and palms against the cool glass, her fingers spread open. Mrs. Whitaker nodded, again dabbing her eyes. "I love you," Sara said aloud. She thought Mrs. Whitaker's lips formed similar words of affection before she waved good-bye.

The cars jolted. The whistle blew again, and the train began to move. She held tight to the carpetbag sitting on her lap. This was really happening to her. She was leaving New York forever to embrace a new life.

One last train whistle bid the occupants of New York City and Mrs. Whitaker a final farewell. Sara wiped another tear from her cheek and whispered a prayer for peace. Now began the long trip to the wilds of northern New Hampshire. A few days ago, inside the shop, Mrs. Whitaker had found a friend who'd been to this state. The woman talked of cold, snowy winters and mountains unlike anything she had ever seen.

"But what about the people?" Sara asked. "Are they nice?"

"They are people from the cities, mostly. They come for a holiday, just like we did. There are plenty of hotels, and the air is so fresh. Many claim it cures them of their ailments."

But the people? Sara wondered again. Instead, the friend talked of the fine hotel she had stayed in, the Sinclair or something like that, and the attentive staff. Sara still didn't know anything about those who dwelled there. Nothing but the letters written by Mr. Haskins. He had sent one final telegram via the telegraph office, telling her what he looked like so she would recognize him. He was tall with dark hair and no mustache. He would have on a tweed coat and hat. And he would be carrying a gift tied with a blue ribbon.

The idea of a gift intrigued Sara. What could he be giving her?

"Most likely it will be your ring," Mrs. Whitaker had said with a laugh.

"It can't be! Not so soon! We don't even know each other. He couldn't possibly be ready to propose when I step off the train."

Mrs. Whitaker just shrugged, the smile still painted on her face. "You never know. A man like that might very well be eager to settle down. I've given him plenty of cause to consider it, after all."

But it also gave Sara cause for concern. Would he like the dress from Mrs. Whitaker, even if it were old-fashioned for the time? Would he like her face? Her hair? Mrs. Whitaker spent tireless hours trying to comb the snarls out of her hair and tying it up in thin strips of cloth to form curls. A few curls came forth the following morning but soon fell out, leaving Sara with stringy hair once more. Mrs. Whitaker then tried to force it into a bun, but again it fell out when the breeze took hold of it. Sara felt her hair now, wishing something could be done to make it presentable. But it was too late. Mr. Haskins would have to be satisfied with the way she looked. And what did it matter anyway? He had already stated that the inside of a person mattered much more than appearances.

Sara listened to the *click-clack* of the train wheels along the metal track. They were in the countryside now. The vivid colors of autumn greeted her at every turn. Between that and watching fellow passengers walk back and forth to other cars, there was plenty to look at and ponder. Opposite her, a young woman about her age sat engaged with a book. Again Sara wished she knew how to read. It bothered her more than her unruly hair or her meager wardrobe.

"Did it take you long to learn to read?" she finally asked the girl.

She looked up. "I've been reading since I was seven."

"Seven! How can you do such things when you're so young?"

"I went to school."

Sara had never gone to school. Mama had taught her some, but she was gone most days, working. She'd often claimed that all Sara needed to learn would come from living day by day. Sara did know a little counting by making change for Mrs. Whitaker at the bakery. She knew the words *bread*, *cake*, and *cookies* from the signs posted on the wall.

"Don't you know how to read?" the girl asked.

Sara shook her head. "I didn't go to school. My mama worked."

The girl thought about it and then, to Sara's surprise, came and sat beside her. She took out a piece of paper and a fountain pen and began drawing letters. "I'll teach you. I want to be a teacher. That's why I'm going to Boston. I'm Lydia, by the way."

"Sara." She tried to still her eagerness in having Lydia show her the letters of the alphabet by concentrating on the lesson.

"If you sound out the letters, you can put them together to make words. All you need to do is learn the sounds of the letters, and the rest will come."

Before the train had pulled into the next station, Sara had mastered the vowels and even some of the consonants. Lydia praised her ability and said she was a quick learner.

"I hope Mr. Haskins will provide me a tutor," Sara said.

"Is he your relative?"

"Oh, no. I am going to New Hampshire to be his bride."

Lydia sat back, startled. "You're going to be his bride?"

"I'm answering an ad he put in the paper. I'm on my way to the town of Bethlehem."

Lydia stared as if unable to comprehend the idea. "I don't believe he asked you to be his bride. Most men in the North expect a woman to at least know proper etiquette and reading and writing. He must be very understanding."

Sara felt uncomfortable. Mr. Haskins didn't know all her limitations. Would he be angry with her when he found out?

"But we are getting a good start here," Lydia added with a smile.

When Lydia bid her good-bye at the depot in Boston, a brief sadness gripped Sara's heart once more. But God was good. He'd sent kind people to help her. And it confirmed His hand on this new path in her life, even if she didn't know the proper etiquette of a fine Northern lady.

Once the train left Boston, Sara watched the scenery change as they headed north. Tall pine trees dotted the landscape. Churches with pointed steeples and white framed houses tucked away in small villages met her curious gaze. There were even covered bridges over rivers. She must tell Mrs. Whitaker all about it as soon as she arrived. That is, if Mr. Haskins would help her craft a letter. Or maybe the maid he had in residence would help. Surely he had a maid or another woman at the house. It would not be proper for her to be alone in the home with him until they were married.

After a few hours, Sara caught sight of something materializing on the horizon. The dark ridge became more defined as the train proceeded. The ridges colored red, gold, and orange grew taller and more rugged. Mountains came into view, one after the other, majestic in appearance. Sara sucked in her breath at the sight. To witness this beauty went beyond description. How blessed she was for the opportunity. She was grateful to Mrs. Whitaker who arranged it all and to Mr. Haskins who placed the ad.

A whistle sounded, and the train began to slow. Sara clung to her shabby carpetbag.

"Bethlehem!" the conductor called out in a hearty voice.

It didn't dawn on her until she stood to her feet how tired and achy she felt. And hungry, too. The bread Mrs. Whitaker had given her did not last. But she put those things aside to bask in the moment. She was here at last!

"I hope my carriage is waiting," she overheard a woman comment. "The last time I came here, there was no carriage to take me to the hotel."

"I'm sure there will be," said another.

Everyone leaving the train appeared to be clothed in their finest and wearing large hats. Sara looked at the women dressed in fancy frocks overlaid by long wool coats. They all looked alike: well-to-do folk from Boston and elsewhere.

Sara felt a blast of cold air enter the train as she inched her way toward the exit. She took out her shabby coat. She didn't know it would be so cold here for October. Once she put the coat on, she immediately felt out of place, but it couldn't be helped.

Sara stepped onto the platform. Carriages littered the area. Drivers assisted passengers and their baggage. She looked up and down. The busyness of the depot surprised her. She expected such activity in a city like Boston or New York, but not here in some village in distant New Hampshire. She felt lost in this sea of people calling for assistance and finding their carriages, intermixed with bags and trunks.

Suddenly her gaze fell on two men in the distance. One held what she thought was a gift, though she couldn't be certain. She waited for a smile. A word of greeting. A hand extended to welcome her and escort her to a place where she might recover.

Instead there came an expression of greeting she never expected....

Chapter Six

....

After weeks of anticipation and glancing at the calendar, the day of Sara's arrival dawned bright and sunny. It was a glorious day indeed to receive the answer to the ad Tom had placed. It seemed so long ago when he took up Edward's suggestion to place an ad in the newspaper. To Tom, it felt like a year had passed. But in his time of waiting, the communications between him and Sara had gone well. He'd received several engaging letters from the beautiful and talented woman, so much so that he couldn't wait to be introduced. He only hoped a woman of the city would like living here in this mountainous region. It would be different for her. He hoped the strangeness wouldn't prove too much. He would do his best to alleviate her discomfort.

A few days ago, his sister Claire had arrived from Springfield, Massachusetts. She had received his letter and was all too happy to help prepare for the new arrival. But, as he expected, she also questioned his judgment.

"I hope you know what you are doing, Tom," she said, carrying her bag while Tom handled her trunk.

"That's why you're here. To help me figure everything out."

The smile Claire gave sealed her willingness. At the house, she pointed out things to him that needed to be done, especially to prepare the room he had reserved for Sara.

"You can't expect a fine lady from the city to live in here," she'd complained, surveying the decorations. "You must buy a new coverlet for the bed and proper bed curtains. A wardrobe for her trousseau would be nice, and she will need a table with a large mirror and cushioned seat."

Tom had obliged, making whatever purchases were necessary to turn the guest room into a place suitable for a new bride-to-be.

"Of course, once you're married, this room will turn into a guest room again," Claire added with a knowing gleam in her eye. "And then we will redecorate your room from a horrid place of a bachelor to one more suited as a marriage chamber."

For some reason, her comment had made Tom uncomfortable. Perhaps if he didn't feel so awkward… Of course the woman who was coming was presumably his future bride. But an uncertainty prevailed whether they would end up at the altar. Especially with the memory of Annabelle Loving's kiss fresh on his mind. And now his friend's words reverberated in Tom's thoughts: *How can you lead on two women like this?*

Tom adjusted the collar of his shirt and smoothed his hair. He pushed the reservations aside to bask in this new day. He held to great expectations for this meeting. Was there such a thing as love at first sight? If so, then there would be no more questions about two women tugging at his heart. The matter would be settled.

He heard the rustling of a skirt. Claire passed by in the hall, carrying a huge vase. He peered out to see that she had filled it with asters and goldenrod.

"A lady must have flowers," her voice echoed down the hall. "Dear brother, there is so much for you to learn. You've been a bachelor for far too long."

"And when do you plan on finding a suitor, Claire?" he asked. He saw her glance back, her face turning rosy.

"Never mind about that."

"Ah, so there is someone? Tell me."

"I had been seeing the son of a prominent lawyer." She stepped back to view the vase she'd placed on the bureau and then fiddled with the bouquet, positioning it this way and that. "But he wanted to go further in our relationship. I would rather take my time and not go headlong into things."

"That's why you're here, too," Tom volunteered. "I also want to take time to prepare for what lies ahead."

"I don't know what you expect me to do. After all, you're the one who advertised for a bride. I assume you will marry her and go on with your lives."

"It's not that simple, Claire. I want her to feel comfortable about the arrangement. And I suppose I want to feel comfortable, too. We need to get to know each other and see if this is God's will. And she comes from the city. She won't be used to life here and the way things are done. It'll take some time. That's why I asked you to come. I'm sure she'll feel more comfortable with another woman here to help her adjust."

"I suppose you're right. I don't want you to rush into a wedding ceremony unless you're certain the choice is correct." Claire nodded in satisfaction at the bouquet and glanced around. "She should be pleased with what we've done in this room. It looks much more suited to a woman of means from the city."

Tom couldn't help but agree. There was something to be said about a woman's touch when it came to decorating a house. While he tried his best to keep up with it, Claire had done more in a week than he had done in years. The home sparkled from a thorough cleaning. It felt fresh with new sets of curtains, slipcovers for the chairs, and a tablecloth adorning the table. It was a place to call home. Sara couldn't help but be impressed.

He looked in the mirror, hoping he appeared as shiny and new as the home. Claire had pressed his shirt. Every hair on his head was in place. His face was freshly shaved. Even his fingernails were clean.

"You haven't much time," Claire reminded him. "The train comes in less than a half hour. Do you have the gift?"

He picked up the gaily wrapped present: a miniature painting he had done of Bethlehem's own little mountain, Mount Agassiz. He thought Sara might like it as a reminder of this place, especially if things didn't go as planned. He chastised himself for doubting this new venture. *Perhaps she will cherish it as a token of her new life.* Instead of the stone and brick of the city, she would see God's majestic mountains. She couldn't help but be refreshed in mind and heart once she saw this grand place.

"Did you eat breakfast?" Claire asked, following him downstairs. "I made pancakes. They are on the stove on a plate."

He went to the stove and grabbed a pancake, folded it over, and began eating it. "I'm sorry. Like you said, time is short."

"I'll see you soon." She gave an encouraging smile, one that lifted his confidence as he headed for the door. While he eagerly anticipated this day, a part of him also dreaded it. What if Sara disliked his looks? What if she thought him too tall? His hair too dark? Or if she didn't like the birthmark on his cheek or the way his nose turned upward from his German descent? He pushed the thoughts aside. He had painted himself the best he could in his letters. Not that he described things well by the pen. He was a man of the brush, revealing what he saw through his paintings.

Even with the eagerness of the day, his steps felt unsure. Looking at the gift he carried, Tom wondered if this was the right decision. But he had no choice now. He must go through with it, as he informed Lawrence many weeks ago. He had done all the planning and invited Claire here to help. Despite the unexpected attention of Annabelle Loving, he would proceed and see what unfolded.

Suddenly, he found Lawrence hovering near the entrance to the train depot. He stopped, wondering what his friend was doing there. His jaw tightened. No doubt Lawrence was interested to meet the competition for his wife's attractive cousin.

"This is the day, isn't it, Tom?" Lawrence announced.

"What are you doing here?"

"To lend support in case you don't want to go through with this."

"Why wouldn't I?"

"Come now. I'm sure you're having doubts. I can see it in your face. If you wish, I will gladly go in your stead and tell this woman that things have changed. If you give me the money, I'll even buy her train ticket back to New York. Though she might need overnight lodging at a guesthouse."

Tom stared and shook his head. "You're mistaken, Lawrence. I have no reason to send her back. Besides, I'd have no peace in doing something like that, even if she's not the right one for me."

Lawrence's eyebrows rose. "What's peace in one's soul than doing what's right? And it may well be the right thing to send her back before things are made worse."

Tom thought on this. Could things turn for the worse if he allowed her to step off the train and enter his home? Then he thought of Edward and Margaret. Their confidence. Their love. "No. I'm going through with this."

Lawrence said no more. Tom knew Lawrence thought him foolish. The things of God did not matter to his friend. Tom had tried at different times to share the gospel with Lawrence, but now was not the time for proselytizing. He had a woman to welcome into his life. A strange twitching in his stomach led to a steady ache. The pancake turned to stone inside. His hand rubbed the nagging sensation.

"Nervous, my friend?"

He shrugged and wiped beads of perspiration from his forehead. Even his palms were slippery. He hoped the gift wouldn't be damaged.

"So is Claire settled?" Lawrence now asked.

"Yes, and I'm glad she's here. She helped ready the house and the room where Sara will be staying. I know nothing about such things." He inhaled a sharp breath, realizing his words sounded tremulous, like a bridegroom on his wedding day. "Were you nervous when you first met Loretta?"

"We were friends for a time, if you remember. We both sang in the church choir. But yes, I do recall some nerves afoot when I first asked her to lunch at the café. I was afraid she would say no."

Tom wondered if that was his problem. He feared Sara would refuse him, a simple artist of the mountains. He considered his gift. Maybe he should have bought her a fine necklace instead. Or a lace handkerchief. "But she didn't refuse you."

"No. In fact, she asked when we might see each other again." He chuckled. "I said to myself, a woman as forward as that is the right woman for me. And she's done well to train me in what I need to do. Finding a good woman is an excellent thing, indeed."

"That's biblical, Lawrence." *Now I just need to know if that good woman is Sara McGee.*

"The train was early today," Lawrence said suddenly, pointing to the travelers congregating on the platform and walking around the station.

"Oh, no!" Tom looked at his pocket watch. To his dismay, he realized he was twenty minutes late. How could that have happened?

"So many tourists are here, ready to enjoy the fall colors." Lawrence paused and glanced around at the busy scene. "I'm not sure how you'll find your lady, Tom. Do you have a description?"

"No, not really. I know she has blue eyes and brown hair." Ladies bedecked in all their finery stood on the platform, many of them looking as if they were expecting someone. Some wore magnificent hats. Others were inquiring about carriage rides to the nearby hotels. A few were clad in less-than-appealing frocks, looking ready to beg coins from passengers or ask for work.

Lawrence laughed long and loud. "What a fine selection, Tom. Maybe you should be introducing yourself to each of them." Suddenly, Lawrence walked up to a woman standing nearby. She wore a large hat over her brown hair; her fine dress was covered by a decorated coat. "Begging your pardon, miss, but are you by chance Miss Sara McGee? The one who answered an ad for a bride in a New York paper?"

"I most certainly am not!" She whirled from him.

Tom contained a chuckle, mixed with uneasiness. How would he find Sara among this flock of peacocks? He'd told her how to find him, but she'd said nothing about what she would be wearing or anything else.

Out of the corner of his eye, he noticed a young woman standing to one side. She was dressed in a shabby coat with holes, buttoned by a single button in front, and stared at him with large blue eyes. Loose strands of stringy brown hair framed the thin, pale face. Her hand clutched a carpetbag. She looked lost or maybe was just looking for money. His feet shifted toward her.

"Well, I don't know what to say, Tom," Lawrence announced loudly, arriving back from his quest. He tipped his hat and scratched his head. "I asked around, but no one is answering to your lady's name of Sara. I guess she decided not to come after all. Probably for the better."

The beggar girl took a few steps forward at this point. She held the carpetbag in front of her like a shield. When Tom caught her eye again, she looked away.

"I'll still wait to make certain. What time does the next train arrive from New York?"

"Not till this evening." Lawrence whirled. "Why are you staring at us, young girl? Are you looking for money?"

"I—I," she began, before turning and shuffling away.

Lawrence shook his head, laughing. "I suppose I should humor her and give her a few coins. Can't be selfish, can I?" He rummaged in his pocket for some coins.

A strange sensation came over Tom as he watched the girl drift away. *It can't be...can it?* Could that possibly be Sara McGee? But how? She was supposed to be a fine woman of the city, nicely dressed. Or was that the portrait he'd created in his own imagination? "Young lady, please wait!" he called out to her.

"What are you doing, Tom?" Lawrence asked, following him.

"I think she might be Sara."

"What? Impossible. That homely thing—it can't be!"

"Stop," he said to his friend. "Don't say that."

"You must stop with this nonsense, Tom!"

Tom ignored him. Suddenly the girl turned, a look of horror overtaking her face. "Please wait!" Tom called again, his steps quickening. "I need to ask you something."

"What's the matter?" The question came from one of two men nearby whom Tom knew from Bethlehem.

"I'm trying to talk to that girl in the worn coat," Tom said breathlessly. "I think she's the one who answered my ad."

The men stared at each other and burst out laughing. "Were you that desperate, Tom?" said one.

"As if Bethlehem doesn't have plenty of fine ladies to choose from," added another.

The young woman whirled. She opened her mouth as if to cry out, but then several people stepped in front of her, blocking her from his view. And suddenly she was gone.

Tom halted. Now there was little doubt in his mind that the young woman was indeed Sara.

Lawrence was panting by the time he caught up to Tom. "I see she's gone."

"She's not gone. She's hiding, I'm sure. And I can't say I blame her. Look at how everyone treated her."

"It's better this way, my friend. Let her go. She's not for you anyway. Leave her some money to go back home and be done with it."

Tom stared at the gift he still held. Never did he envision that a destitute woman of the streets would answer his ad. In his dreams he saw a fine woman like the Astor family, elegant, beautiful, willing to leave the city to come to his doorstep. A fine woman like Margaret who had answered Edward's ad.

Instead, Sara McGee arrived in rags and carrying a dirty carpetbag. What was he to do? He couldn't send her back. She was in desperate need. If nothing else, he must try to help her and be the Christian man he liked to profess to others, like Lawrence. "I have to find her," he decided. "I can't leave her wandering around some strange town. I invited her here to Bethlehem. Her circumstances don't matter. She deserves the same chance at life as if she were wearing pearls and lace."

Lawrence shook his head in disbelief. "Tom, I don't know what to say. I thought I knew you."

"I thought I did, too. But I think I'm about to." *In a way I never thought I would.*

Chapter Seven

....

Dear Lord, what should I do? The pain in Sara's heart was so great,
she felt her heart might fall out of her chest to the cold ground below.
She sat behind the large tree that occasionally sprinkled her with
golden leaves while she sorted out her predicament. She should have
realized that coming here was a mistake, especially after seeing the
fine ladies and gentlemen on the train and at the depot. Maybe if she
had thought to remove her ragged coat and fix her hair, none of this
would have happened. Now Mr. Haskins had seen her for who she
was—a vagabond of the streets. And she'd been the object of scorn by
the man's beastly friends.

Sara's fingers touched the hair that had fallen out of the chignon
Mrs. Whitaker had tried to fashion for her. She'd never considered
keeping herself presentable on the streets of New York. In the days
leading up to her departure, Mrs. Whitaker had become fastidious
with her looks, as if she had some premonition of what might
happen. Sara now stripped off the offending coat, jamming it into her
carpetbag beside her other dress. She looked down at the frock Mrs.
Whitaker had given her. Compared to the other women, the dress
was out of style, even if it was the finest dress Sara had ever owned.
She wanted a new life, yes, but could she find it among people clothed
in fine linen? What about other worthier things? Like kindness? Or
goodness? Mercy? Love?

At least the artist of Bethlehem, Mr. Haskins, appeared to reach out to her in a kindly manner, even if she disliked the snobbish friends who accompanied him. He looked nice, too, from what she had seen of him, dressed as he was in pleated pants, a jacket, and a hat. He carried a gaily wrapped gift that sparked her curiosity. When Mrs. Whitaker had read Mr. Haskins's last letter, it seemed he looked upon the good qualities of a person…those things of worth that existed on the inside. The very things lacking in Mr. Haskins's friends. If only she could trust him.

Sara knew she needed to make a decision. A quick check of her small purse showed that she lacked the money for a train fare all the way back to New York. She had enough to take her to the next station but not even enough for Boston. She sat for the longest time, trying to reason out her dilemma, when she heard a voice.

"Miss? Are you hurt?"

The question startled her. Sara looked up to find a young couple gazing down at her. They were like so many she had seen at the train depot, finely dressed and no doubt here for a visit. The woman held an open parasol; the man carried a cane with a gold head in the shape of a lion. Sara couldn't help but stare at it.

"She must be hurt," the man said to the woman. He offered Sara his hand. "Let me help you up. Did you hurt your leg?"

"Remember how I once hurt my foot?" the young woman said. "There are so many rocks about that it's difficult to walk."

"I'm not hurt," Sara managed to say.

The man withdrew his hand, leaving Sara on the ground, and the couple stared first at her and then at their surroundings. "Are you hiding from someone?"

Sara didn't know what to say as she slowly came to her feet, brushing away the grass and leaves from her skirt. How could she explain that she was avoiding a man who had placed an ad for a bride—because she'd answered it? "Yes," she finally admitted, knowing she couldn't lie. "I came by train. I thought I was waiting for a friend, but he wasn't one after all. I don't have much money, you see...."

"How awful!" exclaimed the woman. She nudged the man, who immediately withdrew a purse out of his pocket. "Please, take a few coins."

"No, no. I won't beg."

They stared back with wide eyes as if confused by her response. "But you must be in need."

"Well, yes. Actually, I was hoping to find some work. Do you know of a place that might need help? Like a maid?"

"There are many hotels and guesthouses. The finest is the Maplewood Hotel. You should have no trouble finding work. Why don't you check there?"

"Thank you."

Again the man tried to give her money. Sara finally accepted a few coins. They smiled, pleased, and bid her farewell. She could at least buy some bread with it. Perhaps there existed an abandoned cellar where she could live for the time being. A chill coursed through her, but she refused to put on the paper-thin coat. It did little to shield her from the autumn weather anyway. Instead, she smoothed out her hair with her fingers and vowed to stand straight and with her head erect. She would try to look her best, or at the least, like a woman with a goal in mind. And her goal right now was seeking employment so she could afford the train fare back to New York where she belonged.

Sara wished she'd asked the couple where this Maplewood Hotel was located. She returned to the depot, hoping to find the answer. Thankfully she saw no sign of Mr. Haskins or his rude friends. The depot appeared empty, as most of the visitors had secured carriages to their destinations. She walked up to the ticket window and asked about the Maplewood.

"Go down the street here, miss. Make a left on Main and walk about two miles. It's a huge place on your right. Can't miss it." He peered over the tops of his reading spectacles. "I can arrange for a carriage, if you'd like. It's quite a walk from here."

"Oh, I'm used to walking. I come from New York City."

"That's a long ways from here. We get plenty of folk visiting here from the cities. Are you up for a visit to see the fine autumn leaves?"

"I'm here for a short time." She hesitated. "Do you, by chance, know a Mr. Thomas Haskins?"

"Sure I know Tom. No finer painter anywhere. In fact, I saw him at the depot today. He was looking for someone." The man peered once more over his spectacles. "You wouldn't, by chance, be the one he was looking for?"

"I…" Again came the urge to lie, but she refused to submit. "Yes, but it's better he doesn't find me. I'm not what he expected, you see."

The man laughed. "None of us are, darling. What was he expecting to find?"

"I'm not sure. Someone in a fine dress, no doubt. A lady of means, not one who has come under hard times. Everyone here is so well-off and sure of themselves."

"Well, you look just fine to me and quite sure of yourself."

She hesitated. "I only wonder…about him. What kind of man he is."

"Aw, Tom's a fine gent. For him to be looking for a woman, that's good news. He could use a good wife and not one who puts on airs. The ladies around here come and go too quickly. They're only here for a spell. So I'm sure it's a fine thing you've come to visit him."

Sara felt her cheeks warm. "Well, thank you for your help. But, please, don't tell Mr. Haskins that I was asking about him." She didn't wait for his reply but turned and made her way toward Main Street. It didn't take long to see that Bethlehem was tiny compared to the giant city of New York. Small, quaint shops stood intermixed with fine hotels and guesthouses. From the middle of Main Street, Sara could already see the end of the town and the vast acreage existing beyond it. But what caught her attention were the mountains surrounding the town—tall, rocky, a few even dusted in powdery white snow. A chill of excitement burst through her. She stopped to take it all in. None of Tom's descriptions had prepared her for this. It was as if she had stepped off the train into another world.

Sara continued. Few people were on the boardwalk. The grumbling in her stomach alerted her to the noon hour, when everyone was at home or the hotels enjoying a meal. She should try to find a bakery that sold bread, if such a place existed here. Bethlehem did not have much in the way of shops. After a bit, she located a small bakery tucked away on the street. Gathering her courage, she entered and encountered the sweet aroma of freshly baked goods. Another woman stood at the counter buying her daily bread. She looked at the woman serving the bread, wishing it was Mrs. Whitaker with her friendly smile. Instead the woman observed her with eyes that weren't unkind…but neither were they friendly.

"May I help you?"

"I'd like a roll please." Sara showed her the coin.

"One roll? Is that all?"

"Three would be fine. And I guess a ginger cookie." Sara knew she shouldn't buy so much, but the woman's perturbed expression spurred her to spend more than she should. She enjoyed the fine morsels anyway and continued her journey along the boardwalk, admiring the many hotels and guesthouses. People here certainly had money. The homes were well-maintained and pleasing to the eye. Nothing was in disrepair. No peeling paint or sagging shutters or broken fences. A shame, she thought, that people's attitudes did not match the mood. Sara tried to quell her emotion with Mama's words, which warned her about the plant of bitterness taking root. *"Once it gets a foothold in your heart, it's hard to pull up. So never give it a place but seek forgiveness."*

"Sara?" A gentle voice greeted her at the next corner.

Sara looked toward the voice and saw the same man from the train depot. His stature reached to the sky. She gazed up at his face that blocked part of the sun, feeling small and insignificant in his presence.

"Sara?" he said again. "You are Sara McGee, aren't you?"

She nodded and wiped her face, hoping she had brushed away the crumbs from her sparse meal.

"I'm Tom Haskins. I'm the one who placed the ad in the newspaper." He offered his hand but not the present he held in the other.

When she did not acknowledge the greeting, he allowed his hand to rest at his side. "I'm very sorry for what happened at the depot today." He paused when a few people walked by and gave them curious looks.

At least Tom's friends were not with him. Still, she didn't know how to respond.

"It's difficult enough coming to a strange place, only to be greeted in such a way," he continued. "I ask for forgiveness."

"It's all right." She fumbled with her carpetbag. "I mean, it isn't all right what some of those men said, especially if they are your friends, sir."

"Those who don't know the Lord say and do foolish things."

Sara stepped back. Mrs. Whitaker was right. Tom Haskins was indeed a Christian man, and a devout one at that. With such knowledge, he deserved forgiveness and more. After all, how many times did she need forgiveness for some folly?

They stood there for an awkward moment. Finally, Tom offered his hand once more, this time inquiring if he might take her carpetbag.

"It's not heavy. There isn't much in it," she confessed.

"Is your trunk still at the depot?"

"I… This is all I brought. It's all I have in the world."

He glanced down the street toward the depot, half expecting her trunk to still be on the platform. He opened his mouth to comment but closed it and took her bag instead.

"I'm sure you weren't expecting someone like me," Sara offered. "I don't look like everyone else here."

"No matter. I'm sure you were expecting someone different to greet you and offer a proper welcome to Bethlehem."

His swift response caught her off guard. "Well, yes, I suppose I was." She admired his fine appearance. He wore the same outfit she had seen him in earlier—the tailored trousers and jacket—and his hair was combed smooth. He carried himself with confidence, nodding at people who greeted him along the way. He was well-known here. If only she looked more presentable, walking by his side. They continued in silence until he inquired about her trip.

"It was fine," she answered. "Boston reminded me of New York."

"You stopped in Boston?"

"I switched trains there."

"Oh yes, of course. I don't travel much. I've lived here all my life. I've never been farther than the White Mountains, actually, although my sister has asked me to visit her in Springfield many times."

Sara wished their conversation wasn't so formal. Maybe it wouldn't be if she didn't feel so awkward after everything that happened at the depot. "Mr. Haskins, if you could suggest a place to stay, I plan to find work at the Maplewood Hotel or someplace like that. I've already seen several hotels here. I'm sure there's plenty of work."

He stopped, turned, and looked her over with a set of dark brown eyes and eyebrows drawn together in concern. "I'm not sure I understand. Why do you need to find work at a hotel?"

"Well, I know I'm not what the letters painted me to be. As an artist, I'm sure you like realistic portraits."

"Actually, I paint landscapes. And, yes, I do like realism. But I'm sure the letters are accurate. You're from New York, aren't you?"

"Yes."

"You've obviously lived a hard life. You love children. You work hard."

"That is all true."

"Then there's nothing to be concerned about. You don't need to find another place to live. Besides, my sister Claire would be very disappointed. She's worked hard all week to make the home presentable. In fact, she traveled here to help me and to serve as a chaperone."

"I'm sorry; I didn't know." Sara fell silent. "Of course, if you've gone to so much trouble, I will gladly stay in your home. I didn't want to be a bother."

"I only hope you won't let what happened this morning keep us from getting to know each other. After all, that's why you're here, isn't it?"

"Yes, yes, of course." Sara's steps felt lighter after that. The previous inhibitions began to melt away. Though Tom was still a stranger, they did hold to the same Christian faith. That fact alone should be strong enough to overcome the differences and spark a ray of hope.

She watched his large hand tighten around the handle to her carpetbag. She liked strong hands willing to take control of a situation. She wondered then what it would feel like to have his hand hold hers. But it was far too early to think about such things. There was so much to learn, after all. She hoped his sister would help ready her for the future and all that Tom Haskins expected of her.

"You will have your own room," Tom went on. "Claire had it made up special. The room used to belong to our parents before they passed away. It's been a guest room ever since."

"I lost my mother, too. She and I were very close. She died of some sickness."

"Mine did, too." He grew quiet.

Talkative and then quiet. A man of deep thought who considered every word before it spilled from his lips. A fine quality to possess. Sara chuckled.

"What's so funny?"

"You're someone who likes to think before he speaks. Mama used to say I should do that. Not to say things unless I considered them first. She said it was a good trait to have."

"It's not one I tend to use very often," he confessed. "But thank you for the compliment. I do hope you come to like it here, Sara. Though it might seem strange at first, give it time."

Warmth filled her. Perhaps, as Tom said, God indeed brought her here for a purpose. This was a time to let the old die and embrace the new, no matter how strange it seemed. Now if only she possessed the strength to embrace it. *Dear God, make me able. Make me acceptable here. Make me the person You want me to be. And may I be the one Tom will love forever.*

Chapter Eight

....

Tom wondered what the future held. The clock had struck noon before he finally found his newspaper bride wandering the streets of Bethlehem. He knew she had been chased away by the comments of his so-called friends, a moment that embarrassed him greatly. He swiftly rebuked the men in his company for their pitiful remarks. Lawrence had given him a sharp look and claimed he had errands to run before taking off. The other men returned sheepishly to their duties. Tom remained at the depot, looking for the young woman in the torn coat and tendrils of brown hair swept up by the wind. She should have been easy to spot among the finely dressed women, but she had disappeared.

For a time he lingered at the depot in the hopes that she might reappear to claim her trunk. If she were anything like Claire, personal possessions meant a great deal to the woman. But time went by and there was no sign of her. Finally he set his hat back on his head and began a slow walk toward his house. If he returned without Sara, Claire was certain to ask what happened. And he could just imagine her response.

"You let those ruffians you call friends mock that poor thing? Tom, what has come over you? How could you invite her here and then let those men say such things?"

He made the decision before God that if he found Sara, he would be nothing short of a gentleman. He would reach out to her and help her—and keep his friends a bay. It was the least he could do.

Finally he saw Sara coming out of the bakery, carrying the shabby carpetbag. She did not run away when he confronted her. In fact, she seemed relieved in the way she sighed and looked at him expectantly. Now they walked together down the boardwalk, saying little. Tom saw neighbors stare in curiosity from their front porches and along the street. A few said hello. Bethlehem was a friendly town, even if Sara had received little of it so far. He hoped in time she would see what a pleasant place this was and that he was pleasant, too.

"You must be hungry," he finally said. "I know a café that serves excellent food. We'll have to go back—it's not far from the depot. I can see about a coach…."

"Thank you, but I'd rather walk. I walked all the time in New York."

He wondered what sights and sounds she must have seen living in a city like that. He'd heard only vague descriptions about it from Mr. Astor, along with some photographs. Large stone buildings, some high like a mountain. Streets teeming with merchants, carriages, shoppers, businessmen. And people like Sara with little money who were all alone. She'd said her mother had died. Did she have any relatives to speak of, save for this Mrs. Whitaker who seemed to care for her a great deal? Did she have anything at all?

"So you've lived here all your life, Mr. Haskins?"

He liked her inquisitiveness. She was a young woman of determination and strength, even if her outward appearance didn't seem to match it. "Yes. Bethlehem was smaller than it is now. Since my youth, many hotels and guesthouses have been built."

"I was wondering why there are so many hotels here. It's such a small town. I don't see how there are enough people to fill them."

"Bethlehem lies on a hill of sorts where the air is fresher. Some say it makes them feel better. Visitors also come to see the mountains. There's no better place to spend a vacation. I should take you on a walk sometime to the fine view from the top of Mount Agassiz. It's Bethlehem's own mountain."

"You mean actually climb a mountain?"

"Of course. Or you can take a carriage to the top. Mr. Corliss offers carriage rides. It has a fine tower where you can see the mountains of the Franconia region. A superb view, worthy of a painting, actually." He realized then the promise he had made to Mr. Astor to paint such a scene. He must do it soon.

Sara paused in her steps as if to comprehend his descriptions. "A mountain with a tower on top? Like a stone tower?"

"Actually, it's made of metal with a huge platform. A perfect viewpoint. I'll take you there sometime." Tom was surprised by the eagerness in his voice. The thought of showing Sara such a site with all its charms excited him. There were intriguing aspects to Sara's character, he admitted. Her rustic appearance lent herself to someone who wouldn't mind an interesting adventure. He would not have to worry about impressing her with pampering and fine things, unlike Annabelle Loving, for example, whom he couldn't imagine climbing to the top of a mountain. Sara would appreciate nice things and a nice view after a hard life in the city. And he would enjoy giving it to her.

They arrived at the café and were greeted by several patrons indulging in afternoon tea. When they looked up and stared at the newcomer with interest, he saw lines of discomfort creasing Sara's face.

"They look at me as if I came from some foreign land," she murmured, settling into a seat opposite him at a small table.

"They're only curious. I didn't tell anyone I was having a guest. Don't be concerned. And by the way, the apple pie here is excellent." He gave her a menu. She seemed to look at it, but then her gaze drifted to the curtains framing the windows, the customers at their tables, and then to a large jar of hard candy sitting on the counter.

"You must have already seen something good?" he asked with a smile.

"Uh…yes, I suppose. This looks like a fine place to eat. I didn't eat out at all in the city. Maybe only a couple times in my life."

The server came by and asked for Sara's selection.

"What kind of soup do you have?"

"It's at the top of the menu there. See? The chicken vegetable and cream of potato."

She searched about but then, noticing the server's look, offered a sheepish smile and a flushed face. "Oh yes, thank you. I'll have the chicken with vegetable…a nice piece of bread with butter on it…and the apple pie."

Tom added, "For two." He noticed the pleased look on Sara's face when he ordered the same, as if she searched for acceptance. He tried to imagine himself in her shoes, as a visitor to the busy city of New York, and how lost he would feel. Without a doubt, the greeting she received when she first arrived must have sent any confidence fleeing. He prayed for the words to say that would help restore what was lost. But what does one say to a young woman—especially one who had come because of a newspaper ad? *Thank you for answering the ad. We will take this one day at a time, with God's help…? By the way, answering an ad doesn't necessarily mean a wedding ring…?* He shook his head, trying to quell any negativity right away.

"You seem upset, Mr. Haskins."

Her observation caught him to the quick. "As a matter of fact, I was trying to think of something to talk about." He chuckled in discomfort.

"Well, since I never really introduced myself, I'll start. Hello, I'm Sara Elisabeth McGee. I'm eighteen, nearly nineteen. I grew up on the streets of New York." She held out her hand.

He couldn't help but chuckle again as he shook her hand. It felt tiny and soft in his rough one. "Pleased to meet you. I'm Thomas Haskins."

"I've lived in the city all my life," she continued. "My father left us when I was a baby. My mother raised me until she died, and then Mrs. Whitaker became like a mother to me."

"This Mrs. Whitaker seems like a kind and generous woman."

Sara's eyes glistened, muting the blue color of them. He admired that shade. It was often seen in the early evening sky, and he occasionally painted it into certain landscapes. "Yes, she is the sweetest person one could know. She's the one who saw the ad in the paper and told me I should come here. She wrote the letters, too."

"She wrote the letters? Why didn't you write them?"

Sara played with her napkin, folding it into small squares. "I–I'm not very good with words. Mrs. Whitaker knows what to say."

"Indeed she does. She painted a glowing portrait of you, I must say."

"I suppose you're disappointed that I'm not what she described."

"I didn't mean it that way. I meant that she has a way of describing things that are interesting to read. I can tell she is very fond of you. It must mean a great deal to you to have her for a friend."

"I owe her so much. My life, really." Sara paused. "After all she has done for me, I need to try to make things work here. That is, if you will give me a chance, Mr. Haskins. I only hope I don't irritate you too much."

Tom had opened his mouth to reply when the server arrived with their steaming bowls of soup, wedges of bread with melted butter, and two slices of apple pie. Tom offered a quick blessing for their food and then unfolded his napkin to tuck inside his shirt. Sara dispensed with the napkin, took up her spoon as if it were a club, and began slurping down the soup with gusto.

"This is good," she said with her mouth full.

Tom stared before averting his gaze. He tried not to let the sight and her sounds aggravate him, but it was plain to see that Sara had no training in table manners. He concentrated on his own meal until Sara picked up the bowl and drank the contents in large gulps. Setting it back on the table, with bits of noodles on her chin, she sighed in content.

"That was so good. I never had such good soup."

Tom tried to keep his attention on his meal but couldn't help noticing the customers in the café staring at them. Whispers began. Sara then attacked her pie, eating with such large mouthfuls that the pie all but disappeared in a matter of moments.

"I guess I was hungrier than I thought," Sara said, sitting back in her chair. She then belched. "Ah, that's better."

The woman at a table beside theirs leaped to her feet. Tom recognized her at once and grimaced. The dignified Mrs. Childress and town gossip. "Why, I never! You could have used a napkin, my dear girl, instead of eating like some pig. Humph." She tossed her head and strode out, her sheepish husband following behind.

Sara sat with her mouth open and her eyes large. Her nervous gaze settled on Tom. "I–I'm sorry. I wasn't thinking. I don't eat in places like this and…"

"It's all right." He tried to finish his meal but found his appetite squelched. The looks, the manners, the life. He could already picture the look of consternation on Mr. Astor's face if he presented Sara as his bride. How could he possibly marry her? She was not Edward's wife, Margaret, even if she came by way of an ad. And she certainly wasn't Annabelle Loving. He admitted he expected a lady to arrive, one of grace and purpose, to be a partner in this lonely life. God must have meant for other things to happen. Perhaps to offer Sara the finer things of life. Maybe to have Claire help with proper table manners and other etiquette of a lady. To offer a fine dress and shoes that fit. Things that Sara would not have, living on the streets of New York.

"I'm sorry," Sara apologized again when they left the café. "I don't know why that lady was upset."

"The ladies around here aren't used to seeing…uh"—Tom hesitated—"someone enjoy their food so much. The ladies here take dainty bites. They use napkins. They hold a fork a certain way. They don't drink out of bowls."

"I'm expected to learn all that while I'm here?"

"It might make you feel more comfortable if you did. After all, this is not the streets. It's different from what you know."

"I've been seeing the differences all day. I wish I had known all this would happen. I might have stayed where I belong and with people who don't care how I eat."

"That's a selfish way of thinking, isn't it?"

His challenge sparked a look of defiance in her eyes. She stopped and put her hands on her hips. "I'd rather be selfish than prideful, Mr. Haskins. I'm not the same as them. I happen to be different. And maybe that isn't a bad thing. Unless you believe it's necessary that I think and act like everyone else."

"Selfishness and pride go hand in hand, Sara. One can still be prideful without means as well as with. You can learn a few things so you don't draw attention to yourself. You can try to fit in with the gifts God has given you."

Sara resumed her pace alongside Tom. She said nothing more and, for now, silence accompanied the journey down Main Street. Tom hadn't anticipated debating a fiery young woman about manners, but Sara had a mind of her own. Doubts plagued his heart. Nothing was as it seemed. And he didn't quite know what to do about it, either.

He was glad to arrive home and find Claire sweeping the front porch. He couldn't wait to give Sara over to Claire's capable hands. Claire would know what to do.

Claire brushed back a swathe of hair from her face and offered a smile. "Why, hello. You must be Sara."

Tom was pleased to see Sara offer her hand in a congenial manner. She did know some propriety, thankfully. Maybe all was not lost.

"I'm Sara McGee from New York City. And you are?"

Both Claire and Sara looked to Tom. He felt a warmth rise in his cheeks. "Sara, this is my sister, Claire, from Springfield, Massachusetts."

"I came through Massachusetts on my way here," Sara said. "I changed trains in Boston."

"I'm sure you must be exhausted from your trip. Come in, and I'll fix you a cup of tea."

Tom watched in relief as Claire took charge of the situation, gesturing Sara into the house. He praised his plan in bringing his sister here to help, especially after what he'd witnessed this day. Sara would need careful tending and a compassionate hand, and there was no one better in that respect than Claire.

He slipped into a wicker chair on the porch to think about his circumstances. After a few minutes the door opened, and Claire came out. "She's taking tea and is interested in a bath. I see she is not well-off, is she?"

"No, she's not."

Claire's eyebrow rose at his stiff reply.

"I mean, she's not what the letter said," Tom continued. "That's not to say she doesn't have interesting traits. She has an excitement for life. She is determined and quite strong-willed. But she eats her food like a railroad worker and has nothing to her name but what she has in that carpetbag. She's unkempt and ill-mannered. She looks as if she has lived on the streets, which, in truth, she has."

"So what does all that mean, dear brother?"

Tom looked at her. "What does that mean? It means we can help her. Give her a home for the time being. Maybe some lessons. Introduce her to a new way of life. Buy her some clothes and feed her good meals. But she is not someone I could ever think of marrying."

"You're deciding all this rather quickly, aren't you?"

He felt his agitation rising. "Did you know she ran away from the depot? I spent over an hour searching for her."

"Why did she run away?"

He hesitated. "You know Lawrence. He made a small comment. A few men snickered."

Claire huffed. "Then she did the right thing. How dare those men make fun of her when she can use all the love we can give. And you, of all people, allowing them to do such a thing."

Tom was cut to the quick. "Claire, I told them it was wrong. And I'm trying to make the best of this situation."

"Good, because you need to stop thinking about your needs and think about hers for now. All you've done the last few years is paint. I know you cared for Father for a time, but now it's time to care for another one in need. Painting some brightness in another person's life, like Sara's, may be just the situation you need in your life." She rose and entered the house, her dress swishing before the door closed.

Tom knew Claire was right. He'd accused Sara of being selfish, but he was the selfish one. He'd wanted the perfect woman to step off the train this morning. Someone like…Annabelle, with refined features, in a large hat and fancy frock to match. Sipping a teacup, looking demure. From the letters, he'd thought Sara was all that and more. So much for expectations. Sara surprised him as much as the reactions surprised her. He wondered if he'd made a mistake by heeding the advice of some couple he'd met months ago in the woods.

Help me do what's right, Lord. He added with reservation, *Not my will…but Yours be done.*

Chapter Nine

....

It didn't take long for Sara to realize that something was wrong with Tom Haskins. He'd never said anything to lead her to this conclusion, but his actions spoke a great deal. After a life on the streets, Sara relied on intuition when it came to people and their responses. Once she had offered to help a man care for his ailing mother. He quoted her a sum of money that nearly made her faint. With that kind of money she could well afford more of a dinner than simple bread and cheese. And maybe even some other things as well, like a new dress. But Sara should have listened to the uneasiness in her heart. The man was not as he appeared. No sooner had she left the store with him than he attempted to have his way with her in a dark alley. Sara managed to escape, but the incident alerted her to never trust a stranger but, instead, to trust in the Lord.

Looking at Tom Haskins that morning at breakfast, she didn't think him a terrible man like the one she'd met that fateful day in New York. On the contrary. Tom had been most giving of his home and his possessions, even if he never gave her the gaily wrapped gift that day at the depot. She wondered who it was for. There was another side of Tom, though, the side filled with displeasure, knowing she was not what he expected. Many mornings he offered few words but only stared at the newspaper. Claire squirmed in her seat, acting as though she wanted to say something but did not.

When he left to perform some errands, Claire sighed with great heaviness. "I don't know what's the matter with him. You've been here nearly a week, and he hasn't so much as spoken but a few words each day."

"He wishes I were someone else," Sara said softly.

"Probably that Loving woman," Claire said with a huff.

"What loving woman?"

"Nothing. She's just...uh, there are wealthy socialites visiting the area. But I don't think he likes her or anyone. I don't think he wants to get married."

But Sara's mind was on the other women of Bethlehem, who would be clothed in fancy dresses and large hats, strolling along the boardwalk, gazing at the colored leaves, flirting with the men, or giggling with other women. To Sara, the women she had seen here all sounded like a gaggle of geese that had lost their way and ended up on the rooftops. Mrs. Whitaker used to tell her they were just resting before they took flight to places she had never seen. Maybe like the geese, the women found rest in Bethlehem before returning to a difficult world.

"I would leave right now if I had the money for the train fare back to New York," Sara announced.

Claire cast a look at her as she carried the breakfast dishes to the kitchen and placed them into a large metal tub. "Now don't start that again. You don't look to me like the kind who gives up easily."

"I wanted to when I first came here," Sara reminded her. "It was foolish, though, to run away like I did. I shouldn't have done it. Your brother will never forget it." *Or the episode in the café with my manners...or my dress...or anything else disagreeable...,* she thought miserably.

"God has His reasons, and there's a reason He chose you to come here. You may be able to accomplish something no one else can."

Sara thought on this, wondering what she could possibly accomplish here in this place. She knew she must cease comparing herself to the wealthy women inhabiting the hotels and think instead of the special woman God had created her to be. He must have a reason for arranging this through Mrs. Whitaker. He had a destiny for her life.

Sara gathered up the remaining dishes. She swiped up the leftover strawberry jam she noticed on a plate and licked her finger. The tangy sweetness left her feeling giddy, like a small girl enjoying summertime.

Claire saw it and stole the plate, shaking her head. "We really need to begin our lessons. You've had some time to settle in now. We can start with some simple manners, such as licking a plate or the silver, as I've seen you do too many times after meals."

"Why should I waste such delicious jam? Or the last piece of bread? In New York I dare not waste anything. And to have strawberry jam, why, it would be like having the finest chocolate."

"That may be, but here we have plenty of strawberry jam and other things. God has brought you to a place of abundance, Sara. You must learn to accept that abundance and not use it as an open door to ill manners."

Sara felt her vexation rise but managed to settle herself. After all, Claire had defended her before Tom when she first came. Claire had arranged her room, a sanctuary that went beyond Sara's wildest dreams. And Claire had even said she'd hoped for a sister to take tea and go shopping with. The irritation vanished as Sara quietly took away the rest of the dishes, even though she had to restrain herself from scooping up the morsel of biscuit she found resting on a butter plate.

"Today I'll show you a fine supper we like to make," Claire said, following her into the kitchen. "New England boiled dinner."

"A boiled dinner for supper?"

"We take a big pot and boil up a nice spiced beef with potatoes, carrots, and turnips. Doesn't that sound delicious?"

"I suppose. I never heard of boiling a whole dinner, unless it's like a soup."

"In many ways it is like soup, only better. You need an apron so you don't ruin your dress." Claire handed one to her. "But first, we're going to make a fine rye bread to go with it. We will make the boiled dinner later."

"How did Mr. Haskins ever live without your help?" Sara mused, tying on the apron.

"I've often wondered that." Claire chuckled as she searched for ingredients.

For the next hour, Sara watched Claire carefully mix the ingredients to make the brown bread flavored with caraway seeds to go along with the boiled dinner. Sara recognized the bread as a variety that Mrs. Whitaker sold in the bakery, but she had never helped make it before. How delighted the older woman would be if she learned Sara was making bread. And even a boiled dinner. Sara would have to write and tell her.

Sara's face warmed. How could she write her? She had yet to tell Claire or Tom she could neither read nor write. It would place a further stigma on her character and be something else for Tom to frown upon and the citizens of Bethlehem to snicker over.

"Sara, the dough! Please knead it a few more minutes. We don't want it to dry out."

Sara worked the dough the way Claire had shown her, giving the sticky mass a quarter turn and then pushing it down with the heel of her hand. When Claire proclaimed it ready, Sara placed the dough in a bowl to let it rise. They spent the rest of the day doing chores around the house, returning to the kitchen to prepare the loaves and put the meat to boil in a kettle. Claire then set Sara to work peeling potatoes.

"I can see now why wealthy women have servants," Sara remarked. "There's so much work to running a household. I could never do it all."

"But you must have done some cooking, sewing, or cleaning in the city."

Sara wondered how much of her life in New York she should share with Claire—like that she subsisted on bread and cheese for the most part, or occasional soup if Mrs. Whitaker invited her over to her house. That once in a while she would be fed a ripe apple or some other gift as a thank-you for helping others in need. That her dwelling for a year had been a forgotten room in a cellar with no stove, let alone a kitchen.

"Didn't you?" Claire pressed.

"I didn't do much cooking. Especially after Mama died. Since it was just me, it made no sense to do cooking and sewing."

"I remember you telling me that she died and you were left alone to fend for yourself. How sad."

"I have a picture of Mama if you would like to see it." Sara hurried off to her room and the possessions she'd shared with no one, save Mrs. Whitaker: the cup and saucer that belonged to her mother and, of course, the faded photographs. She returned with her prized items to show Claire.

"What an honorable woman," Claire said of the picture, to Sara's delight. "I see you both share the same little nose and large eyes."

Sara touched her nose. Was it too small? Did Tom dislike the shape of her nose along with everything else?

"How did she die?"

"From the fever. I think about her all the time."

"I'm sure you do. My parents are gone, too. This was their house, you know. I can still see Mother in the kitchen, making the same dinner we're making today. We never forget what our mothers taught us, do we? They remain with us throughout our lives."

Sara liked Claire more and more as they talked. Maybe they could trust each other with dreams and secrets, things true sisters often shared. A tear glazed her eye at the thought. How lovely that would be. Even if things did not work out with Tom Haskins, to have a sister would be a better gift…and even more reason for her to be content with this new life in Bethlehem and not give any further thought to returning to New York.

But the thoughts quickly vanished when Tom appeared for dinner. Sara proudly placed the bread on the table, but he took little notice of it. She wondered if anything she did would impress him. Perhaps nothing, unless she looked and acted the part of a wealthy socialite. When Claire began dishing up the dinner, he inhaled the aroma. "My favorite," he declared.

"Sara made the bread," Claire added.

Tom's gaze now focused on her. It was the longest he'd ever looked at her, but it seemed to be more out of amazement than appreciation for what he was seeing. "You made the bread?"

"I hope you like it."

"I'm sure I will. It looks good." He cut a healthy slice and slathered it with butter. He took a huge bite, chewed, and swallowed. "Excellent."

Sara glowed with pleasure. She claimed her seat opposite him, cut her own piece of bread, and began to eat.

"I like to put my napkin here, Sara," Claire said gently, showing Sara how to unfold her napkin and place it in her lap. "That way, it keeps spills from staining my dress, and I can use it to wipe my mouth."

"But why not have it right beside your fork?" Sara asked. "It makes no sense to have it in your lap. It's too far away to be of any use. And when it gets soiled, it can stain your dress."

Tom began to choke on his bread and hastily grabbed his glass of water. "I must say, Sara has a good point."

Claire gave him a sharp look, and he returned his attention to his meal.

Sara took up her fork to stab the potatoes and carrots. Claire had shown her how to hold her knife and fork correctly to cut her vegetables and meat into small pieces. In Sara's mind, the slow process would leave her food cold by the time she was done readying it to eat. Why not enjoy the food while it was hot rather than imitate these silly pleasantries? She forced her opinion aside for Claire's sake and cut a piece of spiced beef into five equally sized squares.

"Very nice," Claire said with a smile. "So what did you do today, Tom?"

"I had Ginger shod," he said, slicing a second helping of bread. "And I showed a painting to Mrs. Hunter, who wanted it for her guesthouse."

"How nice. Have you enjoyed the painting Tom did for you, Sara?"

Sara put down her fork. "Painting? What painting?"

Claire looked over at Tom. "I thought you were going to give her the painting, Tom. At the train depot, remember? You had wrapped one up for her."

His face colored. "I was going to, but things didn't go quite as planned."

Sara looked from Tom to Claire. So that was the secret gift in his possession that day. Tom had planned to give her one of his paintings. Why did he change his mind? Did he think her unworthy of his work? Not fit to be by his side, no matter how hard she tried? Tears stung her eyes. Her throat closed over. She stirred in her seat, and the napkin floated to the floor. "I'm sorry you dislike me so," she said stiffly. "But I am trying…."

"You're doing a wonderful job, Sara," Claire interrupted, casting a steely-eyed look at Tom. "I'm sure Tom just forgot to give it to you. It's been busy here."

"Sara, I don't dislike you. I promise I will give you a painting when I have another one to give."

"Another one?"

"You see, that painting was the one Mrs. Hunter bought today." He hesitated. "I didn't think giving you a painting was a good idea right now when you need more important things…like a dress and shoes." He shifted in discomfort. "I'm sorry." He withdrew from the table and slipped into the drawing room.

Sara tried to comprehend this, even as Claire gave her a sympathetic look. "I'm sure Tom thought perhaps you would think a painting useless when you've had little else in your life. I know he didn't mean to hurt your feelings."

"I'm sure," she said, gathering up the dishes and avoiding Claire's gaze. She didn't want her to see the tears gathering in her eyes. Perhaps he was right that she needed other things. But giving her the painting, sharing in his life's work as an artist, his God-given talent, might have signaled a ray of hope for a future relationship.

But what was she to expect, after all? Tom had seemed unwilling to share much of anything since the day she arrived, except for his home and his sister. The inner man, the one God created, remained shut up, unwilling to be exposed, at least before her eyes. That fact renewed the flow of tears as she carried away the bread she'd made. *Dear God, I wish Tom would reveal a part of himself to me. I wish he would think of me as a woman he can share his life and dreams with and not a waif of the streets. Help him see me with new eyes and an open heart.*

* * * *

A few days later, Claire offered to take Sara shopping for a new dress and shoes. Sara all but ran out the door at the invitation. At last she might finally capture Tom's attention, if she looked the part of a grand lady of Bethlehem. While she did appreciate the dress Mrs. Whitaker had given her, it was sadly outdated from the dresses she had seen worn by other women and Claire. She yearned for the regal skirt, the puffy sleeves, and the distinct waistline. And, of course, a large hat to match.

When Sara arrived at the boutique, the clerk wriggled her nose at the garment Sara wore. "I can see you do need help, young lady. That style has not been worn since the war!" She took a dress from a display. "Now here is a lovely frock. Go try it on behind the curtain there."

When Sara stepped out from behind the curtain, the clerk frowned. "I had no idea she was so thin and pale," the lady remarked to Claire. "This will not do."

Sara sighed. Yes, she was pale and spindly, the perfect portrait of a destitute woman. The clerk came with another garment. After three more tries, Claire agreed to an emerald green dress that both she and Sara liked.

"I wish I could pay you," Sara said wistfully while Claire counted out the money to purchase the dress and a matching hat.

"It's a gift, didn't I tell you? Since Tom decided you might prefer a dress, it's your welcome-to-Bethlehem gift."

"I do like it very much." Sara couldn't help but think of the original gift of the painting Tom had planned to give her. But this was far better, she decided. It gave her a sense of belonging and the confidence to walk among the other ladies along the town boardwalk. And she prayed it might turn Tom's attention to her.

She wore the new garment as they walked out to the street. Claire had other errands—to post a letter and visit the butcher for meat. Observing the way the ladies strolled with their head erect and posture straight, with arms curved graciously, Sara mimicked them. The women they passed nodded to her. She nodded in return and smiled to herself. *I'm one of them!*

When Claire came out of the butcher shop with a package of meat, she gazed at Sara. "You look happy."

"Oh, Claire, I am happy. I don't know how to thank you. I'll do whatever I can to help you at the house, I promise. Somehow I'll make this up to you."

"You don't have to do that, though I always welcome your help. I'm just glad you like the dress and hat."

"I do. It makes me feel so…"

"Why, hello, Claire!"

Sara glanced past Claire to see a woman strolling up behind them. Sara performed a small curtsey and nodded her head. The woman gave Sara a brief nod then turned her attention to Claire.

"Annabelle, how are you?"

"Just fine. I was hoping to see that charming brother of yours around. He owes me another outing, you know. In fact, it's his turn to suggest a time and place. I took him on a fine picnic last time. But since then, we've barely spoken."

Disbelief swept through Sara. Claire's gaze darted from her to Annabelle. "I'm sorry; he hasn't mentioned anything. He's been quite preoccupied with our new visitor here. May I introduce Tom's houseguest, Miss Sara McGee from New York City."

Sara could see an icy glaze form in Annabelle's eyes. "A houseguest? Are you a cousin, perhaps? It seems all the cousins are visiting these days. I'm the cousin of Tom's friend, Lawrence. Lawrence's wife, Loretta, actually."

Lawrence. The dreadful, inconsiderate man who had ridiculed her at the depot. "Your cousin's husband is the rudest man," Sara said stoutly.

Annabelle stepped back, her mouth dropping open. "What?"

"A most inconsiderate man. You may tell him for me that he had no right to interfere with Tom's business or my own. And he would do well to stay away, thank you." Sara whirled and walked off. She heard some vague comment from the woman about her inexplicable rudeness, followed by Claire's apology. Then Sara heard the patter of footsteps quicken behind her along the wooden walkway.

"Sara, how could you say such a thing?" Claire said breathlessly, suddenly walking stride for stride beside her.

"I meant every word, Claire. Her cousin's husband was the one who interfered with our meeting. He said terrible things about me, along with other men at the depot. And he planted doubt in Tom's heart."

"Sara, you should know better than to pick a quarrel with someone like Annabelle."

"Why not? You saw what she said. She already has her sights set on Mr. Haskins. And maybe he does on her, too."

"Tom has no interest in her. But you must try to at least be polite, even if you aren't fond of what you're hearing. You're new here. It's best to try to make friends, not enemies."

Sara turned to watch Annabelle walk off, her feminine form swaying in such a manner as to call all attention to herself. "Look at that. Who can't help looking at her?"

"You don't know my brother, then. I hope you will soon."

Sara hoped she would, too, but that hope seemed to dim the longer she stayed here. She feared it might one day vanish altogether.

Chapter Ten
....

Tom trotted along the country road on his horse, Ginger, trying to enjoy this pleasant day. But instead of allowing the autumn breezes to refresh him and the vision of a new painting to fill his mind, he felt instead a reprimand in his spirit. It was as if Mother were alive, standing above him and wagging her finger, telling him how impolite he had been to the family guest. He recalled one day in particular from his youth, when a hoity-toity acquaintance of Father's had come to stay at the house. The man was pretending to be a friend because he knew Tom's father had money and this was all a scheme to steal it. When Tom confronted the man with his deception, Mother immediately took him into another room for punishment.

"You are never to address an elder so impudently, Thomas Edward!"

"Even if he plans to steal from Father? I saw it in his eyes."

Her features turned beet red. "Even so, we are God-fearing people, and we will do what we are asked. And it's God who will watch over our affairs."

Tom wondered what brought that event to mind. Surely Sara wasn't here to take advantage of them—to escape her life of poverty in New York for this fine life of a good home, plenty of food, and now a new dress and shoes to wear. He might have thought so were it not for the first day when she ran away and then claimed she would return to New York as soon as she had the money. None of this lent itself to one looking to take advantage of the situation, but rather someone trying to find her way in life. And he was still determined to do everything he could to help her, just as Mother would have wanted. If only he could keep his feelings out of the fray.

Soon it would be one month since Sara's arrival. Her appearance and manners were much improved, thanks to Claire's careful tutelage. She now made a fine loaf of bread, helped Claire with household duties, and even displayed table manners that would rival anyone at the Maplewood dining room. But in the back of his mind lurked the final goal of all this: a marriage contract. Wasn't that the ad's intent—for him to marry the one who answered it? But so far nothing seemed to point to that conclusion. Sara was young. Immature. Needy. Claire adored her like a sister. And in his eyes, having Sara around was like having another sister. They were a family, in many respects.

Tom continued along the road, glad he made the trip to Littleton yesterday to purchase paints needed for today's work. The day had turned blustery with a hint of winter weather quickly approaching. Soon they would taste the first snowflakes, and once that happened here in the mountains, winter was here to stay. Precious little time of fair weather was left in which to paint. He'd felt the urgency in his spirit recently and thus had made the decision to make the trip to Mount Agassiz today.

Tom patted the saddlebag that bounced on Ginger's rump. He remembered Sara's sadness over the fact he'd sold the painting he was supposed to present to her that day at the depot. He decided to at least make some amends, as a gentleman should, and create another work for her. He would paint the view from the summit of Mount Agassiz, overlooking the town of Bethlehem to the mountains beyond. And he would make a duplicate of the work for Mr. Astor and have it ready when next he visited.

Before heading out that morning, Tom had collected some brushes and a small canvas. In the other room he heard Sara's and Claire's voices. They were engaged in a sewing lesson. He nearly looked in on them but decided he didn't want to interrupt. That is, until Sara suddenly bounded out of the room and nearly collided with him in the hall.

"Oh, excuse me, Mr. Haskins."

"Miss McGee." He kept his gaze averted, though he did admire the lime-colored dress she wore. It appeared soft in the sunlight streaming through the windows. The color reminded him of spring. "I was just gathering some of my supplies."

"You're going to paint?"

"Yes, on Mount Agassiz." He glanced at her and saw her face brighten.

"I would love to go to the summit one day. I remember you talked about the tower there. But Claire plans to show me how to hem a shirt correctly so the stitches don't come out."

"I'm sure we will go sometime," he said, sidestepping his way to the front door. "Good day." He found his way outside, even with the image of Sara's eagerness branded in his mind.

Thinking back on it now, she did brighten up the day in that dress. He could picture Sara in a future landscape, wearing the green dress, perhaps holding a straw hat, with a basket resting at her feet and surrounded by a meadow of flowers.

Now he neared the Maplewood Hotel complex and the path that would lead him to the summit of Mount Agassiz. Suddenly Tom thought he heard someone calling his name. He reined the horse to a slow trot. Again he heard his name and turned about in the saddle.

Lawrence was racing along the boardwalk toward him, waving his hand. Tom pulled back on the reins, drawing his mount to a stop.

"You're getting on in years if your hearing is that bad, my friend," Lawrence said, panting. "And I must be getting on in years when I find myself out of breath from running such a short distance as that."

"I have horse hooves to listen to, the wind, and my thoughts. Sometimes it's difficult to hear anything else."

"Of course you must have a lot on your mind these days… and in your life. So, do tell, how is it with the street urchin? Tell me everything."

"What street urchin?"

Lawrence chuckled. "Oh, dear honest Tom, just like honest Abe. We haven't seen each other in several weeks. I only wanted to hear about life with Miss McGee from the city streets. I ran into Mrs. Childress a week or so ago, and she commented how your guest has the most atrocious table manners."

Tom frowned. "How nice that everyone in town remembers Sara's faults. And what else do they know? Or think they know?"

"Mrs. Childress only meant that the girl didn't seem to know how to act in public."

"She had no family, Lawrence. Or anyone else, for that matter, except the baker's wife. She lived on the street, eating stale bread and taking what she was given from Mrs. Whitaker's hand. I doubt any of us would have endured such a life as well as she did."

Lawrence held up his hands. "All right, enough already. I can see you're taken with her. I thought you were merely providing for her needs and giving her a few lessons until she was ready to go back to the city. I apologize."

Tom, however, wasn't listening. He was caught up in one sentence. *I'm taken with her?* His throat tickled, and he coughed. Ginger shimmied beneath him in response. He drew back on the reins. "Steady, girl. What do you mean, I'm 'taken with her?' "

"Come now, Tom. Listen to yourself. You come to her defense like a conquering hero. Which is fine, I suppose, if that's what you want to do."

Tom decided he didn't want to debate the point anymore. As it was, he'd seen the strain on their friendship the moment Sara arrived. He'd rather salvage what little remained than argue over fruitless points. "So how is business?"

"Business is well, but with the fall season about to end, the visitors are leaving. The hotels are already emptying. But I still get inquiries for work on a coat, especially with the cold weather coming. What about you? Are you off on another painting venture?"

"To the summit of Mount Agassiz. I want to paint the view before the snow comes."

"Ah, perfect. I would accompany you, but a gentleman needs his trousers hemmed. And if I'm not there to oversee the seamstress, the gentleman can get a little anxious. In fact, it seems everyone is anxious these days." His eyebrow lifted.

"I'll see you soon, I'm sure." Tom could hear the disagreement in his voice. He had known Lawrence for a long time, since childhood. It pained him to see their relationship suffer. But then he supposed it was bound to happen. As a Christian, he saw things in a different light than Lawrence did. Maybe one day Lawrence would come to see that eternal light and they would become true brothers in Christ.

Tom made his way up the path and to the gatehouse, the first stop before visitors ascended to the summit of Mount Agassiz. There he was greeted by Mr. Corliss, the proprietor. "Ah, Tom. You still owe me a painting of the summit view for my building here."

"Oh, yes." He said it before realizing he'd intended the painting for Sara. "If I may be allowed to come again soon, that is. I had in mind to paint this one as a gift for a visitor to Bethlehem."

Mr. Corliss frowned before bustling over to address several other visitors eager to make the trip up the mountain for the views. When Tom was finally allowed access to the path after promising a painting as soon as he was able, he made his way on Ginger toward the summit.

In about a half hour he came in view of the newly erected metal tower. Bethlehem was all abuzz with excitement when the structure was first built. Mr. Corliss claimed he built it to offer a view of heaven itself. Tom agreed to the assessment after he mounted the many stairs, while toting his painting supplies. The Presidential range stood before him in all its splendor, as did the Franconia range. Like Mr. Corliss said, Tom felt transported to a city of majestic peaks fashioned by the hand of God. And immediately his heart stirred to bring the scenery to canvas.

Tom set up the portable easel at once and began to sketch an outline. In the next hour he had created the view looking out toward the rugged Franconia range. The higher peaks of Lafayette and Garfield boasted a faint splatter of white from new-fallen snow. He then began dabbing color, bringing out the hues of gray stone and brown-tinged forests flanking the sides. He sat back to peruse the work. Once more he wondered how God guided his hand to create such pieces. He couldn't help but marvel, as he did so often. Not that he meant to wallow in pride, only simply to give God the glory in it.

"Yes, it is indeed excellent," a voice noted in satisfaction.

Startled, Tom looked behind him. A couple stood there, the same couple he'd seen at the gatehouse with Mr. Corliss. They were not commenting on the fine scenery witnessed from the tower either, but rather on his painting. "Thank you. I didn't even hear you come up the stairs."

The man stepped forward and swept off his hat. "I do believe we know you. You're the artist who helped my wife when she hurt her ankle this past July—Mr. Haskins."

Tom stood in an instant, unable to bridle his amazement. "Why, yes."

He offered a grin. "I'm Edward Newkirk, if you recall. And you remember my wife, Margaret."

He shook their hands. "I can't believe we're meeting again like this."

"Neither can we. Here we came to enjoy the view, and we find a famous artist painting it. Quite providential. Now, you cannot refuse me if I offer to buy it."

"Sir, it's only partially completed."

"Then finish it. I will pay you well for your haste in the matter."

"But this painting is for…" He paused. "For a guest staying in my home."

"Maybe even for a nice lady friend, Edward," Margaret noted with a coy smile. "Isn't it?"

"Yes, as a matter of fact, it is. The one who answered the ad for the bride."

"Oh, how wonderful!" Margaret exclaimed. "So you did receive a response." Their faces glowed, accented by broad smiles. "I think it's wonderful to have a painting like that—giving her a bit of your heart through your talent. Quite romantic." She laughed. "I surely didn't know what to do with a wheel, I must say…."

"A wheel?" Tom said, puzzled.

"I oversee a company that makes wheels for carriages," Edward explained.

"In New York City," Tom finished.

"Ah, so you remembered. And now you've found a prospective bride through the ad we placed?"

Tom hesitated on that point. "I'm not certain if she will be a bride. But I am helping a young lady in need."

Edward and Margaret exchanged glances. "Well, we all are needy in one way or another," Margaret commented. "I won't tell you what kind of condition I was in when I first met Edward. And he, well, he barely had his company going then. But we knew in our hearts we were right for each other." She held out her hand. "And I just found out that we will be having a baby come late spring!"

"Congratulations," Tom managed to say.

"Which reminds me, we should be getting back so you can rest," Edward added, taking hold of Margaret's arm. "The carriage is waiting. A pleasure to see you again, Mr. Haskins. Are you sure I can't buy the painting from you?"

Tom looked at the painting and, without another thought, offered it to them when he finished. "You don't need to pay me, either. Your words are payment enough."

The man looked puzzled. "But I would be happy to. In fact, I insist." He fetched his pocketbook.

Tom took the money and watched the couple head for their carriage after he promised to deliver the painting to their hotel that evening. He gathered his own supplies and returned to Ginger, all the while marveling over what had transpired. The couple must be another sign sent by God. A sign not to despair but to have faith and be patient. A relationship and marriage might still be in his future.

Riding down the path on Ginger, Tom wished he could have talked more to them. He looked down the road and at the dust cloud flying behind their carriage and thought of trying to catch them. But instead, he made for the path that would lead him back to his house in Bethlehem. At least now he had a weapon or two of encouragement to battle the doubt that often stalked him.

Tom returned home to find Sara and Claire away on an errand. Just as well. He needed the quiet to collect his thoughts. He wondered what he would say when the women asked to see his painting. Maybe he should just tell them the truth: that the couple who had encouraged him to submit the ad now encouraged him to continue on the journey he'd begun.

A rap came on the door just as Tom had made himself a cup of tea. He opened it to reveal a stunning Annabelle Loving in her dress of pure white and wearing a bright smile on her face. She looked like a bride, of all things. His throat clogged with emotion.

"Why, hello, Thomas!"

"Miss Loving!" he managed to blurt out.

"I hope you don't mind this intrusion. May I come in?"

"Yes, yes, of course." He fought to steady himself as he stepped aside. She brushed by him in a way that brought a flash of warmth. "How are you?"

"I'm well. And yourself?"

"Just fine. Thank you for asking." Her gaze encompassed the house. "What a beautiful home you have, Thomas."

"I owe it all to Claire. There's nothing like a woman's touch."

"I agree. There's nothing like a woman's touch in a man's life, either.

It makes him complete." She laughed coyly. "Did I tell you I saw Claire the other day? She mentioned you had a houseguest, but we weren't quite introduced the way I'd like. She's quite outspoken, I must say. And quite impertinent." Annabelle wandered into the drawing room and took a seat on the settee. She patted the vacant place beside her, but Tom took a seat across from her. Her lips turned downward. "I take it we're alone?"

"Uh, Claire and Sara aren't here."

"Sara, is it? Hmm. Well, I must say, I admire what you're doing for her. It shows your generous and giving heart, Thomas. I'm so impressed. She must be indebted to you."

Tom didn't know if Sara was indebted to him or not. In fact, she had yet to thank them for anything they had done. That mere fact pricked him like a pin.

"Well, there's another reason for my visit besides wanting to see Claire and your little friend. Are you free to take me out to a luncheon today? Lawrence suggested a nice lunch. I'm quite famished, and I really wanted someone to talk to. Perhaps we can go to Rablets'?"

Tom could hardly refuse her charming ways or her sweet smile. In fact, he was hungry also, after his excursion to Mount Agassiz. "I would like that." He fetched his still-warm coat from his mountain excursion earlier that day, along with his hat. Annabelle waited for him in the foyer. Once outside he offered her his arm. He hoped Sara and Claire would not make a sudden appearance on a street corner and see them.

"You seem preoccupied," Annabelle noted. "Lawrence said you were headed to Mount Agassiz to paint. How was it?"

"Excellent. I saw an exquisite view of both Mount Garfield and Mount Lafayette."

"I would love to see the painting when it's finished."

"Can you believe I sold it already? I'm to deliver it tonight to a couple at the Sinclair Hotel."

"You sold it! Why, Thomas."

"They were visiting the tower at the summit. It was the quickest sale I've ever made. The paint wasn't even dry—nor is the painting yet finished." He couldn't help the pride in his voice.

"My, my. It doesn't take long for the public to see what a professional you are. Soon you will be painting for royalty, Thomas." She leaned over his arm and giggled.

"Did you know that Mr. Astor of New York City is one of my principal buyers? In fact, he should be arriving in December. He likes to visit Bethlehem around Christmas."

"Well, how can he not? I mean, it's such a wonderful place to celebrate the season, and it has the most perfect name, too." She snuggled closer. "We must make plans to celebrate the season, Thomas. Can't you just see it? A warm fire, delicious cider, conversation…"

Tom felt warmth begin in his neck and crawl into his face. "I…uh, I'm not certain what my plans will be for Christmas, Miss Loving."

"Now, didn't I tell you that first names are quite appropriate? We're friends now." She paused at the door of the café, allowing him to open it and then escort her to a table.

He couldn't help but admire her ladylike manners, allowing him to remove her wrap, turning ever so slightly, keeping her back stiff and straight as she took a seat. She folded her hands on her lap and continued to sit straight while her gaze locked with his. Her red lips parted in a smile. He compared her to Sara when she arrived, with Sara's rumpled appearance and coarse table manners—slurping up the bowl of soup, the noodles stuck to her chin, and other unsavory noises. Annabelle was the perfect portrait of a woman of means, one who knew all the workings of a lady. The two women were like night and day. But there remained a uniqueness to Sara. Despite her raw ways, her large, expressive eyes and vitality for life drew him. Annabelle didn't need anything nor did she need to change. Her life was found in being worshipped as a fine piece of art. Annabelle sought adoration. Sara sought a new life. And maybe love to go along with it.

"Cat got your tongue?" Annabelle smiled after they gave their selections to the server.

"Sorry. I was just thinking."

"Ah, a man of deep thought. I admire that." She leaned over the table. "So tell me, what are your plans? Will you live out your days as a lonely painter here in Bethlehem?"

"Actually, I would like to travel someday."

Annabelle straightened. Her green eyes grew large. "Really."

"My fondest wish is to see the great artists of Italy. I think it would be an incredible journey to see the real works of Michelangelo, Botticelli, and others. Though their style is so unlike mine." He'd never spoken about his dream until now and wondered why it came out. Perhaps he found in Annabelle an engaging soul with an open heart and ears to listen.

"How grand." Annabelle smiled at the young girl who arrived with their sandwiches and tea and then continued. "I would love a European trip, too. A grand tour of Italy, then on to France and even Spain. Lawrence has a wonderful book on the European artists in his library. I shall bring it by one day for you to look at." She picked up her sandwich, keeping a pinkie raised, and took a dainty bite. She then placed the sandwich on her plate, took a sip of tea, and wiped her curled lips on a cloth napkin.

Tom couldn't help but stare. Sara would have had the meal consumed in a matter of minutes. Not Annabelle. Eating a meal was like art to her. For Tom, he had no inhibitions about finishing his meal after his day on the mountaintop.

"You are certainly a hungry man. I'm glad we decided to come here. One day I shall make you the most luscious berry tart."

Despite his full stomach, the mere picture of Annabelle presenting him with a still-warm fruit tart in her long fingers made his mouth water and his heart beat a little faster.

"So tell me about your houseguest. She is quite opinionated, I must say."

"Yes, Sara is," he declared, more emphatically than he would have liked.

"Is she a cousin of yours? She never did tell me, as she took off without even saying so much as good-bye…after she said in no uncertain terms that Lawrence should stay away. And that he was rude and inconsiderate. I have no idea what that's all about. And Lawrence wouldn't say much either."

What? "Sara is here to…" He paused. "Claire is tutoring her."

"Oh, so she's a student. How nice."

"Claire is enjoying it." *And what about me? Am I enjoying it? No, though I am enjoying the lunch. And talking about Italian art. And maybe fruit tarts.*

"I'm sure your sister will do a marvelous job. Though I think this Sara could use a few lessons in manners. If I can help in any way, let me know. Perhaps she would like to learn piano also? Every well-bred lady ought to play a musical instrument, like piano or violin. Even the flute."

Tom could just imagine Annabelle tutoring Sara on the piano. And then the conversation that would ensue—

Thomas says you're a pupil of his.

Oh, no. I'm here because I answered an ad from Tom to be his bride! Didn't you know?

Then the look of horror on Annabelle's face when she discovered the secret. She would run fast and furious, her face etched in anger, until she encountered him on a dark street. *How could you deceive me like this, Thomas Haskins? It's unthinkable! Why, you cad!*

"Hello?" she said, leaning over, her breath fanning his face. "Thomas, what's the matter?"

"I'm sorry," he apologized. "Annabelle...there's something I should...I've been meaning to say...." He paused.

She fluttered her eyelashes. "Dear Thomas, you don't have to say a word."

"I don't?"

"Of course not. I know exactly how it is. And don't worry. Things have a way of working out just fine. You'll see."

"Well, thank you for being so understanding."

She smiled. "Isn't that what friends are for?"

He breathed easier, thankful he didn't have to tell her about Sara. Lawrence must have said something already. "Well, I need to be getting home. Ginger needs tending to, as she took me all the way up the mountain today. And I must finish the painting for the couple."

"Of course." Annabelle waved over the server and asked that the remainder of her lunch be wrapped and put in a wicker basket. "I hope this lunch helped, Thomas. You just seem so distant these days."

"Too many things on my mind. The trip to Mount Agassiz, the couple buying the painting…." *What to do about Sara. And also you, Annabelle.*

Once outside, they bid each other good day and went their separate ways. But Tom's feet dragged as he returned to the house. He felt as if he were wallowing in confusion. He wished that matters of love and life could be made clearer. Here were two women, each so different but each with characteristics that drew him in ways he didn't understand. One day he would have to settle this once and for all. Though he had no idea how.

Chapter Eleven

....

"I sat on the red *kare*."

"Chair," Claire corrected. "The sound is *chuh*."

Sara bit her lip. "Chair. And I pet the cat until it pur…purred."

"Very nice. Your reading is much better."

Sara smiled. Claire left and soon returned with the large Bible from the table. "This is why we learn to read," she explained. "It's so we can read scripture and learn about God's plan for our lives."

"Mrs. Whitaker would read it to me."

"Yes, but now you can begin reading this on your own."

Claire flipped through the thin pages as Sara pondered her time so far. She'd learned much since the first day she arrived in this town. She glanced down at her dress, stylish and neat. Her hair was swept up in a chignon without a single hair out of place. She sat straight and tall in the seat, her hands folded in her lap. She might look on the outside like a lady of Bethlehem, but inside she was still Sara McGee, the young woman of straggly hair, torn coat, and spindly figure. This outside adornment made her feel like the fine coverings of the windows of Tom's house. Even now, she looked at the stately pieces that hung from rods and ran across the top of the windows. Oh yes, they dressed up the place very well. But once the coverings were removed, plain old windows remained. And as much as Claire had tried to dress her up on the outside, on the inside Sara was no different.

"So let's see how well you do with the Bible."

"But it looks so difficult."

"Just sound out the letters like you've been doing."

Sara began. "I am the *gude* shepherd."

"*Good* shepherd. But you were almost correct." Claire smiled.

"The sheep *her* my…" She paused.

"It's *hear*. Remember that *a* after *e* makes the *e* a long vowel sound. And the *oi* in voice is like the *oy* in boy."

"The sheep hear my voice."

"Very good. You'll remember the rules, Sara. It takes some time. I truly believe that by Christmas, you'll be reading to us about Christ's birth from the Gospel of Luke."

"I'm not sure. How many weeks until Christmas?"

"Oh, not long. It's November already. Can you believe you've been with us over five weeks? My, how time has gone by."

Sara could scarcely believe it either. And despite all she had learned, she was no closer to winning Tom's heart. He appeared as distant as ever, as if he were trapped in one of his paintings. Since receiving a communication from an important buyer, a Mr. Astor, who'd asked for several paintings to give family and associates for Christmas, Tom had been hard at work. It didn't help, either, that an early snowfall had taken them by surprise and left Tom unable to complete one of the required landscapes. For Sara, such early snow was pleasant to see. In the city it did snow, but it never lasted long. Or there would be bouts of frozen rain and icy pellets. She had a distinct feeling that winter here would be quite different in many ways.

"What are you thinking about?" Claire asked as she took up her knitting, a new craft she was teaching Sara. They hoped to make new mittens and hats for the coming winter.

"If Tom can't finish his paintings for Mr. Astor because of the early snow, what he will do?"

"He will finish them. I've seen snow come and go until winter finally decides to stay for good. It isn't even December yet." She then cast Sara an amused glance. Sara wondered what it meant. Did Claire think her too forward in showing concern for Tom's livelihood? Did this mean she missed his presence? Not that he offered her much when he was in the same room, except for a thoughtful look or vague comment. But Sara did like Tom, she had to admit. He was certainly handsome with his dark hair and deep brown eyes. He was tall, distinguished, talented, and he had some money. And he knew wealthy people like the Astors who came from the city. If only she could be his equal somehow, a perfect companion for him, his cherished wife.

Sara took up the Bible once more, determined to read the passage without stopping. Claire put down her knitting to listen. When she finished, Claire exclaimed, "Sara, that was excellent!"

"Thank you. I want to be able to read the Christmas story, like you said. It will be my gift to you all, as you know I have no money to buy gifts."

Claire patted her hand. "It will be a treasured gift, I assure you. There's nothing more satisfying than reading the Bible and learning God's plans for us." She patted the book sitting on Sara's lap. "I remember when I was young and quite foolish. I cared little for what the Bible had to say. I thought, 'It's only an old book written by men.' But then I found a revelation of God in these words, words that helped my wandering soul and planted my feet on the path He'd chosen for me. And suddenly I saw that they weren't just words printed on paper but were living words that brought life. Maybe that's why the Bible is thought of as meat; it's food our souls need every day of our lives."

Sara realized she did not merely hold a book but a treasure worth more than gold. And with each passing moment, she felt an urge to read and write. Not just to become one of Bethlehem's fine ladies, but to be a woman who understands the Bible. "Does this book talk about men and women and about marriage?"

"Oh, yes. In fact, the Bible says how finding an excellent wife is a good thing." Claire flipped through many pages until she came to a section called Proverbs. "Let me share with you what God sees in a virtuous woman." She began reading. " 'Who can find a virtuous woman? For her price is far above rubies. The heart of her husband doth safely trust in her, so that he shall have no need of spoil. She will do him good and not evil all the days of her life….'"

Sara listened as Claire expounded on the characteristics of a godly woman. And suddenly the things she had been learning to do— homemaking, reading, learning about godly strength and wisdom— all were preparations for becoming a virtuous wife. What she'd been doing these past two months was learning to be a keeper of the home, a wife, and a mother. It was true. The Bible was a lamp unto her feet and a light unto her path. And all things were working together for good, if she continued to have patience to the end.

That evening, with Tom called away to a friend's house, Sara and Claire enjoyed their dinner in the dining room where they shared womanly things. Every day Sara felt her bond with Claire strengthening. Claire even claimed that in many ways Sara was the sister she'd never had. They shared secrets and giggled in girlish fashion. Later that evening, dressed in their robes, they sat enjoying the fire. The flames warmed Sara's toes. Normally she would never expose her feet in such a fashion. But here with Claire, she felt uninhibited and at peace. The cup of hot tea Claire had made her felt warm in her hands. "This is so nice," she murmured. "I wish it would never end."

Suddenly the door slammed. Sara bolted upright and instantly spilled the cup of tea across the front of her robe. "Oh, no!"

Claire rushed out, and in an instant Sara heard voices in the hallway. When Claire returned with several towels, Sara blotted the tea from her clothing and the floor.

"Did you hurt yourself?" Tom stood in the doorway, remaining at a distance with his gaze averted in respect.

Sara glanced back at him and was thankful he was not looking at the dark stain splattered across the front of her robe or her bare feet. "I–I'm fine, thank you. The robe caught most of it. I wasn't burned." Her face burned, though, imagining what was running through Tom's mind. She was now clumsy along with being poor and unkempt. She tried to blink back the tears, but they were already making an appearance in her eyes. How she wanted to tell Tom what she'd learned in the Bible—and that she was endeavoring to become a virtuous woman so he would trust her with his worldly possessions and his life. Now the moment was ruined like her robe by the spilt tea.

"Don't let it bother you," Claire whispered, as if she sensed Sara's turmoil. "You were only startled."

Choking back the anguish, Sara hurried out of the drawing room and up the stairs to the bedroom to find a safe haven. It had been such a wonderful day up until this point. "Oh, God, why did this have to happen?" she mourned. "I only wanted You to make me someone Tom will respect and love. To make me the perfect woman for him. And…to make him love me, somehow. And now this had to happen." Everything seemed out of reach. She had a long way left to accomplish the qualities Claire read to her from Proverbs. Too much for Tom to ever truly accept her.

* * * *

A few days later, Sara awoke to a sunny and warm morning. Much of the snow that had fallen the previous week had melted away. At breakfast Tom declared he must finish a certain painting for Mr. Astor. Sara voiced a desire to walk Main Street and see all that there was to see. Now that she had the proper dress and characteristics of a lady, thanks to Claire's guiding hand, she felt certain she could handle the venture with confidence.

"You should escort Sara," Claire remarked to Tom. "You have yet to properly show her the sites of Bethlehem, and she's been here for several weeks."

Tom paused, his fork containing a piece of pancake hovering in mid-air. "I'm sorry, Claire, but I must finish the paintings. Mr. Astor is expecting them." He then added, "I hope you understand, Sara."

"Maybe another time. I know the paintings are important."

Tom finished eating his stack of pancakes then hurried to gather his supplies. Sara stared at her half-eaten breakfast. If only he knew how happy she would be just to accompany him in his work. She began to clear the dishes from the table but felt no joy in doing it. She feared she was only becoming a decoration in this place, like a wooden chest of drawers or a faded picture on the wall that no one ever notices. *Why does he bother to keep me here? Why do I stay where I'm not wanted?*

"Sara…," Claire began, following her into the kitchen, "give Tom some more time. Once the paintings are done for Mr. Astor, he won't be so preoccupied."

"I know." She forced a crooked smile.

"I would go with you on your walk today, but I promised Mrs. Harris I would visit her. She has such terrible rheumatism. I want to bring her some porridge and maybe read to her."

Sara asked if she could be of help, but Claire waved off the suggestion. "Mrs. Harris likes her company one at a time, I'm afraid. But I'll introduce you to her soon."

Sara tried to think good thoughts about the day. At least she was free to roam about Bethlehem wherever she liked. She could enjoy this taste of springtime here in November, even if she must enjoy it alone. She was determined to make this a beautiful day. Despite everything that had happened, today would be different; she could feel it. A new chapter was about to be written in the book of her life.

Sara dressed carefully in the garment she and Claire had picked out many weeks ago, the emerald green dress, complete with a large hat and fitted gloves. Once she came down the stairs, she hoped to garner Claire's opinion but found she had already left to tend to Mrs. Harris. The house seemed empty. Sara wandered from room to room, imagining herself as the lady of the house. She straightened chairs and the paintings on the walls.

"Oh, I must see to tea this afternoon," she announced to no one in particular. She envisioned the parlor filled with Bethlehem's finest ladies, here to discuss the activities of the Ladies' Aid Society and to work on their quilts for the poor. Sara would present tea on a silver platter, along with Claire's famous blueberry biscuits. Everyone would thank her for her hospitality.

"Why, thank you, Mrs. Harris. I'm glad you enjoyed the tea." Sara curtsied and moved in dignified fashion to the mirror in the hall. She looked at her reflection. The green dress suited the day. She turned from one side to the other, convinced that she appeared the part of a fine woman enjoying all that Bethlehem had to offer.

Sara strolled outside, where the warm wind brought the pleasing aroma of mountain air. She took to the wooden boardwalk along Main Street, careful to keep her back straight and her gaze focused ahead. The sumptuous hotels that made Bethlehem an eager destination for holiday travelers materialized before her. She passed the famous Sinclair Hotel and, farther down, the Howard House. Men and women gathered on the front porches to take in the pretty day. They sat in the wicker chairs, rockers, and even on the porch railings, holding cups of tea or reading newspapers. Women embroidered or engaged in conversation with their neighbors. Sara imagined herself on the porch of one of those hotels, indulging in tea while chatting with a handsome suitor. If Tom Haskins refused to look her way, perhaps another man would. She smiled at the prospect.

At that moment, two men walking down the boardwalk slowed their pace as they approached her. They swept their tall hats from their heads and bowed. Sara performed a slight curtsy, which spawned grins on their faces.

"Excuse me, madam," said one of the men, "but surely I saw you at the Maplewood dining room this morning. Didn't I?"

Sara paused, unsure of what to say. "I'm sorry; you've mistaken me for another. I'm actually the guest of Bethlehem's most famous painter."

The two men looked at each other. "I don't believe I've heard of him."

"Mr. Thomas Haskins. Oh, you would love his paintings. They depict the fine land here and the people, too."

"Interesting. I would very much like to meet him and see his work. Where can I find him?"

"On Congress Street. The white house with black shutters and a large porch."

"Excellent. Thank you. A good day to you."

The men moved off, and only then did Sara realize what she'd done. She'd heaped praise upon Tom. She'd encouraged others to buy his work. She truly cared about him. If only he would return the favor by standing with her, offering his support, his encouragement, and sharing in his work. After all, wasn't that why he sent out the ad? Wasn't he responsible for the success of this venture? That is, if he desired it to be successful. But at this moment, Sara wanted it to succeed. She was determined to have it succeed. She would have Tom Haskins fall in love with her. And they would be married.

Sara turned and made her way back down Main Street. Remembering the man's comment about the Maplewood Hotel, Sara decided she must see it for herself. She'd heard what a grand place it was, the largest hotel in Bethlehem. Claire talked of the wealthy people who stayed there during the summer.

She took her time on the journey, savoring the fine air and the grand homes. How simple yet elegant were the homes here compared to the drab buildings in the city. She wished Mama were alive to see this place. Maybe if they had come to this town, away from the dust and air of the city, Mama would have never taken ill. She would have survived to see Sara wed a fine man like Tom and raise a family.

Sara tried not to dwell on such things. If anything, Mama would be glad to know she was away from the city, dressed in fine garments, learning to read and write, and experiencing all that a lady should. She would be thankful to God for Sara's blessings. And Sara should be grateful for this time, too, even if things weren't going exactly as planned. She must thank Claire and Tom for everything…and tell Tom of the fine men she had met and how they wanted to buy his paintings. Then there would be a look of adoration across his face. He would take her in his arms to give her his own message of gratefulness—a loving kiss.

The grand spectacle of the famous Maplewood Hotel soon came into view. Sara stood at a distance, staring for a lengthy time at the unique construction. The long wings with many windows and spiral towers that flanked the ends made the building appear as if it were a palace for royalty. How glorious it would be to have a cup of tea in such surroundings. Perhaps a fine gentleman might ask to sit with her or even engage her in conversation. She felt in her pocket for a few coins, hoping she had enough to splurge on such luxury.

Sara walked toward the entrance of the magnificent building when she noticed a familiar figure in the distance. She stopped short. The tall figure wore a familiar brown hat and carried a wide leather case, like an artist would use to protect a painting. *It must be Tom!* She quickened her pace, drawing up the courage to ask if he cared to have a cup of tea in the dining room, when a woman suddenly intercepted him on the walkway. Sara ducked behind a nearby tree to listen.

"Oh, Thomas, I'm so glad I ran into you! Look what I have for you."

Sara watched as the woman presented him with a large book. "Just as I told you, it has descriptions of wonderful Italian painters."

Tom's joy was evident in his wide grin. "This is magnificent, Annabelle. Where did you find it?"

"Lawrence had it in his library, and I said I would bring it to you. Oh, and I have more news. Delightful news, really. I just received a telegram. Father said that he would help pay for a trip to Italy! You said how much you wanted to go. Isn't that simply marvelous?"

Sara tensed. Cold rippled through her. *What trip is she talking about?*

"Annabelle…" Tom hesitated. "I don't know if…"

"Oh, my father will accompany us, of course. I wouldn't dare presume that we go without a chaperone. That is, unless…" She took hold of his hand. He looked as if he might drop his leather case. "If you would consider making it a wedding trip instead," Annabelle finished. She smiled widely.

Sara gasped and quickly covered her mouth. Tears sprang to her eyes. She whirled and hurried off into a meadow of brown grass. "Oh, dear Lord, I've made such a fool of myself. All this time…I thought he might…" She tripped along, nearly falling as withered blades scratched her and snared her fine dress. *Tom is supposed to marry me. Now it will never happen. Why did I ever come to this place? To be humiliated? Or so Claire and Tom could have the praise of transforming a tramp into a lady? Then put me on display and give themselves an award for their work.*

Sara knew the end of this game. Annabelle had made it clear. Tom never intended to marry her, the waif. Then why should she remain? *I will leave,* she decided. *I'm not meant to be here or to marry Tom. Not now, not ever.*

Sara gathered her skirt and hurried toward the house. She would tell Claire and Tom her decision at dinner tonight, pack what meager belongings she had, and find work at one of the hotels. When she had enough money, she would return to where she belonged, to the people who loved her for who she was. And never again would she set foot in a New England town or answer any man's ad for a bride.

Chapter Twelve

....

Tom stood there speechless, as he often found himself these days. Running his hand across the book that Annabelle had given him, he tried to understand what this meant. Her father was willing to pay for a trip to Italy…but more shockingly, she was speaking marriage. And he hardly knew her.

"Uh…Miss Loving…," he began.

"Annabelle," she corrected, the smile remaining as if she knew she had gained an advantage by this surprise announcement. "This is what you want, isn't it? Your heart's desire?"

He looked down at the book. He should be ecstatic that someone would think to help finance a trip to see the works of the famous Italian painters. But at the same moment, he felt he was offering up his soul on a marriage altar in exchange. He would be beholden to Annabelle and her family. Her father would look to him in anticipation of a marital arrangement. It was too much to consider right now. "Thank you for the loan of the book. As for the trip, I–I'll have to think about it."

"What is there to consider? My father is very intrigued by your work. I shipped home the painting I bought from you at the parade. He was very impressed and says you have wonderful talent. He is more than happy to show you Italy. Thomas, this is an opportunity of a lifetime!"

How well he knew it. Visiting Italy would be a dream come true.

But was this also God's opportunity, or one from a determined woman seeking companionship no matter the cost? He gazed into the meadow beyond and, for an instant, thought he saw someone running. The figure quickly disappeared over a small knoll. He returned his attention to Annabelle's expectant face. "Please offer your father my thanks for his generous offer. But I need time to consider it."

"Well, don't take too long. There are arrangements to be made. And we must book passage on the ship. Now I have to go. I'm meeting several friends for tea at the Maplewood. I'd have you join us, Thomas, but it's women, after all, and you'd be bored with all the chatter."

"I need to be going, too. Thank you again for the book."

Annabelle waited, her face tilted upward as if expecting a reward for all this. A small kiss on the cheek wouldn't harm anything, especially since she had brought him the book. He began to oblige when suddenly she jerked her head, and their lips met instead. He stepped back, flustered. Her cheeks flushed with pleasure, and a smile once more lit up her face. "I'll see you soon."

He watched her walk in dignified fashion toward the Maplewood Hotel. She was beautiful indeed, and she'd offered a more wondrous gift than he could have ever imagined. But how did he dare accept it? A part of him longed to see the sights of Rome and Florence, the works of the Venetians, the grand cathedrals and domes.... *What should I do? Is this a door opening for me? Am I supposed to walk through it?* He considered it as he made his way toward town. If Lawrence found out he'd accepted Annabelle's offer and her hand, the man would sing like a lark up and down the streets of Bethlehem. Mr. Astor would agree to the arrangement with such a fine lady. Claire would wonder what he had done....

And then there was Sara. What about Sara McGee?

He paused. Sara wasn't necessarily the answer to his heart even if she did respond to the ad. She was not like Annabelle Loving or the other ladies who gathered on the porticos of the grand hotels. She was someone Claire had taken under her wing. She was more like a sister living under his roof, and he had treated her as such these many weeks.

But the one who gave him the book was an accomplished and beautiful woman who understood the desires of his heart. And she wanted him.

He hurried toward home, the book in one hand and his leather portfolio in the other. As he did, he began making plans. He would finish his contract for the paintings in time for the holiday season. He would take out the large family trunk and polish it up. It would do nicely for the long voyage to Italy. He would need to consider other things, as well. When would be the appropriate time to ask for Annabelle's hand? Should they make the trip to Italy a wedding tour or simply travel with her father as a chaperone? There was so much to consider.

Tom slowed his pace when he neared his home. Claire stood on the porch shaking a small throw rug in the air. Clouds of dust floated into the late November afternoon. She then placed the rug on the porch floor, straightened, and saw him. She folded her arms across her chest as if she knew what had transpired at the Maplewood. But that was impossible. Still, he tucked the book behind the leather case before he approached.

"How was your day?" he asked, despite the strange look she gave.

"Rather, I should be asking how yours was."

"It went well. I finished another painting for Mr. Astor."

Claire pointed to the porch rockers. Tom opened his mouth, ready to tell her that he had too many things to do, one of which was looking over the fine book Annabelle had given him. Instead, he took a seat and stared off in the distance at nothing in particular.

"I'm sure you're unaware that Sara has been crying for over an hour."

He looked back at her in surprise. "Whatever for?"

"Maybe you should tell me. Something about a marriage?"

He stared in disbelief. "I–I'm not sure I understand."

"She said you are making plans to marry Annabelle Loving."

"I don't understand. How did she hear about that?"

"Maybe in front of the Maplewood Hotel earlier today? After Miss Loving gave you some gift."

Heat spread through his face and singed his neck. "I don't understand how she would know about this. She was there, listening?"

"What does it matter? Is it true?"

"Miss Loving knows my interest in Italian painting and simply brought me a book from Lawrence's library."

"Which ended with some kind of marriage proposal. Tom, how could you do this in front of Sara?"

He sat up in vexation. "I didn't know she was eavesdropping. What was she doing listening to other people's conversations? And what of it, anyway? I never pledged myself to marry Sara just because she answered the ad. Or rather, her nanny answered the ad for her."

"Mrs. Whitaker is not her nanny, just a kind woman who took Sara under her wing when she had no one else."

"I made no pledge of intent. Nor did I make a pledge to Miss Loving…though I'm very grateful she gave me this book and offered me the trip."

Claire's eyes widened. "Trip! What trip?"

His face grew even warmer, as if it were a kettle of soup heating on the cookstove. "Her father offered to pay for a trip to Italy. He admires my paintings and wanted to help. I thought it was a fine and thoughtful gesture."

Claire flew to her feet. "Tom, how could you be so insensitive? You agreed to have Sara come here on the presumption…"

"There is no…"

"…on the presumption," she said louder, "that you would allow her time to embrace the customs of a lady and see if she is the woman you're to marry. But, instead, all you've done is ignore her and throw yourself at Miss Loving's feet—and let that raven pluck at your heart."

Tom opened his mouth to speak, but Claire rushed on.

"Maybe you're too busy to notice these days, but Sara has worked hard to please you and everyone else in this town. She has done everything society requires. Dressed correctly. Worked on manners. Even reading and writing. And this is how you reward her."

"I do not reward with a ring, sister. It's wrong to place that kind of burden on me." He took to his feet and walked down the stairs.

"Then why did you invite her to stay with us, Tom, if you never had any intention of marrying her?"

"I wanted to help her. Is that so wrong? Why am I being condemned for it? Or, rather, put into a corner." He paced about the front lawn, scuffing up the browning grass.

"Then you need to be honest and tell her the truth. And stop giving her hope when there is no hope." The door shut before him.

Tom paused. Was hope for Sara now gone? He had all but sealed it with his words. He looked across the wide field that eventually ended at the Maplewood's doorstep. He wanted to say yes to Annabelle's request. To set his feet on a determined path and not a place in the wilderness. But was he certain the path was meant for Annabelle? Had he allowed Annabelle to bewitch him instead of being patient and waiting to see what the Lord willed for the future? Especially when another young woman entertained hope for a future covenant?

Please, God, he prayed, *make my path known. Not my will, but Yours be done.*

* * * *

The dinner hour arrived, forcing Tom to enter the house and reconcile what had occurred. He prayed for calm and for the right words to say in this situation. An idea for a painting came to mind at that moment, of a deer caught in the throes of a raging wildfire after taking a wrong turn down a woodland path. Its only course of action to avoid being burned was taking a flying leap off a cliff into a lake of water below. Heading into the dining room, Tom decided he must paint such a picture. It was all too telling of what he felt like at that moment.

He waited, expecting Sara to come out with a dish she had prepared, as she did every night. He heard a rustle behind him. He turned and saw a lady bedecked in a splendid dress, her hair neatly piled on her head, with curly ringlets gracing each cheek. She held her back stiffly, moving with grace, to a chair opposite his.

"Can I help you, Claire?" she asked.

"No, thank you, Sara. I have it."

Tom stared. This woman was Sara McGee? Why had he not noticed the changes before now? Her gaze met his then, and in those blue eyes he saw fire. Her lips tensed, and she looked away. She swiped up her napkin, unfolding it to place in her lap.

"Would you like to say the blessing, Tom?" Claire asked.

Tom no more wanted to say the blessing than if he were some heathen. But he bent his head and offered a quick prayer of thanks for the food and the company. He wanted to say more but didn't. May God soon unleash his spiritual man from these burdens of the heart so he might deliver a prayer of thanksgiving and care, one that would bring peace and, most of all, direction.

Sara finished dishing up a modest portion of the chicken soup before handing the ladle to Tom. For a mere moment their fingers brushed as they exchanged the spoon. She jerked her hand away as if he were on fire. The response pained him. He ladled out a helping anyway, determined to enjoy the meal.

Silence prevailed as they each ate their soup. Claire then left the table to bring out the next course while Tom and Sara sat opposite each other, staring at nothing in particular. He wished he could tell her how lovely she looked, or that he was glad they could be of help in providing for her needs. But the words remained locked inside.

Claire arrived with a platter of pot roast surrounded by vegetables. They each spooned servings onto their plates. Again the silence ensued, except for the ticking of the grandfather clock.

"So when do you leave, Mr. Haskins?" Sara asked.

The question came so suddenly, it jarred him. "What?"

"I asked when you plan to leave on your trip."

He slowly wiped his mouth on a napkin. "I have no plans to leave on a trip."

"I suppose the marriage must come first." Sara buttered a slice of bread. "Surely Europe would make a fine wedding tour."

Claire stared first at Sara then at Tom. She seemed uncertain as to what to say.

"I have no plans for that, either," Tom added. "And I'm sorry that somehow you overheard what was meant to be a private discussion."

Sara put down the butter knife. "Well, I've made plans also." She began to eat, allowing the words to hang in mid-air. She chewed, swallowed, then picked up her teacup. "But first I must thank you for everything you've done for me." She set the cup down. "Especially you, Claire. You've been like a sister to me. But even the good things in our lives must come to an end."

"Sara?" Claire laid down her fork.

"This is my last meal with you both. I've already packed my things. I hope you don't mind if I take the dresses, Claire, until I have the means to pay you for them."

"The clothes were gifts, Sara. But I don't understand. What do you mean, you're leaving? Where are you going?"

"Home."

Tom pushed back his chair. "How do you plan to go home?"

"By train, of course. I know this is much to ask, but if you were to loan me the train fare, I would wire the money as soon as I arrived. I'm sure Mrs. Whitaker will oblige. In fact, I plan to wire her a telegram, telling her about my plans." Sara coughed into a napkin. "You see, I've known for some time I wouldn't be able to stay here. Marriage wasn't meant to be." She turned to Tom. "And while I shouldn't have been listening to your conversation, Mr. Haskins, it did confirm what has been in my heart all along. You and I walk different paths. You've been kind to let me stay here and learn, but it's time I moved on with my life and discover my destiny and the man I'm supposed to share it with."

"Sara, there's still so much to learn," Claire intervened. "And we've only just begun with your reading. Remember how you wanted to read the Bible? I'm sure Tom doesn't mean for you to leave…." She cast a warning look in his direction.

"Of course not. It would be good for you to stay."

Sara shook her head. "I can't. I need to find my own way in this world. And if you would be so kind as to lend me the train fare…" Her voice drifted off.

"I don't think it's wise to go back to the city, of all places," he said. "New York holds nothing for you. At least here you have a chance for a better life."

"I will do fine in New York. There I can be myself and not some decoration."

Tom winced at the word she had chosen. When did she ever think she was simply a decoration? "What do you plan to do for money in the city? You can't just peddle with your mother's teacup—or return to rags and sleeping in abandoned cellars. That's no way to exist."

Sara's eyes blazed with a look Tom could not ever remember seeing in a woman. She jumped to her feet, her dress rustling. The table shook. Tea sloshed out of the cups. "I'm sorry you think my existence was so horrible, but it was fine for me. I was happy. And loved. And I will find my own way back." She hurried from the table.

Claire grabbed his arm. "Tom, go after her! Make her see reason. Don't let her leave like this."

"Claire, if she runs from the truth, how do I stop her? She's made her decision. We gave her everything, and yet she feels she must do this."

"If you consider the situation, we gave everything but love and a purpose for her life." Claire rose from the table and left as well. Tom stared at the cold food along with his equally cold cup of tea. He was drifting in a fog like the kind that often blanketed the mountains. Clouds that hid the fine, rocky pinnacles, fooling the visitor into thinking the land was flat. Was he also surrounded in a fog, unable to see what existed before him? Was he truly blind, or was Sara?

A door banged. Footsteps came and went down the hall. He heard voices. Claire was trying to reason with Sara. He took a swallow of cold tea. *Sara won't leave,* he decided. *Either Claire will convince her to stay, or she will realize she has no other place to go.* No matter how tense things seemed now, Tom knew they had a habit of working out. Women also needed each other's companionship.

Again a door banged. Claire came rushing in. "Tom, she's leaving right this moment. Do something!"

Tom stood to his feet just as Sara walked with determined steps into the foyer, clutching her ratty carpetbag and wearing her tattered coat. "Sara, where are you going?"

"I told you my decision at dinner."

"Don't be foolish. You have no place to go. And it's a cold night."

"I'll find a place. I lived on the streets of New York, you know, as distasteful as that is to you. I can take care of myself."

"Please, Sara, don't do this," Claire begged. "Not now. At least wait until morning. Things always look better in the morning."

"I'm sorry, Claire, but I have to go. It's the only thing left to do."

With that, she disappeared into the night. Claire pushed Tom toward the door, ordering him to bring her back. When he ventured out, the night had already swallowed her whole. He returned and closed the door behind him. "I will look for her in the morning, Claire. There's nothing more we can do. I think we all need time to sort this out."

"How could you let it come to this?" Claire wailed.

"Claire, I'm sorry that Sara overheard what happened. But I should not be condemned for the fact that maybe another woman is interested in me. And I in her."

"Annabelle Loving is nothing, and you know it. She's a fancy postcard; a wrapped package with nothing inside. Maybe even an example of that whitewashed tomb Jesus talks about in scripture. You're letting go of someone who is trying with all her heart to be a good wife for you—the woman from Proverbs who wants to be worthy so a man will call her excellent, worthy of his love and trust in everything. Can you really trust in your heart that Annabelle will ever be that kind of wife?"

Tom stood silent. He looked to his heart's response, a heart that longed for someone to share in life, the goals and dreams. Annabelle seemed to be the one, with her words about Italy. But then there was Sara. Sara, who had suffered and worked and tried her best to change with her circumstances. Sara, who had a natural independence and a strong self-will. He gazed out the window into the darkness blanketing Bethlehem and prayed for a new dawn of understanding.

Chapter Thirteen

....

Tom was in no mood to receive visitors, but when two distinguished-looking gentlemen arrived at his doorstep the next morning, he straightened his vest and shirt and went to receive them. The house was strangely quiet this day. As soon as he had risen from bed, he looked out the front window to the street, hoping to find Sara returning and offering an apology for leaving so brusquely. And he, in turn, would have a ready apology on his lips for not being honest about his feelings, for not sharing with her about his friendship with Annabelle, for allowing her hope to be dashed to the ground.

The men at the door removed their top hats and bowed slightly upon Tom's greeting. "Please excuse the intrusion. I'm Henry Wentright, and I'm looking for a Mr. Haskins, Bethlehem's famous painter," said the one.

Tom was at a loss for words. Bethlehem's famous painter? The title sounded like one Annabelle might bestow on him. "I'm not certain I'm famous, but I do paintings, yes. Won't you come in?"

Claire immediately scurried out to see the callers then hastened to the kitchen to put the kettle on. Tom showed them to the parlor. "How can I help you gentlemen?"

"I would very much like to have a portrait made of my wife," Henry said. "It's for her birthday. I think she would like it very much."

"Actually, my specialty is landscape art in the manner of the Hudson River composition."

The men looked at each other. "I thought perhaps you did portraits. You see, we heard you do excellent work. In fact, we heard it directly from the young lady who is a guest in your home. She seemed very eager to share about your paintings."

Tom was cut to the quick. When Claire arrived with the teapot and cups, he gave her a questioning glance.

"Is your guest available? Perhaps she can help clarify what she meant."

"She's quite attractive, I must say," said the second man. "Henry here dares not say such things, as he is happily married. But I'm not, you know. In fact, what is her name? She didn't say."

They must be referring to Sara. And she had captured the attention of two wealthy men. When? Maybe even this morning. He wondered if perhaps they were privy to where she was staying. He stood to his feet. "Her name is Sara. Please, can you tell me where and when you saw her?"

"Why, we saw her on Main Street just yesterday. Didn't we, Henry?"

"That's correct, Stuart. She was taking a walk, enjoying the nice day. And a good thing we were out then, too, as it's turned quite chilly."

Sara must have encountered them before she stormed from this house. They would have no idea where she was now. He sensed Claire's eyes like daggers on him as she poured tea for each guest. "Well, thank you for the information. And I'm sorry I can't help you with the portrait."

"I would like to see some of your work," Stuart asked. "A lady as lovely as Sara must have a good eye for detail. If you don't mind?"

Tom did mind the man's obvious interest in Sara. He hadn't realized how much the idea bothered him until he came face-to-face with it. He went to find his latest painting, still unfinished, of a deer lost in the massive New Hampshire woods.

Stuart exclaimed his interest in purchasing it when it was complete. "It will look perfect in my place of business. In fact, I will give you half the payment now." He withdrew his purse and counted the money. "You'll have it ready by tomorrow, I hope. I leave on the train the following morning."

"Yes, yes, sir, I will."

"Please, no formality. Stuart is fine."

"And I'm Tom Haskins. I'll have your painting done with the utmost haste, sir."

"Stuart," the man reminded him with a smile, replacing his purse. "Thank you for your time."

Tom showed them to the door. When they departed, Claire came forward with her hands on her hips. "So, Sara is quite the vagabond of the street. Here she is, capturing the hearts of eligible bachelors in Bethlehem. The other man, Stuart, had no qualms about pursuing her. And I'm sure there are other gentlemen about as well."

"I never thought she was a vagabond."

"Heavens, you certainly did. And she will become one again if you don't go at once and bring her back. You promised you would."

He glanced out the window. "Where am I supposed to begin looking for her? For all we know, she left this morning on the train… if she was able to find the money for it."

"You could at least inquire at the train station and perhaps a few guesthouses. After all, you are responsible for her well-being while she is in Bethlehem. She is like a sister to me. Would you leave me out in the cold with no money?" Claire paused. "Perhaps I shouldn't be asking that kind of question."

"Claire, you know I wouldn't. Yes, I did promise to look for her, and I will. I'll check around town and ask if anyone has seen her." He went to fetch his coat. "But I cannot be responsible if she decided to leave on the train. Then it's done."

Claire gathered the dishes on a silver tray and moved off in silence.

Tom sighed. How he wished the men had just seen Sara on the street. Then they would know she remained and Claire would have peace. Tom decided he would head for the ticket office and see if the clerk remembered her and then check the neighboring hotels and guesthouses. Or just walk the street and see if somehow their paths crossed.

* * * *

Tom made his way down Main Street, his hands buried in his pockets, as a stiff wind greeted him. On the breath of wind came the raw whisper of snow, ready to make another appearance. December was on the horizon and, with it, Christmas. He had a vision then of Christmas at the house, with a tall tree gracing the parlor and Claire and Sara laughing gaily as they exchanged gifts. He thought suddenly of something pretty to give Sara on that day—maybe some gloves or a fine hat. Or something to replace that worn carpetbag. Or, at the very least, a new coat.

His throat tightened. How could he have allowed Sara to leave like that? He'd invited her here, after all, with the possibility of marriage. Like Claire said, despite what happened with Annabelle, he was responsible for Sara. She had come in answer to his ad. He should have barred the door to prevent her from leaving. Run into the street, calling her name. Search all night if he had to.

But then there was Annabelle. Perhaps things could be made right by returning the book and declining her father's generous offer of the trip to Italy. But he couldn't bring himself to do it quite yet. He felt a certain itch when it came to Miss Loving. She tickled his fancy and aroused his curiosity by the way she spoke to his interests in life. He treasured the book while thoughts of the trip teased him in the night watches. But there remained a nagging question, too. Could one base a lasting relationship on selfish desire?

Tom arrived at the depot, where the daily train had already deposited the new arrivals. The number of visitors to Bethlehem had lessened considerably with the coming of winter. No doubt there would be fresh arrivals on the advent of the Christmas season when visitors found it nostalgic to celebrate the holiday here amid the lure of the fancy resorts and rugged scenery. After all, this was Bethlehem.

"Good morning," Tom greeted the clerk at the ticket counter.

"Ah, Tom. And where are you planning to travel?"

How Tom would love to travel. He'd been nowhere, save this familiar land. Perhaps one day he should visit New York to see where Sara McGee came from. "Actually, I'm here to inquire if a young lady purchased a ticket this morning. She wore a large straw hat with a green ribbon and a fairly shabby-looking coat."

The clerk laughed. "How am I to know which one you mean, Tom? There are plenty of women in hats buying tickets."

"Well, she would have bought a ticket to New York."

The clerk snickered once again. "That's the second most popular destination, my good man, next to Boston."

Tom could see this was going nowhere. He thanked the man and walked along the platform where the train stood. Steam created frosty white curls of smoke in the air. He recalled Sara's arrival that day in early October, with her looking like a lost bird amid the ridicule of the townspeople. Things had changed for the better since then…until recently, when everyone in his life had begun to turn from him. He'd not heard from Lawrence since the day they met before his trip up Mount Agassiz. Sara was gone. Claire would hardly speak to him. The only one who remained was Annabelle. But what did all this say for his godly character? *Help me know what to do, God,* he prayed as his feet walked the street in earnest. *Guide my heart and my mind.*

He considered his next course of action. Sara had talked of finding a place to stay until she could locate employment and earn the money needed for the train fare to New York. Tom headed for Main Street and began combing places she might be, like several of the cottages that housed visitors. He stopped at several of them but none had seen her, though several of the proprietors expressed interest in one of his paintings for their establishment. At least there was a bright side to this—he was certainly drumming up business for his work.

"My work," he said with a sigh. He needed to finish the painting for the gentleman, Stuart. And there remained the work commissioned by Mr. Astor. The man would be coming in a mere three weeks to claim the paintings. Tom had been happy with Mr. Astor's confidence in him. Now he worried he would have many unhappy customers if he didn't return to his work.

How will I accomplish it in light of what's happening? Painting required freedom of the mind, heart, and spirit. He could not simply sit and draw on a whim. It had to come forth from his innermost being, and right now that being felt trapped by circumstances of his own making. *I have no choice. I need to find Sara and make certain she's all right. I have to talk to her and tell her about Annabelle. I have to talk to Annabelle, too, and tell her about Sara. I need to straighten out this messy affair and see what is left in the end.*

The morning went badly, and by late afternoon he reluctantly returned home to paint. Claire ignored him the rest of the day and at dinner. He struggled as best he could to finish the painting and then left that evening to deliver it to Stuart.

On his way back, he stopped at another guesthouse, though knowing the answer to his inquiry. He knocked on the door, stomping his feet to keep warm. The cold began to seep through his coat and chill him. His feet felt numb. He would need to return home soon and make some tea.

A large woman holding a broom answered the knock. "You need a place to stay?"

"No. I'm here to inquire about a certain young woman. Her name is Sara McGee."

"Uh-huh. What about her?"

Tom felt an instant surge of excitement. *Blessed be the Lord.* "I have an important message to give her."

"Sorry, she's not in right now."

"Do you have paper and ink so I can leave her a message?"

She looked at him, twisted her lips, and then strode off, but not before she placed the broom against the wall. "You can come and use the desk there in the hall." She placed the writing implements before him.

"Thank you." He rubbed his cold hands together, staring at the blank piece of paper. He had no idea what to write. Should he confess everything? Or share just enough words to bring her back home? The woman nearly standing over him didn't help his concentration.

"If you want my suggestion, young man, just tell her how you feel. I'm guessing that's why you're here, right? That's what I told the other man."

He put down his pen. "There was another man here calling on Sara?"

"Oh, you're about the third caller she's had. She's very much admired, this young lady. In fact, just last night she received a gentleman caller right here at the cottage. They sat over there." She pointed to a couch barely wide enough for two people. "He certainly looked interested in her."

Tom gritted his teeth. Stuart was wasting no time, was he? In fact, when Tom had delivered the painting this night, the man boasted about having dinner with a special guest. Tom felt his blood run cold and not from the winter's day. It was something he'd never experienced before. It was the cold sensation of jealousy in his veins.

"I'll be in the kitchen if you need anything." She shuffled away, leaving Tom to his mess of jumbled thoughts. It was plain to see Sara was no longer ordinary. She was a lady and entertaining gentlemen callers. And he needed to figure out if they had a future before one of those callers swept her away.

Dear Sara,

I'm not certain what to say. I know we did not part on good terms the other evening, and for that I'm truly sorry.

He dipped the pen in the inkwell, thought for a moment, then continued.

Claire misses you dreadfully, and I will say with my heart that I do, too. The house has been quiet without you. I pray to God for His will in this and in what the future holds. I ask you to reconsider coming back to us. I need to talk to you about what happened. If I'm too late, I understand. But I wanted you to know, and I pray you will reconsider.

> *I am yours truly,*
> *Thomas Haskins*

He read it over and sighed. It was the best he could do under the circumstances. He had just placed the pen in the inkwell when the portly woman returned.

"So you're finished?"

"I am. Thank you very much for allowing me to leave a note."

"Of course. I'll leave it right here for when she comes in."

Tom looked at the note and then at the woman before placing his hat on his head. "Do you have any idea if she's found a job at a hotel?"

The woman stared and burst out laughing. "What? She doesn't need a job. She has all the money in the world. At least I think she does. She gave me a nice fancy tip the other day."

Now it was Tom's turn to stare. How had Sara come by money so soon? Perhaps Stuart had lent her some. "This *is* Sara McGee we're speaking of."

"Sarah Manley, yes."

"No, I mean Sara McGee. She was carrying a carpetbag that was very old. She's from New York City."

The woman shook her head. "I'm afraid you have the wrong lady.

This Sarah has her own carriage and team here in Bethlehem, and she's from Connecticut."

Tom issued a loud sigh and pocketed the letter. "I do have the wrong lady. I'm sorry."

"I am, too. I hope you find who you're looking for."

Tom left the house, never feeling lower in his life. He paused to reread the letter. A feeling rose up within him, a longing for her to read this and see his true heart. "Sara…where are you? Please don't tell me you went back to New York. I'll never forgive myself if I let you go off without making certain you're all right…allowing you to escape without knowing God's will in this situation." He folded the letter and put it into his coat pocket.

Shivering from the cold, he could do nothing else but return home. Gray clouds had thickened and lowered. A few flakes of snow began dancing in the air. A storm was brewing and Sara could be out in the middle of it, huddled in a barn or worse. And it was his fault.

He walked back to the house, his steps tentative. Claire would be waiting for any news, hoping beyond hope that he had found her, and he had nothing to offer. But with God there was hope. God knew where Sara was. He could make their paths cross, giving them another opportunity to understand, to forgive, and to accept the future, whatever that future may be.

Claire stood in the foyer when he entered. She studied his reaction as he slowly took off his coat, which she kindly took from him. "You still haven't found her."

"I thought I did, at the Highland Cottage. Until I learned it was another woman staying there with a similar name. I'd even written a letter before I discovered it was the wrong woman."

"May I read it?"

Tom handed the note to her and left to fix some tea. He had already put the kettle on the cookstove when he heard the rustle of a dress entering the kitchen.

"What a beautiful letter, Tom." Tears glazed Claire's eyes. "I'm so happy you want to know God's will."

"It's all I've ever wanted, Claire. But I didn't let it be known like I should. And I kept things from Sara, especially about Annabelle. I guess I thought it would never work out between us. Sara was from a different life. I couldn't see how the two of us could become one. But I should have been honest and not given her false hope."

Claire slowly sank into a chair. "I've been thinking while you were away this evening. Sometimes I felt I forced my way of life on Sara and didn't allow her to be the woman God made her to be. I once told her that God had a special reason for her being here and that He would reveal it. But then I also wanted her to learn what I thought was right. To dress fashionably. To act ladylike. I suppose those are reasonable virtues—but there are more worthy virtues. Peace. Joy, loving-kindness, self-control. Good and godly fruits that are not man-made."

"Claire, none of this is your fault. It's mine."

"No, it's both our faults. God is trying to teach us things through having Sara here. We only thought we were helping her; really she came to help us. She came from a place of hardship to teach us that there's more to life than a fancy dress or good manners or a nice lifestyle."

Tom couldn't help but give Claire a hug of reassurance. She wept softly on his shoulder. "I miss her so much. She was like a sister to me."

"Claire, I'm sure she misses you, too."

"I wish that were true. I so much want to believe it."

"It is true. And I have faith that somehow this will work out. That we will see her again. God will make it clear to us what He wants us to do. And if that means we allow Sara to go home, then we do that. Or if it means that she is to become my wife, then I will do that, too." And he meant it with all his heart.

If only he knew where to find her...

Chapter Fourteen

Tom thought long and hard about the conversation with Claire and everything that had happened. When a week went by with no sign of Sara, he decided she must have returned to the city. He had no choice but to let her go and continue on, somehow, someway. Though he tried to make peace with his heart, his spirit remained troubled. His ability to paint anything fresh on a snow white canvas was also stymied. The flowing waters of creativity had been dammed up. Today he sat frozen, as he had the past few days, staring at the empty canvas before him and thinking how it mirrored his heart—absent of color or anything else. But despite how he felt, he had commissions to fulfill. Only two weeks remained before Mr. Astor would return for the Christmas holiday and expect the paintings to be ready.

Tom sighed, forcing himself to mix the paints for his palette. December ought to be a time of good cheer and plenty of creativity. The town was already preparing for the array of visitors to arrive. Cottages and hotels were decorated with cheerful wreaths, garlands, and huge red bows. Even with Sara's departure, Claire talked of decorating the house for Christmas and what she would prepare for Christmas dinner. She had even suggested inviting relatives they had not seen in years.

Tom only grunted and wondered privately how they could celebrate.

"There's nothing more we can do for Sara," Claire had said. "We must think about the future. And I think it would be nice to have Mama's sister and her husband from Maine for Christmas."

"I'm not in the mood for entertaining."

"Nor should we stare at each other and mourn the past. Sara has made her decision. We may have made mistakes, but there's nothing we can do." She then drew in a quick breath. "Would you like to invite Annabelle Loving over?"

Tom had looked up, nearly dropping his cup of hot tea. Even now as he reflected on the conversation, he shuddered. "I can't believe you're suggesting such a thing," he'd said.

"I saw her the other day at the mercantile. She talked about you and said she missed you. And she hoped perhaps we might get together for Christmas Eve."

"So you've given up on Sara completely? I'm surprised, Claire."

"I've surrendered it to God, Tom, as you should. And I'm thinking of your welfare. I do love you, you know, and I want what's best for you."

Is Annabelle Loving what's best for me? he wondered pensively. He stared at the empty canvas, trying to picture Annabelle sharing Christmas with them and what it would mean. It seemed more akin to rubbing salt into an open wound. After all, the conversation Sara overheard between Annabelle and him at the Maplewood Hotel had first spawned the disagreement. And it also led to the question, Was Annabelle even right for him?

Tom imagined then a dip in the refreshing waters to escape the fire of trial and indecision. He took up the brush and began painting a river scene. He painted a log floating downstream, as if it were ready to rescue someone unable to swim. He added a few small birds listening to the play of music as the water rushed by. Then some bushes flanking the river's edge with swift strokes of the brush dipped in green.

He murmured a prayer, thanking God for the grace at least to accomplish one small work. But Mr. Astor still requested one work in particular, a painting of Franconia Notch in the winter with the famous Old Man of the Mountain. He must venture there soon to refresh his memory of the scene. And with snow already gracing the land, he would need to borrow Lawrence's sleigh for the trip. He rested the brush on the palette. No doubt Annabelle would insist on joining him in the venture. Maybe there was another way for him to venture to Franconia Notch without having to ask Lawrence for his sleigh and risk further encounters.

Claire raced into the room then, panting. Her wide eyes and flushed face met his startled gaze. "What is it? What's the matter?"

"He's here!" she said breathlessly.

"Who?"

"That man from the city…the one who buys your paintings…Mr. Astor. Did you know he was coming?"

Tom flew to his feet, and when he did, he upset the green paint. The color of a deep summer forest now decorated the cloth protecting the floor. Green droplets had splattered across his shoes. *What is he doing here?* The man was not due to arrive for another two weeks. What if Mr. Astor demanded his paintings now? Or wished to see the works in progress? "What am I going to do?"

"You'd better come right away. He's in the parlor. I need to make some tea. Thank goodness I baked some blueberry biscuits this morning." She scurried away to fulfill her duties as hostess while Tom took a rag and tried to wipe the green paint off his shoes.

He then looked in a mirror, smoothing back a small tuft of dark hair that had fallen across his forehead. Worry lines creased his brow and surrounded his eyes. He was the perfect portrait of a man about to enter into battle for his livelihood. He tried to smile at the reflection to drum up his courage, but anxiety persisted, confirmed by the pounding of his heart in his ears.

He picked up the still-wet painting of the river and entered the parlor, where Claire had just begun to serve tea. "Mr. Astor, what a pleasant surprise." He offered his free hand.

"Thomas." The man rose and shook his hand. He appeared as dignified as always, in a stiff, starched white shirt, black tailored trousers, and a short coat. "I see you're hard at work. Excellent."

"I thought you would like to see my newest creation. I call it *The Wandering Soul*." He did not elaborate that he had just painted it an hour ago and that it mirrored his own soul.

"Yes, of course. Please excuse my early arrival, but my business did not allow me to venture here during the time I wanted. I sincerely hope you have the other paintings ready or at least in their final stages of completion."

Tom felt his face turning hot like a burn sometimes suffered in the summer heat. He walked over and took a seat, conscious of the man's gaze on him. "Well, sir…," he began. He looked at the painting of the river lying against the wall, feeling more and more like that log being swept away by the rushing water.

Mr. Astor stirred a sugar lump into his tea. "Is there a problem, Thomas?"

How he wanted to tell Mr. Astor everything…especially that his suggestion of marriage had caused more trouble than he ever imagined. And that with all the distraction followed an inability to create anything worthy of the man's attention.

The spoon clinked inside the cup. "I can see from your face there is."

"Yes, there are several problems, sir. I'm not exactly sure how to explain them…."

"I see. Perhaps we can meet over dinner tonight at the Maplewood and discuss them."

"Uh…that's kind of you, sir, but…"

He took a sip. "Six o'clock. And this is the Maplewood, you understand. Have you a decent suit to wear?"

"Fair enough, I think."

"Plan to arrive at five o'clock. My assistant, Alfred, will be there at my room with a suit of clothes for you. Room 211."

Tom shifted in his seat. "Well, thank you sir, but…"

"We'll talk business and find out why you're lacking in artistic skill. It's a terrible thing to abandon one's talent for frivolous matters." He drained his cup before rising to his feet. Claire, who had been eavesdropping, quickly scurried forward to give the man his hat and cane. "Thank you, miss. I have great plans for you, Thomas, but we can't have your work interrupted by other matters. I've invested too much time in you. I've told fellow businessmen of your work and showed them your paintings. Especially the one you painted for me last summer, the Old Man of the Mountain. They are very interested in having the painting duplicated."

"I understand, sir."

"I won't have them disappointed. You must embrace your destiny as a master artist, Thomas. There's too much at stake." He again thanked Claire for her hospitality, nodded to Tom, then walked out the door that Claire held open for him.

Closing it, Claire whirled to face him, concern etched in the lines running across her face. "He didn't seem happy at all, Tom."

"Well, he's not supposed to be here. He told me he would arrive on December eighteenth. I had two weeks to finish the paintings. Now he expects me to have the Old Man ready by tomorrow night?" Tom waved his hand in the air. "I haven't even traveled to Franconia Notch to sketch it."

"Of course he doesn't mean you must have all the paintings completed at this moment. He only wants assurance that you're keeping your obligations. And I must agree. You need to keep your commitments, Tom, in everything."

"In everything? What's that supposed to mean?"

"It means you need to examine yourself and see what is happening. What the future holds. You must admit you've been distracted, as Mr. Astor fears."

"This situation with Sara hasn't helped matters. I'm no closer to Mr. Astor's wish that I find a wife. It was folly to try this ad-for-a-bride notion, even if it did work for that other couple. And I have no idea what will happen with Annabelle. If he asks what I've done in the area of marriage, what will I say?"

"Just go to supper tonight and see where things stand. Let the matter of marriage lie. And with your work, tell him you will do your best to finish the paintings in a timely manner."

He nodded and walked off to think about the upcoming meeting. He stopped short when he saw the mess he had left, the puddle of green paint still on the floor covering. He remembered the spill and glanced down at the green smears decorating his shoes. What would Mr. Astor think of him wearing these shoes to a fine dinner at the

Maplewood? That and hearing his woes concerning his work of late? Mr. Astor would think him a disorganized mess like the room before him. The man might cancel the paintings altogether and find himself another artist.

Tom had no choice but to be honest with Mr. Astor—to tell him what he had done in the matter of relationships, that he had heeded the man's advice but things had gone astray. And to tell him about the struggle in his heart. Ask for advice. He was his mentor, after all. He had told Tom about the importance and stability inherent in marriage. *Some stability.* Tom groaned. He'd encountered nothing but rocks and ruts since walking this path.

Tom sat down at the easel once more. How he wished he could paint what Mr. Astor desired. But the only image he saw was Sara McGee's wide eyes staring at him from across the table. Large, soft blue eyes conveying her vulnerability but yet a ray of hope. He could do nothing but pray for guidance in the meeting to come. Then he set to work removing the green from his shoes.

* * * *

Mr. Astor smiled in approval when Tom arrived in the stately dining room. "You look fine, indeed. Alfred does wonders."

Tom tugged at the snug collar of his shirt and hoped the tight fit of the coat wouldn't bother him. But seeing the men and women arriving for dinner, dressed in fine array, he was glad Mr. Astor had suggested the change of clothes. Everyone looked as if they had stepped off a fashion plate in their fancy dresses and black suits. He and Mr. Astor waited until they were directed to a table in the corner of the vast dining room. The last time Tom had been here, sipping tea with Mr. Astor, they had discussed great plans for his work. The mere thought made the shirt collar tighten like a noose. He ran his finger underneath the neckline before smiling sheepishly at Mr. Astor.

A young waiter poured them water and asked for their drink orders. Mr. Astor ordered a scotch. Tom declined.

"So tell me what's happening in your life, Thomas. I'm interested in seeing you succeed in your work."

"Thank you, sir, for giving me so many opportunities. I would be a floundering artist at best if not for your support."

Mr. Astor laughed as the young waiter arrived with his drink and the menus. "Ah, do you see this fine menu? That's why I prefer dining at the Maplewood. They offer more choices than one could possibly eat. For a hotel in the far reaches of the North, I have yet to find such exquisite cuisine."

Tom joined him in a survey of the delectable entrées offered. Maryland chicken. Breast of duck. Leg of lamb with mint sauce. All accompanied by endless vegetables, breads, and desserts. It did look excellent.

"May I take the gentlemen's order?" the waiter inquired.

Mr. Astor wasted no time. "I'll have the lamb with mint sauce. And you'd do well to order it also, Thomas."

Tom followed suit, ordering the leg of lamb, though he had never been very particular about it before, along with vegetables and bread pudding for a dessert. "Thank you, sir, for this meal."

"No trouble at all. But I do intend to find out what is keeping you from your work."

"Well, sir, in a way it's you."

Mr. Astor sat back. "And just what do you mean by that, young man?"

"I'm sorry, sir, I didn't mean for it to come out that way. I was trying to be humorous. What I meant is, do you remember the day when we met this past summer and you talked about my finding a wife?"

"Certainly. Whatever happened with that, by the way?"

"I've had several prospects, actually. And one came from an ad I placed for a bride."

Mr. Astor sat still, his eyes wide. "Really. I never would have considered such a method."

"But she's not quite what I expected."

Mr. Astor chuckled. "Are they ever? A woman is an enigma. While the wrapping may look as if it contains a fine good, one never knows what lies within. And one might receive a wooden crate in appearance but inside find exquisite china."

"She arrived quite destitute off the street and in great need. Not that such a condition is bad, mind you, but again she was not what I expected."

"So this is keeping you from concentrating on your work?"

"In a way. You see, I've also met a fine woman from Boston. She is a gifted musician and well-versed in etiquette. And I've found myself…"

"Caught in between." The bread basket arrived, and Mr. Astor helped himself to a crusty roll. "How like a book of relationships when one is tested multiple times. And here you had no such prospects just this past summer." He laughed as if finding great humor in Tom's predicament. "I was once in your place with two different women of different backgrounds. I decided the one that remained to enjoy all the seasons of life was the right one for me."

Tom reasoned this. "Well, the one who answered the ad, Sara, found out about the other woman and left our house, determined to return to New York."

"Then it seems you have your answer. If she's gone, then what about the woman from Boston?"

"She has remained, at least for now." He considered then if Annabelle would remain with him through the summers and winters of life. The more he thought about it, the more unsettled he became.

"If a bird is determined to live free, then nothing you can say will hold it back. If you try to keep it caged against its will, it will struggle until it dies. You don't want that to happen here."

"Sara didn't struggle until she witnessed the passing friendship I had with Miss Loving. I'm not convinced that she did not have feelings for me. Otherwise, why would she take flight?"

"A sound observation." He began to eat while Tom stared at his butter plate a few moments. "If this is meant to be, she will return. If not, you must seek another answer, perhaps with this other woman. But for now, until matters are settled, you need to give attention to your work. You cannot allow your talent to be wasted. Use it instead while you are waiting. Give attention to finer details. And I must insist that the painting of Franconia Notch and the others be done as soon as possible."

Tom tensed. "While you are here?"

"No, I'm leaving in a few days. But I will leave you money to have the works shipped to New York. Oh, and you may keep the river painting you showed me. I didn't like it much, I'm afraid. Not enough scope."

Tom nodded. He didn't mind the man's frankness. Mr. Astor

proved to be a father figure in many ways, setting his mind on the things he must consider in life. He buttered his bread and looked up, slowly taking a bite.

He stopped in mid-bite.

It can't be.

He nearly choked on the bread before remembering to chew and swallow. Quickly he gulped water to wash it down. "I don't believe it," he sputtered. *All this time...and I never thought to look here!*

"Thomas? What are you mumbling about? Speak up, young man. I can't hear you with all this noise in the dining room."

Tom didn't answer Mr. Astor. Instead he wiped his eyes to make certain he wasn't seeing some vision of his own making. But he wasn't. Sara McGee stood three tables over, putting dirty plates and glasses into a large tin basin. "Excuse me, sir. I'll be right back." He laid down his napkin and hurried over.

"Sara?"

She whirled and nearly dropped a plate. He reached out to grab it before it fell, and when he did, his hand brushed hers. Her cheeks reddened. She wore a simple cotton dress covered by a white apron, her full brown hair concealed by a white cap. Her eyes remained as intensely blue as he remembered. And her features just as rigid with determination.

"Sara, what are you doing here?"

"I'm working, of course. What are *you* doing here?" She looked around. "Meeting someone, I suppose?" She turned from him to gather up the remaining dishes.

"Yes, I'm having dinner with Mr. Astor...the gentleman from New York who buys many of my paintings. He's here to help me succeed with my work...like Mrs. Whitaker wanted for your life." He paused to see recognition pass over her face. "Sara, I want you to know, I've been looking everywhere for you the past week."

"I don't understand why. I said I could take care of myself. And I have."

Tom wanted to say more but caught sight of Mr. Astor and the perturbed look on his face. "I'm sorry; I have to return to my table. Will you meet with me at eight o'clock so we can talk?"

"I can't. I'm still working then. And Mrs. White expects me home right afterward or she worries."

"We need to talk. I need to tell you something, something I should have said a long time ago."

"There isn't anything left to say." She returned to her work. Tom waited. When she moved on to another table, he reluctantly went back to his seat.

"I take it you've found your lost bird?" Mr. Astor observed. "Is she the one who answered the ad?"

"Yes. And her feathers are too ruffled. She will not even speak to me."

Astor chuckled. "Thomas, let the matter settle." He pointed to their lamb with mint sauce that had just arrived. "Enjoy your dinner, and think about your work. It's all you can do."

My work, he thought. *A work that is only just beginning.*

Chapter Fifteen

Sara could not get the vision of Tom Haskins out of her mind, even as she cleared away the remaining dishes from the tables that evening. She saw his face everywhere—the dark eyes, raised eyebrows, and lips parted in inquiry. The way he asked to speak to her. Yet the memory of the conversation between him and Annabelle Loving still raked her. Why had he tried to find her? Didn't he already have Annabelle at his beck and call? An accomplished and beautiful lady, ready to fulfill his every desire?

Perhaps Claire had a hand in this sudden meeting. After all, she and Claire had grown quite close. She was indebted to Claire for the love she'd shown. Her heart ached at the thought of their separation. Many times Sara wanted to send word to Claire, explaining why she could not remain in the house. She had come to Bethlehem for one reason: to answer an ad for a bride. But when another woman entered the scene, it made no sense for her to stay. She had to move on with her life the best way she knew how.

Sara carried a stack of plates back to the kitchen, where young maids bustled about, washing plates, cups, and silver. Sara took up a towel to begin drying the mounds of dishes. Her arms ached, and her fingers soon turned to lumps of wrinkled flesh. *I'm just a servant,* she thought bitterly. *Perhaps that's why he came here tonight—to witness my true status. To confirm his decision regarding Annabelle and all the things she promised him.*

"So who were you talkin' to out there?" a young girl named Rachel inquired. "Saw ya there in the dining room with some fine gentleman."

Sara looked over at the young girl not much older than she. Like Sara, many of the help were unlearned and poor. They worked to put bread on the table. Some worked to pay off debts. Others worked for the reason Sara did, to provide for some untold future.

"A man I met some time ago."

"And why would some fancy gentleman be interested in any of us?" Rachel hooted. "Do you think they're lookin' at us in our aprons and caps?" She began to strut about the room like a lady of means, her hand pointed at an angle, her nose in the air. "Why, thank ye, man, I'll have this dance." She performed a clumsy curtsy. "Oh, but please pardon the cap an' apron."

The other girls burst out in laughter.

Yet the image convicted Sara when she thought about how she'd tried to become such a lady like that, full of airs. She once had the appropriate dresses and hats, courtesy of Claire, but had sold the garments to pay for her lodging. "Did you know I actually lived with him at one time?" Sara said.

At this, the girls in the kitchen stopped their chores and turned to look at her. "Mercy me, you lived with a man?" said one. "How did you dare?"

"How improper," said another.

"Why not, if he's providin'?" added a third.

Sara felt a flush in her cheeks. "I didn't live with him alone. I lived with his sister and him, in their house."

"Why are you working here, then, if you had such a fine life?"

It seemed as if everyone wanted to hear her sad tale. Sara obliged, sharing with them her life on the streets of New York, answering Tom Haskins's ad, and her arrival here in Bethlehem.

"And he dared court another woman while you were here?" Rachel said in dismay, shaking her head. "Why if I saw him, I'd tell him a thing or two. Shameful."

"I'd tell him to go his way," declared another.

The others agreed and shared sympathy over Sara's plight. She should welcome it with open arms, except she couldn't forget the memory of Tom's sad countenance this evening in the dining room. Thinking on it, it seemed as if he missed her company. But why? He had no reason to, with the accomplished Annabelle available to entertain him—with a grand wedding trip…living a lavish lifestyle with a beautiful woman on his arm…everything a man could want.

And what did Sara herself have to offer him? She could barely read and write. She worked as a maid peeling potatoes and washing dishes. She had no money, no fame, nothing but disheveled hair and dark circles under her eyes. And one shabby work dress. Yet he appeared relieved to find her. And he wanted to speak to her. There was little doubt he still cared about what happened to her, but he was more likely looking after his charge out of obligation.

Sara moved to dry more dishes until they were finally done. By then it was nearing nine o'clock and weariness had set in.

"Now if you need me to go and talk to that man, you let me know," Rachel told her.

Sara smiled. "Thank you, but I'll be all right." She had taken care of herself among all sorts of strangers and friends for many years in New York. Surely she could do it in a tiny town like Bethlehem and with a man like Tom.

Sara left the kitchen and went to fetch her ratty coat. The garment did little to shield her from the New Hampshire cold. She had considered buying a coat, but that would put her further behind in saving enough money for the train ticket to New York. Oh, how she wished Tom had just lent her the money to leave. Why he wanted her to work herself to death and nearly freeze in the process, she did not understand. He could have done the right thing and sent her back to where she belonged.

Sara ventured outside and found that a fresh layer of snow had fallen while she worked. The new snow soaked her leather shoes, numbing her feet. She looked carefully where she walked, hoping she wouldn't slip and fall.

Suddenly she heard a cry from the darkness. She paused. Tingles shot through her arms and down her back. She squinted until she saw a small child walking about in the snow, crying. Sara hurried over and found a young boy in distress. "My goodness, what are you doing out here in the snow this late at night?"

"I–I'm lost!" he cried. "Please help me."

"Shh, it's all right." Sara crouched beside him. "What's your name?"

"S–Sammy," he said in a shivering voice. "Sammy Turner."

Sara looked about at the houses with the soft glow from oil lamps filling the windows. "We will go to the next house and see if anyone recognizes you." Sara took his small hand, which gripped hers soundly. As they started down the street, she thought of the times she'd helped lost children wandering about the city streets. Some were reunited with their parents but others she had to take to the orphanage and leave them there. It nearly broke her heart. How well she understood what it meant to be alone in the world with no family save God.

"I—I don't know how I got lost," the boy mumbled. "I went to fetch some sticks for the fire. Then I couldn't find my way back. Please help me find my house."

"Shush, it will be all right." How the little boy's anguish mirrored her heart. She, too, wanted to find her way back home. But where was home? Bethlehem? New York? Maybe nowhere.

They stumbled their way along, and finally she saw a house barely visible in the whirling snow. "Let me ask here." She knocked at the door.

"Well…what do you want?" answered a gruff man smoking a pipe. "It's too cold to be out begging for money. But if it's money you need…"

"Please, this little boy is lost. His name is Sammy Turner."

"Ha, you're lost again, Sammy?" the man exclaimed, shaking his head. "He does this often, miss. He lives two houses down from us on the right. Picket fence out front, if you can see it in the snow. I'd help you, but I have a bad knee. Can't risk falling. But wait…" He left and soon returned with a lantern. "This should help."

"Oh, thank you, sir." Joy filled her heart at his kindness. She coaxed Sammy down the snow-covered walkway until they came upon a group of people with flickering lanterns.

"Sammy!" a voice shouted. A man grabbed him up in a hefty hold.

"S–sorry, Papa. I got lost when I went to get sticks from the woodpile."

"I'm so grateful someone found you." The man then looked at Sara. "Thank you so much, miss. We realized he was missing an hour ago and began looking around town. I should have known he might head for the Maplewood Hotel. It's the biggest place around, and he likes going there. Especially since they put in that newfangled bowling alley."

"I like bowling," Sammy said solemnly, wiping his runny nose with the back of his hand. "You knock over milk bottles with balls."

Sara smiled, though by now she could barely contain her shivers. "I–I'm g–glad he's back with you, s–sir."

"We shouldn't be standing out here in the cold. Please, come to our house. I insist. My wife will want to thank you, and we will get you something warm to drink."

Sara accepted as numbness began to settle in her hands, joining her cold feet. She followed Sammy's father to a house that was but a hundred yards away. When they burst inside, a woman stood in the hallway as if expecting their return.

"You found him! Oh, thank You, dear Lord!" She gave Sammy a hug, nuzzling her face in his hair. "I was so worried."

"Addie, this is…" The man paused.

"S–Sara."

"Sara found Sammy out on the street and brought him back to us. But she is very cold."

"Oh my, come right in," Addie invited. "Sit close by the fire." Sara found an abundance of warmth and love in the words and kind gestures as she was led into the main sitting room where a huge fire was kindled in the fireplace. "Sit here and warm yourself. Elisa," she addressed a young woman who ventured in, "go fetch Miss Sara a nice, hot cup of tea. And bring Sammy some warm cider." Addie then went to find them blankets.

Sara snuggled under the blanket that brought instant warmth while the heat of the fire warmed her cold feet. Likewise, Sammy rested nearby, wrapped in his own blanket. For the first time in a long time Sara felt warm and secure, surrounded by the attention of a kind family.

"Please stay as long as you like," Addie said. "In fact, please stay the night. We have a spare room."

"Oh, I can't stay long. I must go back soon, or Mrs. White will wonder what happened to me."

"You can leave when you're warm. Henry will be glad to walk you to wherever you're staying." She glanced at her husband. "Henry, I'm so thankful for the way our neighbors came out in the snow to help us."

"Our town is like that when difficulties happen," Henry said, taking a seat near Sara. "We see many wealthy people come and go. But the real wealth is found when we come together and help each other. We can't close our doors to people's needs…."

"Or our hearts," his wife added. "You're welcome to come here any-time, Sara. Even stay with us if you need to. Oh, listen to me, I haven't even properly introduced myself. I'm Adelaide Turner, and this is my husband, Henry. These are our children. Elisa's the eldest, and she's eighteen. Susan is twelve, and of course you know Sammy, who's five."

Elisa brought her a cup of tea. Sara took a sip, even as the three children sat nearby, staring at her. She immediately engaged them in conversation, asking each one about themselves and what they liked to do.

"I love snow!" declared Sammy. "Except when I get lost in it. But I have a new sled that Papa made for me."

"I would rather do my embroidery," Elisa said. Sara could tell there was a certain maturity about her. She wondered if they might be friends someday.

The middle child, Susan, sat still and silent. Sara asked what she liked to do. Prompted by Elisa, she finally talked about her enjoyment in reading.

"I'm learning to read," Sara said. "I didn't have much schooling when I lived in New York."

Suddenly members of the family were interested in hearing her adventures in the big city.

"I always wanted to visit New York," Henry mused. "You must tell us about it."

"Yes, and why you came all the way here to Bethlehem," asked Elisa. "You aren't here for a holiday—just to work?"

"I…" Sara didn't know what to say. For some reason, trying to explain to the family about Tom's ad for a bride seemed rather foolish. In a way, she felt foolish, too. "Let's just say I came seeking a new life. And nothing has gone as I expected."

The family exchanged glances but said no more. As the hour drew late, Adelaide ordered the children to bed while Henry drew on his coat. "I suppose we'd better get you back home now, miss."

Sara thanked Adelaide for everything and followed Henry into the cold. When they arrived at the guesthouse, Sara offered her thanks.

"No, I should thank you. You saved my boy's life. And since we don't live too far from Maplewood, you're welcome to visit anytime. Even board with us, if you wish."

"You have a lovely family, sir. Thank you again." Sara managed a smile before venturing inside. When she walked into the living room, a tall figure stood there. He whirled to face her.

It was Tom Haskins.

Her heart felt as if it might stop. *Oh no! How did he find me? Dear Lord, not now. After all I've been through tonight.* She shivered once more, this time from nerves.

Tom came toward her, his dark eyes wide with concern. "Sara, I was so worried! Mrs. White said you were very late. You usually come home a little after nine, and it's nearly eleven! I even went to the Maplewood looking for you."

"I'm sorry, but I—I can't talk now," she managed to say, walking past him. "I don't know how you found me."

"You mentioned staying with a Mrs. White. I knew of the guesthouse. And Sara, I…" He followed her to the stairs.

"Tom, I can't. I–I'm so tired. It's late. Go home. I'm sure Claire is worried about you."

Tom took another step forward then stopped.

Sara stumbled her way up the stairs and to her room, where she collapsed on the bed. "Oh, dear God, what am I going to do?" She buried her face in her pillow. *I can't think. I can barely breathe. But You, dear Lord, are kind even still. You have helped me. You have sent people my way, not only for me to help but to help me, too.* She began to relax. *And for some reason, You have sent Tom back into my life. I don't know why. I pray, please help me rest so I can figure out what to do tomorrow.*

* * * *

Morning arrived all too quickly. At least Sara did not have to report to work at the Maplewood until the afternoon, in time for the busy dinner hour. She spent the morning assisting Mrs. White with housework in exchange for a reduced rate on her room. Her cheeks tingled in the cold air as she stood on the back stoop, beating out rug after rug. She'd also promised to wash the kitchen floor before noon.

"Oh, Sara, you have a guest!" Mrs. White called out.

Who would be visiting her? Sara heaved a sigh as she dragged the rug back inside. She stopped short.

Tom stood before her once more—tall, dark, distinguished, and ever-curious about her circumstances. He took off his hat. "Good morning, Sara."

"Why do you keep following me?"

"I couldn't very well stay away. You looked as if something terrible had happened last night. As it was, I didn't sleep all night for worrying."

She folded the rugs. "I helped a little boy who was lost in the snow and returned him to his family. It took longer than I thought, visiting with the family after it happened. With the long hours at work and then the boy, I was quite exhausted. But they were a kind family. I was very glad to meet them."

"There are many fine people here in Bethlehem. They are not all the sordid kind you've seen in recent months."

"I never thought they were."

"I didn't mean it to come out that way. But I was thinking…with you working so late at night at the hotel, I don't like the idea of your walking home alone. I would very much like to be your escort, if you would allow me."

Sara stared in amazement at his offer. "Oh, come now. You're not truly going to walk me back each night at nine o'clock?"

"It would be my pleasure. And we can talk, if you wish. Or we can just walk."

Sara gave him what she hoped was a suspicious look. *Why in all the heavens would Tom want to do such a thing?* "Why are you doing this?" she finally asked, going to a closet to retrieve a bucket and scrub brush.

"Why?" He hesitated. Sara wondered if he knew the reason himself. "Because it's the right thing to do." He stood silent while she filled the bucket with water and added soap flakes. "And because I would never forgive myself if something happened to you."

She paused in her work to see the sincerity in his face and the same dark eyes that were looking quite handsome at that moment.

"And I want to know you better. I want to meet the woman who saved a little boy's life last night."

"Humph." She worked the water into a lather. "You had plenty of time to get to know me when I was a guest in your home, but you hardly gave me the time of day."

"I know, and for that I'm truly sorry. " He stepped forward.

Sara tensed, wondering if he was going to reach for her hand. Instead, he reached down and picked up the bucket. "Where do you need it?"

Without a word, Sara pointed to the kitchen floor. Something had changed within the heart of Tom Haskins...and maybe in her heart, as well. After last night, walking home in the snow, she was eager to accept and enjoy the companionship. She knew Tom would protect her, even after all that had happened. He wouldn't be here now if he didn't.

"So will you allow me to walk you home at night?"

"All right. I leave the kitchen at nine. And...thank you."

He nodded. "I'll see you then." He placed his hat on his head. "Oh—I have something for you." He took an envelope out of his coat pocket. "I will see you tonight."

Sara wiped her damp hands on her apron, watching him move toward the front door before she examined the letter. She worked to unseal the envelope. Inside was money and a simple note. She began to sound out the letters.

For your train fare, so you may leave whenever you wish.
Tom Haskins

Sara closed her hand over the envelope. What did this mean? Did he want her to leave? If he did, then why would he ask to walk her back from the hotel each night? How she wished she could read the unspoken words behind the simple note to reveal Tom's heart.

Sara sighed and tucked the envelope into the pocket of her apron. Today might well be her last day here in Bethlehem. She could have her few belongings packed and be on the train tomorrow morning. Yet she had no peace with such a plan. She had begun to find a special place in her heart for this town. She liked the beauty of the area and the pastor of the church where they attended. She had friends: Mrs. White…her coworkers at Maplewood…even the new family she met last night…Claire…maybe even Tom Haskins.

After Sara finished scrubbing the floor, she returned to her room. On a small table beside the cup and saucer that had belonged to her mother rested another letter. Tom had sent the letter to her in New York shortly before she came to Bethlehem. She took it now and compared it to the handwriting on the note she'd received today. The handwriting was the same, but the contents were much different.

Thank you very much for your recent letter. I was happy
indeed to hear more of Sara and her kind heart. How we need
such people as her to bring joy into the lives of those who have
none. And I must say I'm more than eager to meet her and
share that joy. And you have written wise words when you
say that beauty is found inside. That is the beauty I cherish,

too, and hope to share. Please don't think anything of Sara's circumstances, for they mean little in the grand scale of life. We will have much to do and share when we meet. I look forward to it with all my heart.

When Mrs. Whitaker read it to her, she'd commented, "It's a letter of love, for certain."

Sara shook her head. "It is a mockery, to be sure. None of what he wrote matched what he has done or how he looks at me. He has only ever judged the outside." She chuckled in scorn, folded the letter, and put it away. Yet her heart remained unsettled, yearning to know where his feelings stood now. And more importantly, what God's will was for them. How would she know the right answers if she chose to leave prematurely?

They would begin the journey again with Sara accepting Tom's offer to escort her to the guesthouse each night. They would walk the path together and see where God led them. And if it did not work out, he'd given her the freedom to leave whenever she wished. Sara opened the envelope and counted out the money. "All right, Mr. Haskins, you shall have your walk. I shall have my escort. And we shall see what comes of it."

Chapter Sixteen

....

Tom could hardly concentrate the rest of that day for thinking of Sara. He'd learned even more about last night's escapade with the lost boy when he arrived at the mercantile to buy some items for Claire. Everyone was talking about it. When anything happened among the Bethlehem townspeople, it became news. He was glad then he had stopped by to see Sara earlier that morning. Yet he couldn't help but wonder what might happen. By offering her the money so she could return home, it might well signal the end. Sara could leave this very afternoon if she wanted. But he hoped she might choose differently. She did, after all, accept his escort for this evening. Perhaps something new would spring up between them.

Now he tried to return his thoughts to his paintings. With the weather more favorable, he set up his easel in a large field, hoping to paint Mount Agassiz blanketed in freshly fallen snow. But the white canvas stared back at him as if to challenge him. Again the mood for a painting had fled. Mr. Astor had left a few days ago, reminding Tom of his commitment to have the paintings sent to New York in time for Christmas. But at this rate of progress, Tom would never make the deadline. Other things continued to hold his creative touch captive.

Finally he forced himself to sit before an easel and mix paints. He must paint something, no matter how he felt. Just then several children arrived with sleds to ride down the hill before him. He watched the playful scene unfold: the screams of delight as the children raced each other then turned into miniature snowmen after rolling off their sleds. Suddenly he had the urge to capture the simplistic but meaningful image of children enjoying a winter's day in Bethlehem. Even when the children left an hour later, Tom continued to paint until his fingers grew too cold to hold a paintbrush and the paints turned thick and sticky. With the scene emblazoned in his memory, he could finish the rest of it in the warmth of his home. He began to pack up his supplies.

"Hello, Thomas," came a familiar voice.

He turned and saw a feminine form plodding through the snow, dressed in a stylish coat, with hands buried inside a woolly muff. Annabelle Loving withdrew her hand and extended it to him. He hesitated to take her hand at first. Her red lips twisted into a pout, distorting her otherwise chiseled features. Finally he took her hand and kissed it lightly.

She smiled. "I haven't seen you in so long, not since the day we met at the hotel. Did you like the book on Italy?"

He didn't admit to her that he'd forgotten about it, but a perturbed look on her face formed anyway.

"What's the matter?" she asked.

"I'm just busy, Annabelle. Mr. Astor was here for a few days, demanding his paintings. I'm severely behind in my work."

"I'm sorry to hear that, but I'm delighted that Mr. Astor wants your paintings. Is that why you're out here in the cold? I'm surprised to find you painting in a big snowy field like this."

"I can no longer feel my fingers," he admitted, flexing them.

In a graceful move, Annabelle took his cold hands in hers, made warm by the muff, and began rubbing them. She drew nearer. "Does this help?" she whispered in a sultry voice.

Tom withdrew his hands and turned away. "Thank you. I do have to get my paints inside before they freeze."

"Of course. I only wondered what's happening. I thought…" She paused. "I thought things were going so well between us…and then suddenly I heard nothing from you. Are you angry with me?"

"Of course not. Why would I be?"

A smile lit her face, and her eyes glistened. "I couldn't begin to imagine why. We are so perfect for each other, Thomas, with our love for the arts. Then there's the trip to Italy Father has planned."

"I can't go to Italy," he said quickly, continuing to pack his paints.

She didn't seem to hear him. "I just know it will be a wonderful trip. Perfect for an artist. Can you see it? The painted domes. The cathedrals. And of course, the romance of Rome. Maybe we could even get married in Rome itself! A dream come true, just as you once said."

He froze. Again came the words about a marriage proposal. But the way she said them, he sensed for the first time the error of it all, offering the fulfillment of a dream in exchange for a marital commitment. A relationship formed like this would never last, especially through the trials of life. "Annabelle, I can't go on the trip. I should have said this to you sooner, but…there's someone else." He glanced up in time to see her face redden.

"What?" Her laugher reached a crescendo. "You can't be serious. Don't tell me it's that simpleton of a girl who used to live in your house. I heard how she ran off as soon as she learned about us. Lawrence told me she was some newspaper bride, of all things. How silly. It's better she left. I mean…" She laughed once more. "You can't possibly see yourself married to such a woman, can you? She's a strumpet from the street. No matter how much Claire has tried to dress her like a lady, she never will be a lady. You must know it."

A silent rage began to fill him. His face began to heat. "Sara is a fine Christian woman, Annabelle, and *not* some harlot. And I will no longer judge by outward appearances. That was my mistake in the beginning. It's the inner person, the quiet heart, that matters. The Bible even says not to put on airs like jewels but to adorn oneself with a gentle and quiet spirit."

She opened her mouth to interrupt, but he continued.

"Talk with people at the mercantile on Main Street, and you will learn how Sara helped a young boy who was lost in the snow last night. If she had not found him, he would have died. And I must say it's that gentle spirit of humility one finds attractive. And likable."

"So are you saying I won't help others? Why, I helped you, in case you don't realize it. More than you know. And this is how you thank me, by giving me some kind of Bible lesson, like I'm in Sunday school?"

"Annabelle, you can't base a marriage on selfishness. Using trips or money to buy your way to happiness will never work. You will still be miserable, no matter how hard you try."

Annabelle jerked backward as though she had been slapped. "How dare you. I've never been so insulted!"

"I didn't mean to insult you. But I've given this plenty of thought recently. And I can't go on a trip, nor can I marry you." He paused. "And please tell Lawrence that I will return his book." He continued packing up his paints. By the time he finished, the only image of Annabelle that remained was hurried footprints in the new-fallen snow, heading toward town.

Tom felt as if a great boulder had been lifted from his shoulders. He didn't know why; he had nothing now. Annabelle was no more.

Sara remained distant and even angry with him. *But I have peace. I couldn't have been happy with someone like Annabelle. Why I didn't see it until now, I don't know.* He paused. *I may be too late for Sara, too.* Still he felt at peace with the situation. Somehow, someway, he was on the right path and no longer fighting through a hedge of choking briars.

For the first time in many months, Tom felt light on his feet, even if they were temporarily dragged down by his trudging through snow drifts. He returned to the house, whistling a favorite hymn, "How Great Thou Art."

A startled Claire greeted him with a confused look. "So what's the reason for all this gaiety today?"

"I've found freedom, Claire."

"Freedom from what, dear brother? I must admit, I'm almost afraid to ask."

"Freedom from selfishness and criticism."

"I don't understand."

He entered the study and began setting up the easel. Claire followed. "Annabelle found me while I was painting, and we talked. But as she spoke, I realized my own mistake—valuing the outward appearance. Criticizing those beneath us. But now I'm free from it all. And from Annabelle. Neither of us was good for the other."

Tom felt the strength of Claire's embrace, and with such force, he nearly lost his balance.

"Oh, Tom, this is an answer to prayer! How I prayed God would direct all this and open your eyes. I can't believe it's happened."

Tom couldn't quite believe what had happened, either. But he knew he was finally in the right place in his heart. "And tonight I'm seeing Sara. She tried so hard to fit in, to find her way in a world that rejected her and left her alone. And I want her to know that she does fit in this place, better than anyone, even those who supposedly have everything."

"I know you said you saw her at the Maplewood in the dining room when you met Mr. Astor. What happened after that?"

"We didn't talk much last night. I returned to her guesthouse this morning, and I found out she was responsible for rescuing the little Turner boy out in the snow. The news is all over town."

Claire's eyes widened.

"I didn't like the idea of her walking home alone every night, so I offered to be her escort each evening after work. And you may as well know this, too. I gave her the money for the train fare back to New York City. If she still chooses to go."

"You did what?" Claire grabbed his hand. "But we don't want her to leave. Whatever possessed you to do that?"

"I would rather she leave than be a servant in a hotel dining room all because I wouldn't give her the money. I want her to be free to choose the life she wants. It's better this way."

"Then how do you know she won't take the train tonight? If she has the money, she has no reason to stay."

Tom knew that could happen. He'd given her no reason to stay except a hope that he'd shown her some fragment of his heart—one willing to be there for her and help her. He wished he could go right now and tell her of his encounter with Annabelle. That his eyes were opened and he'd thrust the relationship aside. That he'd even told Annabelle there was another. "I suppose if I arrive tonight and she's not at the hotel, I will have my answer."

"Oh, Tom. Can you live with the fact that both these women might be gone from your life forever?"

He thought about it before slowly nodding. "As long as I have peace. And there is always my work. My only prayer, Claire, is that I'll be in God's will."

Claire shook her head in amusement. "Oh, Tom, I was so worried about what would happen. I'm glad God's hand is in this. You truly are a dear brother."

"Sometimes I think I've been quite foolish."

She hugged him. "Look at you. For a man who had no prospects a year ago, you've certainly had a share in the fire of relationships these many months. Who would have thought?"

Tom chuckled as he set up his paints. "It was more than I ever expected. Now I can value what matters most and leave the rest behind." *All things worked together for good,* he realized. And, as in the way of life, God was taking him through the maze step by step. He only prayed that Sara was still on a similar path. He prayed she had not purchased the train ticket today. He prayed even as he began finishing the painting of Bethlehem's children enjoying a winter's day. *God, if she will only remain here. Please...give her a reason to stay.*

* * * *

Tom's nerves were on edge at dinner. Normally he couldn't wait to wolf down Claire's fine cooking, but this night everything tasted the same.

"You haven't taken your second helping," Claire observed with the hint of a smile, as if she knew the anxiety inside him. "You're acting like a nervous bridegroom."

Tom felt his face flush. "Hardly. I'm just curious, I suppose, to see what Sara has decided. If she did leave to go back to New York, you're free to return home to Massachusetts. You've done so much here already. I never really thanked you for it, either."

"Oh, I would never leave before Christmas! We only have each other, Tom. Nothing is waiting for me in Springfield. In fact, maybe I'll even come back and settle here again."

Tom picked up his teacup. "Really?"

"I'm finding I like Bethlehem very much after many years of being away. I have friends in the sewing circle I gather with every Tuesday. I've become close to cantankerous Mrs. Harris, believe it or not." She chuckled. "I like the church we attend. And, of course, this is a beautiful place. Who wouldn't want to live in a town called Bethlehem?"

"I'm glad you feel that way. I only wish Sara did."

"She does."

"You seem confident of that."

"All Sara ever wanted was someone who cared about her. You're showing you care by offering to walk her home. She won't leave."

"I hope you're right." He took a long drink of the now-lukewarm tea. Claire would be privy to the goings-on inside a woman's heart and especially the woman she thought of like a sister. She would know Sara's thoughts.

The hands of the clock took forever to move. He decided to go earlier than planned, especially with the snow falling in earnest once again. Not that it was unusual in the White Mountains to find snow steadily rising with each storm until it reached the window frames. He did not want Sara herself lost in the snow or anywhere else. He wanted her here, safe, away from danger, away from anything of life back in the city.

The remainder of the evening he tried to stay occupied with mundane activities. Reading the latest edition of the *White Mountain Echo*. Considering his next painting—which must be the Old Man of the Mountain—if he could summon the courage to ask Lawrence for his sleigh. He tapped a tune on the armrest of the chair, imagining how that would go, especially after the confrontation with Annabelle.

Claire glanced up from her sewing and smiled. "What a jittery soul you are," she mused.

At last the clock struck eight. He began to bundle up in his coat, scarf, and hat and took a cane to assist him in navigating the icy walkway.

Claire lit a lantern for him. "I pray it goes well, dear brother," she said, standing on tiptoe to kiss his cheek.

If nothing else, Tom thanked God for his relationship with Claire. Stepping outside, a blast of cold air chilled his limbs, but his heart soared with expectation. In just a short time he would know whether Sara remained in town and if a future awaited them. He took cautious steps on the slippery walkway. No one was on the streets this time of night. He could barely see, with the snowflakes swirling in his face and collecting on his eyelashes. He hoped the lantern would not blow out in the wind.

At last he saw the familiar spirals of Maplewood. Soft yellow light filled the hotel windows. The hotel stood like a place of refuge in the snowstorm and gave him courage. He arrived in the lobby, cold and shivering, and stomped his feet to rid his shoes of the snow.

One of the stewards approached. "Good evening, sir. Do you require a room?"

"I'm here to escort one of your maids from the dining room."

The man looked at him rather strangely. "The dining room is down the hall to your left, sir."

Tom brushed the snow from his coat, smoothed his damp hair, and headed for the dining room. Only a few guests remained, lingering over their glasses of cognac. He saw several servants moving about, clearing tables. He approached a petite woman in an apron and small cap and inquired of Sara's whereabouts.

"Sara? She's not here anymore. She left."

In an instant all hope drained out of him. "She must be here. I told her I would walk her home tonight. She was expecting me."

"You're too late, I'm sure. You men are always too late." The young woman moved off to clear another table.

Tom stared after her. How could this be? Claire had been so confident that Sara would be here. And he'd been, too. It seemed inconceivable that she would leave. Did that mean she left Bethlehem as well?

There was no time to waste. He hurried out into the cold once more, headed for Sara's guesthouse, praying that she was there and her belongings were in her room. When he inquired at the door, Mrs. White shook her head. "She packed up everything she had this afternoon. She didn't say where she was going, either, but paid her bill and disappeared. I'm sorry."

Tom offered a meager thank-you and stumbled into the snowy night. His throat clogged with emotion. He forced back the tear or two teasing his eyes. Sara had taken the money and gone back to Mrs. Whitaker and the lonely streets of New York. *It's my fault. I was so blind, so stupid. I let her think I didn't care. Now I will be a bachelor the rest of my days…and I deserve it.* At that moment, Tom truly disliked the outcome of all this—and himself in particular. There was nothing else to do but return home.

He arrived there so burdened he could barely keep himself upright. Claire was busy trimming the Christmas tree with delicate ornaments when he collapsed into a chair in the drawing room.

"Tom? What's the matter?"

"She's gone, Claire. Sara left and went back to New York."

"How do you know?"

"She no longer works at the Maplewood. I stopped by Mrs. White's house, and she said Sara left this very afternoon and took everything with her. It's too late for anything. I'm too late."

"I'm so sorry, Tom."

"No one ever told me the hard lessons learned when placing an ad for a bride. I should have taken further counsel from Edward and his bride. It wasn't enough just to try their plan. I needed to learn what to do and how to act appropriately."

"There's nothing more you can do. Sara made her decision."

He thought for a few minutes, analyzing it all. Suddenly, he flew to his feet. "There is one thing I can do."

"What?"

"I have the address for that woman, Mrs. Whitaker. I'll leave tomorrow and head for New York. If I can find Mrs. Whitaker, I will find Sara."

"But why? She made her choice."

"She doesn't know everything. What happened with Annabelle… the decision I made concerning us… She needs to know."

Claire stared. "But travel all the way to the city? Tom, you've never even been out of New Hampshire! Are you sure you want to do this?"

He was never so sure in his life as he strode off to pack a bag. Something, or rather, *Someone* drove him to do what a short time ago would have been unthinkable. Even with all his faults, he prayed that God would give him another opportunity to make things right. To find Sara and see if she would return to him.

Chapter Seventeen

Tom immediately thought of Sara's arrival to Bethlehem as the train rumbled along the tracks. She'd taken this same ride to come to him, traveling far to come to a strange place. She must have been as nervous as he, removing herself to a foreign land filled with strangers. Stepping off the train in Bethlehem to see all the ladies in their fineries while she herself wore a ragged coat and clung to a carpetbag—he had to admire her courage, remembering the picture.

Tom leaned close to the glass, his breath fogging it, while he observed the countryside frosted in white. Why had it taken him this long to venture from Bethlehem and his roots? He thought then of the gospel, of Mary and Joseph leaving their small village to venture to the city of Jerusalem for the Passover. Now he was going to a big city also, but this time it was to beg Sara to reconsider and return to Bethlehem with him. He wished then that he had a gift to give her, but his departure had been so hasty, there wasn't time. He could only offer the gift of his heart. "God, I pray I'm not too late," he whispered.

After long hours of travel, the train chugged into Grand Central Depot in New York City late that afternoon. Tom had never seen a place like it. Tall gray buildings immediately caught his attention. Numerous carriages and coaches clogged the muddy streets. Peoples of all sizes and backgrounds rushed by. Many accents filled the air, some unfamiliar, others difficult to even understand. Standing on the platform, Tom realized that this foreign place was also Sara's home. What she once experienced in Bethlehem, he was now experiencing as a stranger in a strange land.

Just then he felt a tug at his pocket. He whirled and found a young boy trying to pull his pocketbook out of his trouser pocket. His grabbed it just in time, even as the boy with large eyes backed away from him. "What are you doing?"

"I need money." The boy sniffed and wiped his nose with his shirt sleeve. "And you got lots. I can tell from your fine clothes."

Tom glanced at his attire, thinking that he did not look at all wealthy. Mr. Astor had even found the suit unfit for dinner at a hotel. But here things were different. He set down his bag and took some coins from his pocket. "Here, and don't steal anymore. It's against God's law." The boy looked at him strangely then took the money and ran off into the crowd, no doubt looking for his next target.

Welcome to New York, Tom thought grimly. He couldn't recall a single instance of pickpocketing in Bethlehem. What kind of place had he entered? He reached down to pick up his bag only to find an empty walk at his feet.

The boy! While he had been engaged with the boy, another one must have made off with his bag. He looked around, trying to find the rascal who'd stolen his possessions. "Have you seen a young boy with a black bag?" he asked a bald-headed gentleman passing by.

"Of course not," the man snapped. "People are everywhere."

"Someone just stole my bag! It had my clothes in it."

The man grinned. "You sure don't know the city, do you? Got to look out for your money and your possessions."

At least Tom still had his pocketbook. He reached inside it for the slip of paper where he'd scribbled Mr. Whitaker's address. "Do you know where this is?"

"I know it. You can take a carriage there. It's quite a few blocks away."

"Quite a few blocks?"

The man wrinkled his forehead and began to chuckle. "Where are you from, anyway? The farmlands? Europe?"

"Actually, Bethlehem."

The man hooted. "Bethlehem, eh? No such place, except in the Bible. Maybe you belong in the hospital."

"I beg to differ, sir. There is such a town, in New Hampshire."

"Bethlehem, New Hampshire. Never heard of it. Next thing you know, someone will be telling me they're from Jerusalem, Ohio." He laughed once more and shouted to a friend. "Walt, you have to hear this. This fellow says he's from Bethlehem."

Walt strode over, his eyes wide and a ready smile on his lips. "Well, if that isn't just the place to be for Christmas. Donkeys and mangers and shepherds in their fields keeping watch over the ol' flocks."

"Bethlehem, New Hampshire, is a nice place to visit," Tom said evenly. "If you don't believe me, perhaps you can ask my friend, Mr. Astor. I'm sure you've heard of him?"

Both men ceased their snickering. "You mean of *the* Astor family?"

"I'm his professional artist. He visits Bethlehem quite often on holiday."

The men looked at him in disbelief and even took a step back. One removed his hat. "Well, pardon us," Walt said hurriedly. "We didn't mean anything. It's just we've never heard of such a town."

"Anyway, take a carriage, and you'll find the place you're looking for," added the first man. Both men tipped their hats and scurried away.

Tom thanked them even if he still burned with resentment over the reception he'd received…until he remembered Sara at the Bethlehem depot, enduring taunts from those who did not understand her. His steps slowed. *God, was this what it was like for her? I never understood it until now.* He inhaled a swift breath, feeling humbled already, and he'd only been here an hour. In that time, he'd had his belongings stolen, his money nearly taken, and his hometown mocked. "Blessed be the name of the Lord who knows that pride comes before the fall," he whispered before striding off to find a carriage.

At least the carriage driver proved to be interested in hearing about Bethlehem when Tom mentioned the town's name. He asked many questions about the area and the people. When Tom also dropped the name of Mr. Astor into the conversation, the man looked at him with the same stunned surprise that Tom saw on the faces of the men at the depot. The driver then took Tom on a short tour of the city, pointing out the various buildings. At the end of the journey he sat waiting in expectation, his hand wavering. Tom obliged with a healthy tip and thanked him for the ride.

"Thank you, sir. And if you need me again, I come by here frequently."

Tom nodded and stared at the busy street before him. He wished then he had the company of Mr. Astor to help him navigate this place. But the man didn't even know he was in the city. Tom was supposed to be in Bethlehem painting the man's requested landscapes. Instead, he traveled the long and noisy streets of New York in his quest to find a pale young woman who could be any of the women he saw on the street. He passed many who appeared frail and dressed in ragged clothes. But others were clad in fine apparel, like those who inhabited the Bethlehem hotels. The contrast proved startling.

He felt strange, standing here on the sidewalk with nothing but the clothes on his back and some money in his pocket. He didn't know what he would do for personal possessions or where he would even stay. He left these things in the Lord's care, as Sara must have done. She, too, trusted God for every provision. Shelter. Food. Clothing. A friendly face. And he was about to do the same.

Tom paused before the bakery owned by Mrs. Whitaker, looking for the words to say. He wasn't ready to propose to Sara, certainly, but he did want her to come back to Bethlehem with him. At least until they discovered God's will for their future. He entered the shop. People stood in line, waiting to be served. He found a man there, taking bread out and serving the customers one by one. Tom waited patiently until his turn came at the counter.

"What'll it be?"

"Actually, I'm looking for someone. A young woman. Sara McGee."

The man shook his head. "Don't know anyone by that name."

Tom glanced down at the address on the paper and read it aloud. "That's this address, but I don't know any Sara McGee."

"What about Mrs. Whitaker? Is she here?"

The man shook his head. "She ain't here. Look, are you going to buy something or not? I've got customers waiting."

Tom selected three rolls, which the man hastily wrapped in paper and shoved toward him. Numbed, he took them. *Sara, where are you? I don't understand why you're not here! It's like you've vanished.*

He walked out the door and plopped down on a nearby stoop, ignoring the cold stone beneath him. No doubt he looked the part of some lost soul of the street. He ate slowly, enjoying none of the bread, all the while wondering where Sara could be. He felt certain she'd taken the train here. And this was the address where he had sent the letters; the place was even confirmed by the man inside the bakery. None of this made sense. It was as if door after door were shutting before him, no matter how hard he tried to walk through. *What am I doing wrong?* he wondered. *Maybe I'm supposed to accept the life of a bachelor...painting my works, selling them off to rich people like Mr. Astor, making a name for nothing.* But what good was any of it if he shared it alone? Didn't the Bible even say that two were better than one? Didn't Mr. Astor, Lawrence, even Claire agree that marriage was important?

"You look like you could use the warmth of a friend," came a soft, feminine voice. "It's so cold out here."

Tom glanced up from his contemplation to find an attractive face peering down at him. Her painted lips curved upward in an alluring smile. Furs lay wrapped around her shoulders, with a plunging neckline that revealed her bosom. Heat flooded his face. He stood to his feet and walked away, refusing to look back even as she called to him. *Is this the kind of life Sara was forced to endure on the street, living among people of ill repute? Surrounded by sin and depravity? God, why couldn't I have been more patient and understanding of her plight?*

He returned to the bakery window, this time noticing a portly woman outfitted in a tight apron manning the counter. Hope soared within him. He bolted through the door. "Mrs. Whitaker?"

She paused in arranging the fresh baked goods in the glass case. "Yes, can I help you?"

Thank You, blessed Lord! "You've never met me...but I'm Tom Haskins from Bethlehem, New Hampshire."

A tray of baked goods clattered to the floor, scattering freshly baked rolls.

"Forgive me, I didn't mean to startle you." Tom tried in vain to find a way behind the counter to help clean up the mess.

"Whatever are you doing here? Is Sara all right? Oh, please, don't tell me something terrible has happened to her!"

"No... I—I was wondering if you had seen her. I talked to the man who was working here, and he didn't seem to know anything about her. I feared I was in the wrong place."

"My helper, Harold, is new here. He doesn't know Sara. But why would I see her? She left to be with you, back in October. I know she made it there safely. I've received a few letters since then, but nothing recently."

"She... Well, she's gone, Mrs. Whitaker. She left. I assumed she came back here to New York to be with you. I was hoping to find her and talk to her."

Mrs. Whitaker opened her mouth to inquire when several customers walked in. He waited, trying not to fidget, until they were served and left the establishment.

"Why did she leave?" Mrs. Whitaker asked him as she stooped to gather up the rolls that had dropped on the floor.

"If I had an evening, I could tell you the whole story."

"Hmm. Have you a place to stay?"

"No. I just arrived on the train. And, sad to say, I have nothing to my name here, either, except my pocketbook. Some boy took off with my bag at the depot."

Mrs. Whitaker shook her head with a look of concern evident in her large gray eyes. "You poor man. I'm sorry that happened to you, but New York is not for the faint of heart, I must say. I would invite you to stay with us, but my husband is rather grouchy. And he disliked Sara very much."

"I'll find a place to stay. There must be a hotel nearby."

"Yes, just around the corner is a fine one. Will you at least come for dinner?"

"Thank you. I appreciate it."

She studied him for a moment or two more before a smile creased her face. "I must say, though, you're a handsome man, Mr. Haskins. I could tell that from your letters, but to meet you face-to-face like this…it's indeed a pleasure."

He smiled sheepishly and thanked her before venturing once more onto the frantic streets of New York. Yet his heart still wondered where Sara could be hiding.

* * * *

"I'm glad this is the night my husband plays cards," Mrs. Whitaker mused as she poured tea for Tom. "We can talk for a long while."

Tom sat still as he tried to work through this confusing scenario. While he had shared with the woman about the time in Bethlehem with Sara, he still mourned the idea that his quest had been futile. "I thought for certain she would be here with you. Where could she be?"

Mrs. Whitaker's head tilted in a look of sympathy. "Don't worry. I'm quite sure she's still somewhere in Bethlehem."

"Why would she be? She had no reason to stay. I told you how I never gave her any attention. Instead, I found myself chasing after something that wasn't meant to be. A 'postcard' is what my sister called the other woman."

"Sometimes God has to wake us up to what's important in life. Just as you received this knowledge, you must give Sara time to receive it, too."

"I thought she did, and that's why she left."

"Perhaps. Sara sometimes takes things too much to heart. She allows people to wound her and then holds onto it instead of letting it go. I've told her many times to give her wounds over to God, to forgive and go on. It's almost as if she feels she must conquer it herself, as she's had to do living here in New York after the death of her mother. It's been difficult for her, going on after losing the most important person in her life. And I'm sure when she saw you with the other woman, she saw the loss and the abandonment happening again. Her determination to go on rises up to cover the hurt and the pain."

Tom slowly fingered his cup. "I never really appreciated what a kind friend Sara had in you. I, too, have a mentor who believes in me. In fact, he lives somewhere in the city. Mr. James Astor."

Mrs. Whitaker straightened. "My goodness, you know the Astor family? Why, they're probably the wealthiest family in all of New York!"

"I paint for him."

She looked about her humble home. "I'm so sorry for this simple place, Mr. Haskins. Dear me, I can't believe you know the Astor family." She rose from her seat and began tidying up the room.

Tom couldn't help but chuckle. "Please, I'm no one in particular. Did you know that Sara took it upon herself to tell visitors to Bethlehem that I was the town's famous painter? Do you know what it's like to have to fulfill that kind of obligation? I'd rather be a humble carpenter like Jesus."

Mrs. Whitaker returned to a seat opposite him. "Yes, you're right. We're just ordinary people in God's eyes. But I had no idea what influential friends you have. Or how important you are. And here you've come all this way to find Sara. Oh, if only she could know."

"Know what?"

"That an accomplished and wealthy man loves her."

Tom looked at her in surprise. Did he love Sara? The words seemed foreign to him.

"Why else would you spend precious time and money traveling here to find her, if you didn't? Even if you did give her the train fare, which in itself tells me a great deal. You put her needs above your own. It's the first step in true love."

"I've never done anything like that, I'm sorry to say."

"It takes time. We're born to selfishness, looking out for our interests. Sara is no different, though I daresay she has tried hard to slip out of that mold and become someone. And I know she will. I also believe you will find her, Mr. Haskins, safe and sound in Bethlehem."

"Thank you, Mrs. Whitaker." Tom took out his pocket watch. "I suppose I'd better head back to the hotel. I have an early train to catch in the morning."

"I'm sorry this didn't work out for you."

"On the contrary, Mrs. Whitaker. This trip is the best thing to happen to me in a long time. Not only have I been humbled beyond measure here, but I've seen where Sara comes from. I can understand a little more about her and about the woman who cared so much that she took it upon herself to send Sara to me. For that, I thank you."

Mrs. Whitaker dabbed her eyes with the corner of her apron. "I really do care about her. She's like a daughter to me. I had no children of my own, you see. I so wanted to help take care of the poor orphans on the street, but my husband would have nothing to do with them. Then Sara came along, so needy, and I told God that I wanted to help her any way I could. I saw your ad as a way for her to have a new life. Not a life in a cellar, looking for odd jobs just to buy bread, but a real life in the beauty of God's world."

Tom grabbed her hand then and shook it. "Mrs. Whitaker, I believe the best thing you ever did was answer that ad for her."

"You are a kind man. I believe it was the right thing, too. Now if Sara would only believe it."

Tom hoped for this as well. He offered a pleasant good night and returned to the hotel. The street still teemed with wanderers and others of ill repute roaming the streets. He sat inside his room and pondered the evening's conversation with Mrs. Whitaker. Somehow he felt connected to Sara in this place. He had taken a short journey into Sara's past and sensed a new bond with the knowledge he'd gained.

Armed with a new understanding, he desperately wanted to find the young woman who was slowly capturing his mind and heart. He prayed that Bethlehem held the answer.

Chapter Eighteen

....

"Sara, help me tie my shoes! Please!"

Sara had just tied her apron across her dress when young Sammy rushed into the room, the laces of his shoes dragging along the ground. "You're such a big fellow, why don't you learn to tie them?"

"No one ever taught me." He sat on the edge of her bed, his feet dangling off the side.

Sara sat beside him and took his foot in her lap. "I'll show you. First we're going to make a rabbit ear."

"A rabbit ear?" He giggled.

"See, you make a rabbit ear with the lace. And then you wrap the other lace around the rabbit ear and poke it underneath like this. Now you have made two rabbit ears, and you're done."

"Let me, let me!"

Sara watched as he tried to mimic the instructions with the other shoe. When she looked up, Adelaide Turner stood in the doorway, shaking her head. "Sara, I'm so glad you decided stay with us. It's as if new life has come into this house. Everyone is enjoying having you." Adelaide moved to the stairs.

Sara was glad to be here, too. Not long after Tom left that one morning, she remembered the friendly invitation extended by the family for her to stay with them. She went at once to inquire if she might live with them while doing household chores to earn her keep. Adelaide pounced on the idea and invited her at once. Since that time,

Sara found the love and acceptance of a true family and the example of a loving marriage, watching Adelaide and her husband interact. When the couple thought no one was looking, they would sneak a kiss or exchange tender caresses. Sometimes Sara imagined her and Tom exchanging a kiss with their little ones scattered around the table…until a pain in her stomach silenced the scene. Tom had not been seen at the Maplewood since he asked to be her escort. She had left word with a worker the first evening that she was leaving early, but Tom had chosen not to follow through on his promise. No doubt Annabelle Loving was to blame for his distraction. The fact burdened her so much, she nearly cried. But he had made his choice, and now she'd made hers.

Sara immersed herself in the lives of the Turners, who filled her days with joy. Elisa and she sewed gifts for Christmas. She read with Susan famous works like *A Christmas Carol* by Charles Dickens. And Sammy and she played in the snow and built a snowman. The days were exciting until Sara was obliged to dress for work at the Maplewood.

Today was no different as she took a comb to her hair then twisted it up into a tight chignon suitable for work. Maybe she would look forward to work if Tom had kept his promise to escort her. Several times she thought of walking by the house to see what had happened to him, but the constant snow and ice forced her to stay close to her job and the Turner home.

"I hope you have a nice evening." Adelaide offered a smile when Sara descended the stairs.

"Thank you." Sara took up her disheveled coat, which she slipped on as she left the home, though it did little to shield her from the cold. It didn't take her long to arrive at the Maplewood. The number of visitors to the hotel and town were growing with the approaching holiday season. Only a week remained until Christmas Day. She'd been invited by the Turners to their family celebration when relatives gathered at the home to share in brunch and gifts. "You're family, too," they insisted when Sara opened her mouth to decline and say she didn't want to intrude. Silently she thanked God for intersecting her path with the family. Maybe this was His way of easing the pain in her heart over Tom's lack of interest in her welfare.

The evening went by quickly, with many customers enjoying the fancy meals. Sara carried out pan after pan of dirty dishes until her arms began to ache. When it was time to leave, she was thankful to say good night to her fellow workers.

"You look tired," said Rachel, carrying one last armful of dishes to the kitchen.

"Yes, I am. Very tired. And still upset, too."

"Upset about what? Did Mr. Akins shout at you again? He said I was too sloppy with setting the silver. I know he's looking out for us, but he could have been a little kinder."

"No. I was…wondering about someone."

"That man? The one who came here a few days ago?"

Sara whirled. "He came here? Tom? You saw him?"

"Well, some man was lookin' for ya. He didn't tell me his name."

"What did he look like?"

"Oh, he was handsome all right. Real tall, too, with dark hair and eyes. I told him you'd left. He just took off then. I haven't seen him since."

Oh no! Sara had told James at the desk to inform Tom she'd left early that day to move into the Turner home. She wished then she had also mentioned something to Rachel. It might explain his absence, thinking she didn't care about him or their plans for a nightly walk.

Sara headed for the coatroom to find her ratty garment. At least it warmed her heart to know Tom had come looking for her—that he did care about the arrangements, that he'd not forgotten her. She paused. But why hadn't he come back? If Rachel had told him she was gone and then he went to Mrs. White to hear she had packed up and left…perhaps he thought she'd left for good. *I had the money for the train fare he gave me. He might have assumed I returned to New York!* "Oh, I have to tell him I'm still here!" There was no time to waste. She would go at once.

"Sara?"

She turned, expecting to find Charles or James. Instead it was Tom. He swept off his hat, staring wide-eyed. "It's true. You're still here. God be praised, she was right."

"Tom, you—you look like you're seeing a ghost. Maybe you are?" She chuckled uneasily.

He came forward with his arms wide, looking as if he couldn't wait to take her into his embrace. Oh, how she'd imagined a time like this, relishing the touch of his arms holding her close. She held her breath when he did come and slip his arms around her, but it only lasted a moment. Still, he felt warm and strong to her, as if everything would be all right.

Tom released her and stepped back. "I thought—I thought you had left for good. That's what everyone said."

"I did leave early the day you came here, but I left a message for you with James of where to find me. I was moving in with the Turners. They're the family whose little boy I helped that other night."

"Thank You, God." He uttered it as if he meant every word, that he was truly thankful to God Most High that he had found her. He seemed to be looking her over carefully. First he stared into her eyes with his own dark brown ones in a manner she found quite appealing. Her mousy brown hair flowed over her shoulders, having fallen out of the chignon due to her labors that day. Her face was no doubt quite flushed from this unexpected encounter. And she still wore her tattered coat.

He now pointed at it and frowned. "You are not wearing that anymore," he said, beginning to remove his own coat.

"Don't be silly. You can't give me your coat. What are you going to wear? It's snowing…again." She shook her head. "It's always snowing here."

"I don't care. You need a coat. You can't wear that thing."

"And I will not have you freeze."

They looked at each other and suddenly broke out in laughter. Laughter of freedom, as if they enjoyed this little game. To her, the laughter reminded her of the freedom when hurt and pain were gone, and they could move freely in life and in love.

"I will ask James if he knows of any coats that have been left by previous guests," Sara suggested. She went to inquire while Tom remained with his coat in his arms.

She returned with a large coat. "It's another man's coat and far too big for me. Maybe even for you, though you're quite tall."

"Then you will take mine, and I will take this. As it is, my coat is short on me. "

She agreed and put it on. The sleeves covered her hands and the coat reached to mid-calf. Yet Tom seemed to relish seeing her slight form nestled in the confines of his coat. She felt warm and happy, more than she ever thought she would.

He picked up his lantern and offered her the cane. "It's to steady yourself. It's very slippery outside."

"But I have your arm to help me in that matter, don't I? That's much better than a cane."

He smiled when she placed her slender hand around his arm. He patted it as if thanking her for trusting in him. And Sara did want to trust him, more than anything.

"Tom! What are you doing here?"

Tom stopped and turned. It was his friend Lawrence standing in the hotel lobby. The joy drained from Tom's face and was replaced by grimness.

Sara's hand slipped off his arm. She felt light-headed and weak. Tom looked at her in concern as Lawrence came forward to greet them.

Lawrence looked from one to the other. "What brings you here this time of night?"

"I'm walking Miss McGee home from work."

"Ah, the famous heroine of Bethlehem. It's all over town, still, how a certain maid from Maplewood rescued a young boy lost in the snowstorm earlier in the week. I had to come here and see for myself."

"Yes, it was Sara." Tom couldn't help boasting about it to his friend. He then went on, making her out to be so courageous that it seemed as if a statue ought to be erected in her honor. Sara stood in stunned silence, listening to it all.

Lawrence gave her an inquisitive look. "Well, I'm sure the Turners are indebted to you, Miss McGee."

"More than indebted," Tom added. "You make it sound like she simply found a misplaced trinket. She saved their son. That little boy could not have survived much longer in the cold and snow. And now they have asked her to live with them."

Lawrence took off his hat and bowed. "May I offer you my congratulations, Miss McGee."

"Anyone would have done the same," she said, uncertain how to answer the man who once thought her a feeble-minded waif of the street who begged for coins.

"I often wonder if that is true or not. But I do know the people of Bethlehem help in times of need…except perhaps when strangers arrive who we do not anticipate. Bethlehem is known for having quite the fancy and frolicking crowds here for their own pleasure. But to have someone different gracing our town, it does make people take notice."

"And I didn't come by the usual means, either."

Tom interrupted. "Although we would like to talk, we must be going, Lawrence. The hour is late." Tom offered his arm once more to Sara.

Sara took his arm, grateful to finally be leaving.

"I do have something to ask." Lawrence followed them to the door. "Loretta, my wife, would very much like to know you better, Miss McGee. Perhaps you can join us for dinner after church this Sunday? You too, Tom."

Sara blinked, taken aback by the invitation. "That's very kind of you. Thank you."

He tipped his hat and offered them a congenial smile. Tom nodded in return. As they made their way outside, he sighed loudly. "Would I be wrong to say that a burden may have been lifted tonight?" she asked tentatively.

"Sara, you can read my thoughts. Lawrence and I have not seen eye to eye these past few months."

"I could tell."

He looked at her briefly before turning his attention to the snowy road before them. "I thought we might be ready for another confrontation at the hotel tonight. But despite everything that's happened and my many mistakes, God is redeeming the time and restoring relationships."

"What would God have to redeem unless there were people with faults?" Sara said softly. "He works His best in us when we can say to Him, 'I can't do it alone.' "

"I've never been able to do any of this alone," he admitted. "Even when I thought I could—in my paintings, in finding a good and godly wife—I knew it couldn't come from me. I needed guidance."

Sara walked along in silence, trying to decide how best to answer him. "I never needed true guidance, I thought, until the day Mrs. Whitaker encouraged me to come here, and suddenly I had to trust God for my future. Especially in a strange place where the people didn't know me. Since I've been here, I've learned so much. And I've grown fond of the town, even if my first few weeks were difficult."

"We have plenty of room for people of means, but I have been wrong not to have room in my heart for you." He stopped suddenly and lowered his head, staring at the white snow at his feet set aglow by the lantern he carried. "I'm truly sorry for not accepting you for who you are."

Sara had the urge to tell him that it didn't matter, that all was forgotten. But she allowed his words to remain unanswered. They continued until they arrived at the Turners' door. "Thank you for walking me back, Tom. You don't have to come every night, you know."

"I would be happy to, if you'll let me. I'm not looking for a reward. It's just something I believe would be good for both of us."

"All right." She turned to head into the house.

"Sara." His voice sounded so gentle and kind that her heart leaped at the sound of it. "Are you planning to leave?"

"Leave?"

"Bethlehem. To return to New York. The money I gave you. I—I just wanted to know your plans...so I can tell Claire. She's been asking about you."

Sara hesitated. "I'm not sure, Tom. I haven't made up my mind."

He nodded, though she could tell he desperately wanted to know her answer. But at that moment, Sara didn't quite know herself.

"Good night."

Once inside, she looked through the parted curtains, watching the lone light of the lantern fade in the distance as Tom headed for home. Her fingers tightened around the window covering when she thought of his dear sister and how all this must have hurt her. She would consider moving back there if they would have her, but Tom had not offered. Maybe he remained entangled by Annabelle Loving. Perhaps he only did this walk to satisfy a request of Claire's. Sara sighed, wishing it were true that he did care about her. That the real reason he returned was to draw her to himself.

For the next few days, Sara went to work at the Maplewood Hotel, and Tom escorted her home evenings. Because the Turners' house wasn't far from the hotel, they had only a short time to converse. She still didn't feel comfortable inviting him in, and he didn't ask, either. But his nightly presence on the front stoop of the house finally roused Adelaide's interest.

"Are you seeing the artist?" she asked one day, while Sara was mending a damaged tablecloth.

She looked up, startled by the comment. "The artist? You mean Mr. Haskins?"

"Of course. I see him walking you home every night, though you leave him out in the cold. It's fine with me if you invite him in to get warm."

"Oh, he's only walking me home from the hotel."

"What a kind thing to do. Do you realize he's famous?"

Sara flinched when the sewing needle pricked her skin. She soothed the finger in her mouth. "I'm not sure what you mean."

"I was talking to a friend, and she told me how he paints exclusively for that rich Mr. Astor of New York. Having a wealthy man like that interested in his work must make Mr. Haskins famous. He'll soon be known all over the world."

Sara bent over her stitching, trying not to think about it. If this were true, why would Tom want anything to do with her? Annabelle was much more suited in that respect—a well-to-do, accomplished lady of Boston. They would make a handsome couple.

That afternoon at the Maplewood, Sara considered Tom's status as she cleared tables and did the dishes. She grew nervous when she noticed the clock nearing nine p.m. and thought of Tom's pending arrival. The hour came and went. She thought of leaving, but just as she was ready to depart he arrived in the hotel lobby, his breathing labored and the lantern swaying.

"I'm sorry, Sara," he apologized. "Time got away from me. I was having dinner…"

Probably with Annabelle Loving. She tried to quell her jealousy.

"…with Claire, and we were talking about Christmas."

Sara breathed easier. During the walk home she said little, only offering one- or two-word responses to the few questions he posed.

"Are you angry I wasn't there on time tonight?"

"No. I'm just wondering—why do you bother doing this every night? I'm sure there are many others who must be more interesting to walk home."

She felt a gentle tug of his hand on hers as he stopped walking and turned her to face him. "I don't want to walk with anyone else, Sara. I want to walk with you."

"I don't understand. You're a famous painter."

He laughed with a sound that startled her.

"Yes, and I heard how you made my name famous in this town, telling strangers about my work. Did you know that two men came knocking on my door? They claimed to have talked to you about me. And one of them even bought a painting."

Sara had forgotten that day when she boasted about his work to the two men she'd met on the road. Her thoughts became muddled under his bemused expression. She gazed at his laughing brown eyes, rugged complexion, that crop of dark hair with its swath to one side, the bit of sideburns…. "I mean, Mr. Astor, from one of the wealthiest families in New York, is interested in your work. Think how it will open doors of opportunities for buyers and art shows, even world tours…." She halted.

"Do you think that's what I consider important in life? I love to paint, that's all. God gave me the talent to use for His glory. And if others praise the work, they are praising Him. I paint His creation, after all. His colors and textures. His touch. His landscapes."

Sara felt foolish making such a commotion about his work. He truly was a humble man and, yes, handsome, too. She buried her hands inside her new coat, a fine lady's coat Tom had bought her the other day. "I suppose I should go inside. Adelaide says I should invite you in for a cup of tea."

"Actually, I need to be heading back. You remember that this Sunday is the dinner invitation with Lawrence and his wife…? Are you ready?"

"I suppose. I've certainly learned how to eat like a lady, thanks to your sister."

Tom chuckled. "You'll do just fine. I'll see you then."

Sara watched as he meandered down the walk. He paused then and turned. They exchanged a lengthy look, a silent communication—of what, Sara didn't know. But something was happening between then. A bond was forming. A closeness that was unmistakable. *Oh, what to do?* her heart wondered. She could do little but pray and see what came of it.

Chapter Nineteen

Sara took time to ready herself for the church service and then the dinner afterward with Tom's friends. Sara shivered, wondering what would happen. She had not been to services since she left Tom and Claire's. And Lawrence, after all, did not approve of her. He was the one who wanted Tom to marry his wife's cousin and send Sara back to where she belonged. She dismissed her anxiety over the dinner and reflected on her evening walks with Tom this past week. She thought about how their relationship had turned around so quickly. Brushing out her long hair before fastening it into a chignon for the occasion, Sara had to admit she was searching for the answer Tom sought. Many times she looked at the money in the dresser that Tom had given her for the train fare. She wondered if she should stay in Bethlehem and if they would wed one day…or if her destiny lay elsewhere.

Sara was finishing her primping when Elisa hurried into the room. "Your beau's here, Sara. He's waiting in the parlor."

My beau. If only it were so. She patted down a stray piece of hair with a mind of its own, grabbed her coat, and hurried downstairs. Tom stood in the foyer, looking as fine as she had ever seen him. The clear image of him delighted her senses. His recent appearances had been muted by the darkness during their evening walks.

Tom, too, seemed to look her over with new appreciation. He offered his arm, which she took. The day was clear but snowdrifts were everywhere. Sleighs dashed by as couples rode back and forth between the hotels in Bethlehem. Christmas wasn't far away. Sara knew she would spend it with the Turners. And though she should be happy about the plan, the thought saddened her.

"You're quiet," Tom noted. "If you're nervous about the visit with Lawrence and Loretta, please don't be."

"Actually, I was thinking about Christmas and family."

He hesitated. "I'm sure you miss Mrs. Whitaker."

"No…yes—I mean, of course I do." She felt a blush beginning. "I mean, I was thinking about how I will spend the day."

"Claire and I were talking about that, too. We hoped you might be able to have Christmas dinner with us. Consider this your invitation."

"That's nice of you to ask, but the Turners have invited me to their family gathering. They ask all their relatives to come for a fancy brunch and to exchange gifts."

"I see."

Now Tom turned silent. Sara wondered about it, but they arrived at the church momentarily. People greeted Tom while giving Sara curious glances. And then she saw a familiar face coming toward her through the crowd of people.

"Oh, my dear Sara! How I missed you." Claire gave her a warm embrace.

Tears filled her eyes. "I missed you, too." When they parted, she saw Claire's eyes glimmering. "I've been practicing my reading. Susan Turner has been helping me. She's been reading to me Charles Dickens's *A Christmas Carol*. And I was even able to read the letter Tom had written."

"Oh, really?" Claire gave Tom a curious glance as he stood among the congregation talking to several men. "I'm not sure what letter this is. Do you mean the letter with the money to return to New York?" Her face suddenly dropped, and her eyes glistened again.

"Claire, I have no plans to go back to New York. In fact, do you think Tom would mind if I use the money to buy a few personal items?"

Claire grabbed her hand. "Oh, Sara, you don't know how happy that makes me! Of course you can use it to buy whatever you need. I see that Tom bought the coat for you, too. I told him which one to get at the mercantile."

Sara smiled, happy for Claire but surprised, too, over what had just come out of her mouth—that she would not be leaving Bethlehem. What had caused her to come to this conclusion? Was it the emotion of seeing Claire? Looking out over the congregation that filled the pews, Sara realized it was more than that. It was the community. The Turners. The people she worked with at the Maplewood. And, yes, Tom.

When they began to assemble in the pews to sing the opening hymn, Tom stood on her right. Sara cast a glance at him out of her eyes. He was staring straight ahead. What was he to her? A brother? A friend certainly, but perhaps one day, dare she think it—a husband?

After they had sung a few hymns, the reverend spoke on the preparations for Christmas, encouraging each of them to likewise prepare for the arrival of the Savior in their hearts as they embraced His love this season. Sara felt Tom's fingers brush across her hand, and she relished his touch.

When the service concluded, Tom led the way outside to await Lawrence and Loretta. Tom shifted about, rubbing his hands together. Sara found little comfort in seeing his anxiety. Her stomach tightened when Lawrence arrived with his wife and the tall, stately form of

Annabelle Loving. Sara thought she might faint under the woman's piercing gaze. Annabelle's lips pressed together in a thin line, and she nodded curtly at Tom before looking away.

"We'll be having dinner shortly," Lawrence said. "I need to take Annabelle to the depot."

Annabelle looked with disdain at both her and Tom.

"You're leaving us?" Tom asked.

"I'm sure that comes as no surprise to you, Mr. Haskins." She drew on her gloves. "It's been quite illuminating here, I must say."

"I hope you do well with the conservatory in Boston."

"I suppose I should continue with my piano. At least there I will be appreciated for my efforts." Her gaze then turned to Sara. "Take care of him, darling. He's quite a talented man in some areas, but not in others, I'm sorry to say." She whirled away, her head high, and strode off in the direction of Lawrence's sleigh.

Sara was speechless, as was Tom. She looked to him for an answer, but his face appeared stony and unreadable. What had become of the two of them? Did this mean that he had relinquished Annabelle?

Loretta tried to give them an encouraging smile and waved her hand. "Please, come with me. We'll go on to the house. Lawrence will be back shortly."

Everything seemed awkward, yet the knowledge of Annabelle Loving's departure renewed hope for Sara. Could it mean…was it possible to even think…? She looked at Tom, but he appeared sullen, with his gaze focused on the ground. She instead chose to wait and be patient.

Inside the Boshens' fine home, Loretta told them to make themselves at home while she finished dinner. The array of paintings on the walls captivated Sara. Most of them showed a style similar to

Tom's artistic flair, depicting the White Mountains in all seasons.

"Did you do these?" she asked.

He nodded as she studied each work. One showed a couple strolling in a meadow filled with wildflowers; another showed a train climbing a mountain. "What is this one?" she asked Tom.

"It's a painting of the Cog Railway. It's a train that goes up the side of Mount Washington."

"A train that climbs a mountain!" Sara stared in amazement. "I didn't know trains could do that."

"It's quite an engineering feat. Of course, the train isn't running in the winter, but in the summer it takes tourists to the summit of the highest mountain in the state. Maybe you would like to see it sometime."

"Oh, I would love to!"

Tom's grin widened as they continued their examination of the paintings. He took pleasure in explaining each one and where he painted it, along with the story that inspired him. Sara enjoyed this time of sharing in his work and his enthusiasm.

The front door slammed. Lawrence walked into the drawing room, rubbing his hands together. "Well, she's gone back to Boston," he told Loretta, who had come from the kitchen upon his arrival.

"She will be much happier there, I'm sure. She needs to use the talents God has given her and not stay here, pining away in Bethlehem."

"I suppose you're right. I thought it would be nice to have family here, especially with Christmas coming. She could have at least stayed for that. I don't understand why she…" He paused when his wife shook her head, as if to remind him of Sara and Tom's presence in their home. He smiled meekly and led the way to the dining room, where they gathered for dinner.

Sara remembered all of Claire's instructions concerning table manners, using the linen napkin properly, cutting her meat into dainty portions, and taking care to chew and swallow without causing undue attention. She even refused second helpings, though she yearned for more of the delicious Yorkshire pudding. Tom and Lawrence discussed the snow and possibly going snowshoeing. Tom asked if he might borrow Lawrence's sleigh for a trip to a place called Franconia Notch. Sara only stared at the fine china, the burning candelabra, and the glimmering silver.

"So where do you live now, Sara?" Loretta asked.

She glanced up. "Oh, I'm living with the Turner family."

"We heard how you helped that poor Turner boy who was lost in the storm. Do you plan to stay with the Turners permanently?"

"I…" She paused. "I have no other plans at the moment. But plans can change very quickly."

"Too quickly," Lawrence piped up. "One moment we think a marriage might be coming and the next it's gone…."

"Shush, Lawrence," Loretta said.

"I meant no harm. I was only agreeing with the young woman that times and seasons are forever changing. But it seems, Miss McGee, that you're adapting quite well to the life of a New Englander."

"Time helps, sir. And the excellent tutelage I received under Claire Haskins."

"She is a wonder," Loretta agreed. "A sweet woman. We have talked at the sewing circle. She misses you dreadfully, Sara. It makes no sense for you to be spending your time and money living away from her. What do you say, Tom?"

Sara found herself at a loss for words. She bowed her head and stared at her lap, waiting with baited breath for his reply.

"Sara is quite settled where she is now," Tom said without looking her way. "She likes the Turners very much, and they like her."

"Of course." Loretta smiled and went to bring out the dessert of bread pudding and rum sauce.

Though the dessert looked delicious, Sara had no appetite for it. She considered the statement Tom had made. He apparently didn't want her living in his home. All the hopes that had been building since Annabelle's departure were quickly falling apart. There seemed to be no future even still. Tom Haskins would never love her. There would never be a marriage. They would continue with this shallow existence, the nightly platitudes, the occasional glances. He still felt her unworthy of anything more. She would forever remain a maid in a fancy hotel, grieving over what might have been.

Oh, why did I tell Claire I wouldn't use the train fare?

* * * *

For the next two nights, Tom did not come to walk her home from her job at the Maplewood. Sara tried to put the disappointment out of her mind but couldn't. He'd been cordial and kind this past week, even seeing to her safety, that is, until the dinner at the Boshen house. A part of her dearly wanted to be with him. She enjoyed his company. If only he felt the same way.

She spent a quiet night after work looking out the window at the dark street of Bethlehem, her fingers clutching the envelope of money. She had no reason not to take this money right now and go to the depot to buy the ticket. If she did, she could be back in New York in time for Christmas. Wouldn't Mrs. Whitaker be surprised?

But she'd be unhappy, too. What would Sara do once she arrived there? Mr. Whitaker would never allow her to stay at the house. She would become a vagabond on the street once more, having to find lodging and scrounge around for work to buy food. How could she return to that kind of existence after all she'd experienced here?

Maybe, if she stayed in Bethlehem, another man would come into her life. She'd already captured the attention of several men. She was no longer beholden to Tom or the ad in the newspaper. She could continue living with the Turners and wait to see whom God would bring.

Sara sighed. *Dearest Lord, I pray that You would show me what to do in this matter of the heart. Make it clear to me which path I should take. And help me to not become bitter over Tom's decision.*

Meanwhile, another snowstorm doused Bethlehem, adding six more inches to the total they had already received. Sara had never seen so much snow in all her life. Occasionally New York received a few snowstorms, but not one after another like this. And there were many months left before spring graced the land. She wondered what the White Mountains looked like in the spring and summer. She'd seen Tom's paintings and others in the Maplewood Hotel that displayed the beauty of other seasons. At that moment, her heart suddenly yearned to see spring come to this place. *How can I leave?* she mused. *Even if Tom and I must go our separate ways, Bethlehem is now my home.*

The next day, Sara rose to dress as usual. Today was her day off, but she had agreed to help Mrs. White, her former proprietor, with some duties. The woman had stopped by the Turners' and asked if Sara might do a little work for extra pay. Sara obliged when she heard that other boarders had come in for the Christmas holidays and Mrs. White was beside herself with everything that needed to be done.

"How could you move away and leave me at a time like this?" Mrs. White moaned when Sara arrived. "I'm so glad to have your help."

The home was fairly bursting, with visitors roaming about. One gentleman, an older man, stopped in the hall when she entered. He immediately swiped off his hat and bowed. Sara remembered him. He was a visiting lawyer from Boston whom she had met when she lived in the guesthouse.

"Miss McGee, a pleasure to see you again. I hear from Mrs. White that you're now living elsewhere."

"Hello, Mr. Dickerson. Yes, I found a place with a nice family, though today I'm helping Mrs. White prepare food for her guests."

"I see." He hesitated. "I would love to have an escort while I'm here this time, to show me the sights of Bethlehem. Perhaps you would do me the honor? We were unable to meet the last time I was here, as I was too busy with my clients. And I regret it."

Sara's face grew warm with his suggestion. "But I'm new here, too. I've only lived here since October myself. The only places I know are the depot, the store, and the Maplewood Hotel. And the café in town."

"Then perhaps we should discover it together. And I will even treat you to dinner afterward at this café."

Sara felt her face grow even hotter. "I—I shall think about it, Mr. Dickerson. Please excuse me."

He nodded and moved off. Sara watched him slowly ascend the steps, stiff and formal, so like a fine gentleman. But he was much older, with gray in his sideburns. She knew little about him except that he was a lawyer from the city. But what harm was there in finding company on a cold day in Bethlehem? It would do her good to get out rather than stay home and mourn for a relationship that would never be.

Sara climbed the steps after him, preparing to agree to Mr. Dickerson's offer, when a voice called to her from below. "Sara!" She turned to see a tall figure in a black coat. A familiar set of brown eyes stared at her. She started and nearly slipped down the stairs. "T–Tom, what are you doing here?"

"Mrs. Turner said I could find you here. I'm so sorry I was unable to walk you home these past few days. Claire took sick, and I felt it unwise to leave her. Did you get my message?"

"No." Once more, a worker at the hotel had failed to give her a much-needed message. Sara scolded herself for having thought he'd abandoned her and even guiltier for nearly accepting a stranger's company rather than the man she yearned to know with all her heart. "Please don't apologize for not coming. Is Claire better?"

"Yes, much, and she all but ordered me to find you. There's a painting I must complete today, but it requires a trip to Franconia Notch. Are you free to go with me, or do you have plans?"

"Actually, I'm doing work for Mrs. White."

His face fell with a disappointment she had never seen before. Just then Mrs. White hurried into the hall to discover who had arrived in her home. When Sara told her about Tom's invitation, the woman smiled. "Oh, you must go, Sara. If you can stay until noon, that will be enough."

"Are you certain?"

"We all need a day to refresh ourselves. It's a beautiful afternoon for a sleigh ride…and with a fine gentleman, too."

"Then would you do me the honor?" Tom asked in eagerness. "I would very much enjoy your company."

"All right, I'll go with you."

He smiled, and when he did, his white teeth stood out in sharp contrast with the dark appearance of his clothing and dark brown hair. He tipped his hat. "I'll see you at noon, then." Tom excused himself to perform errands in town.

Sara scurried to finish the tasks for Mrs. White, feeling giddy for the first time in her life. Once or twice she caught sight of Mr. Dickerson in the drawing room and thought of Tom's invitation. She should feel honored that two men desired her companionship. What a distant cry from the days when she first came here and received those jeers. *Have I changed that much?* Perhaps in appearance, but that same spirit to survive, to make it day by day, to be the woman God wanted her to be, *that* had not changed.

At noon, as she was preparing to leave, Mr. Dickerson intercepted her. "Have you considered my offer, Miss McGee?"

"I'm sorry, Mr. Dickerson, but I have another errand to run today."

"Let me come along, then."

She nearly laughed. "I'm sorry, but I'm accompanying Bethlehem's famous artist, Mr. Haskins. He needs to complete a very important work. Would you excuse me?"

She hurried into the hall and found Tom waiting patiently for her. She followed him outside, where a sleigh stood and horses exhaled clouds like smoke into the frosty air. "There are plenty of wool blankets here to keep us warm," he told her. "Lawrence made sure we had enough."

"So you were able to borrow it from him without any trouble?" She climbed aboard the sleigh and arranged the blankets across her lap.

"He's offered it to me many times, actually. But I'm thankful I could have it today. I must get this last painting done for Mr. Astor. I only hope my paints don't thicken up in this weather, or painting will be difficult."

"I'm sure the work will be excellent all the same, Tom." She enjoyed saying his name, and he appeared to like hearing it—at least the small smile on his rugged face said so.

Tom flicked the reins, and the sleigh moved easily along the snowy street. They rode for a time before he inquired, "So who was the gentleman you were talking to in the parlor?"

"The gentleman?" Sara caught her breath, realizing that he had seen her with Mr. Dickerson. "You mean Mr. Dickerson?"

Tom nodded.

"He's a guest of Mrs. White. A lawyer from Boston, I think. I met him while I was staying at the house."

"A lawyer, eh? He seems quite taken with you."

It was a simple statement, yet a revealing one. "I...well, perhaps. He wanted someone to show him around town, but I know so little about Bethlehem. I know the train depot and the Maplewood Hotel. Besides, I'd prefer a nice sleigh ride on a fine winter's day."

He sighed. "Good. I'm glad to have you."

It never dawned on Sara that Tom might be jealous of her contacts with other men. The thought rather pleased her. She then remembered how she felt seeing Tom with Annabelle Loving and the attention they gave each other. Perhaps she and Tom were more alike than she had considered.

"Something is making you smile," Tom noted. "What is it?"

"How similar we are, you and I."

His eyebrow lifted. "Really. How so?"

"We would rather be in each other's company than someone else's."

"I'm glad you prefer my company," he said, so softly she could barely make out the words above the swish of the sleigh in the snow and the snort of the horses. "I've given you little reason to, after all."

"Why do you say that now? You've been a fine and considerate gentleman. Anyone who would accompany a tired spinster night after night from her duties at the hotel is worth high praise."

"Sara, what you are doing at the hotel is just as worthy as if you were keeping house. You've worked hard all your life. You survived both New York and the unpleasantness of living here among society. When we begin to make comparisons about those who are worthy and unworthy, it's when we fail to see the true worth of the person within."

"Maybe I'm thinking this way because my time here didn't offer much hope for anything else. Until lately, that is."

"Well, I can't argue with that. But I hope you'll be able to rise above it and one day find it in your heart to forgive my stupidity of those days. Please know that I very much admire the woman within and without."

Sara burrowed deeper into the blankets, considering the sincerity of his words. Yes, she did need to forgive. The conversation pointed to wounds that still existed over past hurts, even here in Bethlehem. The jeers of the men when she arrived…the looks of disgust at her unseemly ways at the café and the dinner table…the contempt in Annabelle's eyes…Tom's indifference until something stirred him to life.

"Do you realize, for instance, that our Lord would rather invite guests in rags to His wedding feast than ones finely clothed?" Tom confirmed. "That He gave them wedding garments to wear when they arrived?"

"Yes, but…"

"Many people of means feel they are above the call to come and dine. But without the riches, there are no such pretenses. You've needed to rely on the Lord for your provisions, for helping you day by day in New York. Even here, by finding a job and a place to live, and in helping a little boy in need. You're far richer than anyone I know, Sara. Including me."

His words jarred her. "I—I never considered that. Here in Bethlehem, it's so easy to overlook the simple things when you're surrounded by wealth."

"It's all fleeting. But some things are not." Tom nodded toward the scenery of the chain of mountains appearing before them. "See that? Think of the way God made His creation, so rich and interesting. The mountains. Deer and birds. Even the flowers, which the Bible says are more finely clothed than Solomon, who was a wealthy king."

"It is beautiful." One after another the mountains grew before them until they flanked the narrow passage that became Franconia Notch. Sara gazed up at the craggy tops covered with snow. How steep and rugged they were, yet majestic, too. They did not compete for attention. They stood on their own merit, in their own beauty.

"Just you wait." They continued until suddenly he brought the sleigh to a stop before a small lake. "Ahead of us is Profile Mountain." He reached behind him to a sack of belongings and withdrew a set of binoculars. "Take a look at the side of the mountain before you."

Sara brought the glasses to her eyes. "What am I supposed to see?"

He gently tilted her face and the glasses, bringing the mountain summit in view. "Do you see anything now?"

"Why, it looks like a man's face made out of rock!"

"He's the Old Man of the Mountain."

"Oh, Tom. From here in the snow, he looks like Saint Nicholas."

Tom laughed long and loud. "That would make a fine painting," he said, rummaging for his supplies. "The Old Man as Saint Nicholas, for Christmas."

"Is this the face you plan to paint for Mr. Astor?"

"Yes. And if it goes well, it might even be made into a Currier and Ives print. Mr. Astor has tremendous plans for my work. So pray that I can capture this scene to his liking."

"Yes, I will. Oh, it will be grand." Sara studied the face projecting outward from the side of the mountain. It looked as if the man of rock surveyed the land before him. The rocks were attached in such a way as to form the perfect image of a face. She had never seen such a sight. How she wished Tom could paint another picture of the scene so she might have it for her very own. But she dare not ask, as he had much to accomplish just in capturing this splendid scenery for his mentor.

Tom set up the easel in the snow and arranged the canvas. Sara helped him retrieve his paints and even held the containers so he could mix dabs of color on the palette with his brush. He made a simple sketch first and then began to fill it in with white and gray. Shades of blue followed, for the crop of winter sky and the lake below. It didn't matter that the cold was steadily invading her feet and hands. Sara only watched in fascination as he captured Profile Mountain and then the details of the Old Man.

"I'll make mostly an outline," he explained as he painted, "and then fill in the rest of the color when I return to Bethlehem. It's too cold to stay out here much longer."

"You do beautiful work, Tom."

"Long ago, Daniel Webster thought highly of the Old Man. You know how businesspeople put out certain signs depicting the work they do? Such as a tooth for an extractor, or a book for a printer?"

"Yes."

His hand flicked the paintbrush this way and that to create the rugged sides of the mountain and then dabbed a mixture of black and white to form the gray rocks. "Well, of the Old Man, he said that up in the mountains of New Hampshire, God Himself has displayed a sign that here He makes men."

Sara gazed once more at the face of rock before her. God Himself had hung a sign for all to see; that these were His mountains and in them He establishes man. And yes, He could even establish the destiny of a lowly woman from the streets of New York.

"The clouds are coming in. It's getting colder." Tom cast a glance in her direction. "And you're starting to shiver. We need to leave."

"I'm fine. I'm trembling over what you just said. But I'm getting a little cold, too."

Tom put down the brush. "This is good enough. I have the scene pictured in my mind. Come. We'll return and get you before a roaring fire with plenty of hot tea."

The mere image flooded Sara with a warm sensation. She folded up the small chair while Tom took down the easel. Her feet and fingers were clearly numb by the time they had everything packed away, but she would not exchange this time at God's mountain for anything. "Tom, this has been wonderful," she declared, snuggling into the blankets once more. She closed her eyes to envision it all. The snow-covered mountains, the Old Man, Tom painting so magnificently, when she felt an unexpected warmth. Flicking open her eyes, she saw Tom's face over hers. His lips sought hers, and to her surprise, she responded.

Finally she drew back, breathless. "Tom?"

"You are so beautiful, Sara," he murmured, his hand cradling her face. "Please, can I hold you once more?"

"Tom, we need to go back. We don't have a chaperone…." She turned away. They were both vulnerable, alone in this country scene and in search of warmth that should not be kindled at this time, as tempting as it was.

He withdrew his hand. "You're right. I'm sorry. You looked so beautiful against the backdrop of the forest." He took up the reins and ushered the horses to the road. "I—I have never felt this way," he confessed. "You've done something to me, Sara. I almost lost myself."

"Surely you must have felt that way when you were with Annabelle, didn't you?"

She saw his hands tighten around the reins. Immediately she regretted her words.

"I had no such feelings for Miss Loving. And if I did have any, they were shallow at best. She may have wanted me to feel differently, but it was not meant to be."

"Did you ever take her to see the Old Man?"

"No. This was *our* trip of discovery, Sara. Ours alone."

Sara couldn't help but agree. The Old Man had been wonderful, but so, too, was the kiss…only now, she wondered what would come of it. Surely the contact spoke of a turn in their relationship. A distinct change. She didn't know what to think or even say—so she said nothing. She just listened to the sound of the horses in the snow and felt the cold wind that numbed her face and waited on God for an answer.

Chapter Twenty

....

Tom relished the tender time they had shared at the Old Man as he drove the sleigh back toward Bethlehem. It was more wondrous than he had ever expected. He'd never considered kissing Sara until the moment when he saw her in the sleigh, her red lips inviting, her head tilted back. No, the kiss had not been proper, as she said. He should have restrained himself. But maybe it spoke more than words could ever do. That he cared. That love was overcoming whatever obstacles they had faced in the past. That he wanted them to take the next step.

But for now his thoughts turned to the trip home that was taking longer than expected—especially with the clouds gathering from the west and, with it, darkness seeping across the land. Snowflakes soon fell and the wind began to pick up. He felt a shiver race through him and wondered about Sara. "Are you cold?" Tom called above the wind that howled through the mountains flanking both sides of the notch.

Sara said nothing at first as the wind drove through them. She huddled beneath the blankets. "I'm all right," her voice trembled.

Her feeble response concerned him. "I wasn't expecting a storm to blow in like this. I should have been prepared. Here in the White Mountains, we take nothing for granted, especially the weather." He shouted his observation in competition with the howling tempest.

"How far are we from Bethlehem? Can you tell?"

The lantern flames flickered in the wind and suddenly went out. Tom drew the horses to a stop. "I'm not sure. The wind is picking up, as is the snow." He tried to halt the fear rising within. Caught in a snowstorm in the midst of the mountains and with a woman he was responsible to protect, anxiety tried to assail him. He calmed it with a silent prayer, knowing he must remain clearheaded.

"You do know where we are, don't you?"

He didn't answer but searched through the driving snow for a recognizable landmark. He rarely traveled this route in the daylight, though, much less in the ravages of a winter storm and during the night. "We shouldn't have left so late in the day," he muttered.

"I had promised Mrs. White my work, and…"

"Sara, I'm not blaming you. It's my fault. I should know that storms tend to come in later in the afternoon. I should have picked a day when we could have left in the morning." He heard her sniff then and felt the touch of her hand on his arm.

"I–I'm sorry, Tom. We just have to make the best of it."

"It will be all right. We'll be home soon. I promise." Though at that moment, home seemed very far away.

He urged the horses onward, praying to God for help. Tom dearly wanted Sara to find comfort in his confidence, but right now, he lacked what he needed. He was an artist—not a skilled mountaineer used to being in these conditions—with a sleigh that didn't belong to him and a woman who had just begun to trust him. Tom could only hope that somehow they were still on the road to Bethlehem. He knew there was one turn left to make before reaching Bethlehem proper. If he missed it, they could find themselves in the midst of the mountains without knowing exactly where they were. And they could not spend the night like this in the sleigh, exposed to the elements. They would freeze to death.

God, help us through, he thought silently. He wiped away the snow that had gathered on his face. Even the horses struggled to keep their footing in the wind. He tried to keep his frustration at bay. It had been such a perfect day before the Old Man, too, and then the feel of Sara's lips on his…. The bond between them had strengthened, and so, too, had their trust in each other—until now, when everything teetered precariously on a snowstorm. Was this God's test for them? To weather life's storms so they came forth even stronger?

"Do you know where we are yet?" asked Sara's feeble voice from beneath the blankets.

"I'm sure this is the road to Bethlehem," he answered, though he wasn't certain about anything. All he saw was white without any discernible markings. He knew there was a dilapidated wooden sign at a road crossing, pointing the direction to Bethlehem…if only he could find it.

"I can't feel my feet or hands," Sara complained. She shifted about and pulled the blankets closer.

"We'll make it. Hold on." He wished he had more words of hope to offer. He needed to get Sara before a warm fire, and soon. But time seemed to go so slowly, which often happened in a crisis.

"I—I don't know how m–much longer I can be out here, T–Tom." Sara's voice grew fainter each time she spoke.

"Sara, just keep talking to me. It will keep us both warm and alert. Tell me how you met Mrs. Whitaker. She's a kind woman who cares so much about you."

"I—I don't want to. I'm so tired, Tom. I'd rather sleep."

He panicked when he heard these words. Sleep was one thing she could not do in this weather, for that meant her body was getting too cold. He shook her with his free hand. "No, don't sleep, Sara. Tell me about New York."

"I—Mrs. Whitaker is such a fine person. She—she found me on a stormy night when it was raining. I had no coat. I was so cold." Her voice drifted away.

Tom looked down to see her nodding off. Fear gripped him with a heavy hand. *What am I going to do, God?* Again he shook her. "Sara? Wake up!"

Suddenly, through the whirl of snow, he caught a glimpse of a strange light off to the right. He didn't know if it was his imagination or if it was real, but he turned the sleigh toward it. As he drew near, he made out the image of a cabin tucked away in a grove of pine, and he thanked God for the shelter.

Bringing the sleigh to a stop, he flew out of it and fell into a snow drift. Snow covered him from head to foot. He stood and stumbled his way to the door, pounding on it. "I need help! Is anyone here?"

The door creaked open. Through bleary eyes, he saw a weathered man with a beard hanging down to his chest. "What do you want?"

"Please, sir, my—my fiancée is freezing. I need to get her into shelter."

The grizzly man grabbed for a coat made of animal skin and followed Tom to the sleigh. With effort, he and Tom managed to carry Sara's still form into the cabin.

"She's out," their rescuer said matter-of-factly.

Tom piled blankets upon Sara as she lay still in the bed, her head tilted to one side, her eyes closed. "Sara, please wake up. You have to wake up."

"Give her time to get warm." The man added a log to the fire and stirred something in a large iron kettle. How could the man be so calm with Sara lying at death's door? Tom stroked her damp hair, murmuring a prayer for her. He began to shiver himself, realizing how cold he, too, had become in the storm.

"Go grab yourself some stew," the man said. "You look like you need it. I need to get your horses to shelter. And don't worry, she's gonna be fine. She's just sleeping now."

Tom moved to the fire, warming himself by the flames, thinking on the day that had begun so wonderfully and now ended with such grave uncertainty. He then remembered the painting still in the sleigh, likely covered in snow. All his hard work could very well be ruined by the elements. Tom looked in on Sara and saw her moving about, her eyes flickering.

"Sara?"

"Tom. Tom, are we safe?"

"We're safe. Are you all right?"

"Just sleepy. Can I go back to sleep?"

He nodded, stroking her hair while telling her he must leave for a moment to rescue the painting from the snow. He went for his coat and wet shoes and headed out to see the older man walking about, carrying a lantern.

"What are you doing out here?"

"My—my painting," Tom's voice shivered. He groped around in the back of the sleigh until his cold fingers touched the square package; the picture was encased in leather skin to protect it. He thanked the Lord he had thought to keep it wrapped, as he stumbled back to the house, barely able to keep upright in the wind. He then felt the grip of the man's hand on his arm, leading him. He shivered so much, he could hardly move. His fingers were numb once more. But he managed to unwrap the painting and found it intact, having suffered no damage in the storm.

"So is that what you do?" he asked, acknowledging Tom's work. "You're one of those fancy artists? I've seen them around these parts, looking to paint the Notch."

"Yes. A gentleman from New York requested it as a Christmas gift. I have one day left before I must send it to him. That's why we were out today, so I could paint the scene."

"Needs some more work, but I'd say you've done a good job. You make the Old Man proud."

Tom nearly chuckled at the thought of the stony face congratulating him for the image he'd painted. "I never did get your name, sir."

"Harvey Spears. Lived here all my life."

"Tom Haskins. I have, too. But Sara here," he said, pointing to her as she slept peacefully, "she just came from New York City a few months ago."

"You two plan to get married soon?"

Tom eyed the sleeping Sara once again. "I'm not sure. I want to, but I don't think she's ready. I wish she was."

Harvey laughed as he lit his pipe and relaxed in a chair positioned by the fire. "No one is ever ready to marry. Save yourself plenty of trouble, friend, and live alone."

"I've often thought of that." But being with Sara, enjoying the day at Franconia Notch and enduring near calamity with her in this snowstorm, he only felt an urge to love and protect her. To keep her from harm. To make a home and a family with her. But did she desire the same thing?

"She's had herself a good sleep," Harvey observed as Sara stirred in the bed. "Told you she needed to get warm. Go get her some warm stew."

Sara's eyes flicked open, the blueness of them reflecting the soft glow of the lamp that stood on a nightstand. "Tom? Is that you? Where are we?"

"I found a cabin in the woods, Sara. Mr. Spears was kind enough to take us in."

She struggled to sit up until her gaze fell on Harvey, who sat calmly by the fire adding some more wood. "Thank you so much, sir."

"Well, glad my cabin was here. Don't think you two would have made it much farther. And it would not have been pleasant to find you both frozen solid out there tomorrow. Gotta respect these mountains here. Too many fancy folks go riding around and then the storms blow up." He paused for a moment. "I lost my son in a storm."

Tom whirled to look at the man. "What?"

"He was an adventurer, that boy. He went climbing Mount Washington a few years back. He never got over his mother's death. Anyway, he was looking for a good trail to climb up there, and he fell into a ravine."

Again, the man seemed matter-of-fact about it all, but Tom knew it was more than that. Loss was difficult. And certainly the loss of a son must have been devastating. When he looked back at Sara, her blue eyes glimmered with tears. "I'm so sorry to hear this, sir," Tom said.

The man shrugged. "It was his choice. I warned him not to do it, but he had to. That's why you need to know what you're doing out here. With you being a painter, I know you've seen it. The mountains are pretty and all to look at, but they hold something wild, some power that can take over a man's soul and kill a man, too."

"I was sharing with Sara about Daniel Webster who said the mountains are where God makes men."

"Yep, He can make men. And He can take them away, too."

Tom came to Sara's side to see if she needed anything. She only buried herself in the blankets, her blue eyes wide with anxiety. "Must we stay here, Tom?" she asked in a worried voice. "I want to go home."

"We're safe and warm here, Sara. By tomorrow the storm should be gone, and we can find our way back to Bethlehem then."

"I don't know…. For all my wandering in a big city like New York, this is the first time I've really been frightened." She paused. "H–he's right, you know. The mountains are wild and unpredictable. And they can kill. I never realized that until today."

Tom wondered if Sara's fear also led to doubt about staying in these mountains. She had seen how they could be beautiful but also deadly. "But God watched over you, Sara. There's nothing to fear."

"He sure did, indeed," Harvey said. "Like I said, if you hadn't seen the cabin here, there's no telling what might have happened. And you were sleepy, miss. That means you were on your way to freezing to death."

Tom closed his eyes, wishing the man wouldn't say these things. Sara was struggling as it was with what happened. Now other things were grabbing hold of her heart. Fear, worry, doubt… *It will be better come morning*, he reasoned. *When Sara sees the sunrise, it will be a new day. She will forget this.* He prayed it was so.

Tom endured a fitful night on the hard floor, wrapped in a blanket. He waited for hours for the first rays of daylight to pierce the window. When the dawn finally came, he looked out on a world of pure white with a blue sky and bright sunshine. He thanked the Lord for life to enjoy another day. He and Sara would be able to find their way home now. He looked back to see Sara slowly awakening. She rose and joined him at the window.

"My goodness, a lot of snow fell. Will we be able to find our way home?"

"I'm sure Harvey can tell us where the road crossing is. It can't be that far. Isn't it pretty, though? See how the trees look?"

She didn't seem to care about the sight but only went to collect their belongings. "I've never seen anything like this in New York," she admitted. "I've been cold and wet, but never was I so close to dying as I was yesterday. No one ever told me a place like this could be so dangerous."

"Don't give up, Sara. Today is a new day, and the sun is shining."

"I'm not giving up, Tom. But I'll be glad to get back to Bethlehem and the Turners. I'm sure they're very worried."

Tom looked about the cabin, wondering where Harvey had gone. He helped himself to some bread and cheese laid out on the table. They ate quietly until Sara declared it was time to go. When they put their coats on, Harvey came back carrying a milk bucket.

"Had to do the chores," he said "Your sleigh and team are ready."

"I can't thank you enough, sir." Tom reached into his pocket for his purse.

"No, I won't take money. We need to help one another as the Good Book says. Just make sure you take care of each other. Don't do what I did and let it all slip away."

"Thank you. Can you tell us where the road is to Bethlehem?"

"Yep. Just continue down the road and make a right turn in about fifteen minutes. You weren't too far from town, actually. Once you get to the road, you'll see Mount Agassiz, and then you'll recognize where you are."

"Excellent. Thank you again for everything." He offered his arm to Sara, which she took, and he slowly led her to the sleigh. "Do you see, Sara? Everything is fine. And we weren't far from town after all. He says we will soon see Mount Agassiz. "

She said nothing as he helped her into the sleigh and tucked the blankets around her. If only he could read her thoughts and, most of all, calm the remaining doubt about this place and about him.

* * * *

The ride was quiet—the only sounds made by the sleigh moving swiftly over the fresh snowfall and the labored breathing of the horses. When they arrived back in Bethlehem, Sara was once more numb from the cold. Tom insisted they stop at his house to warm up before he took her back to the Turners. She leaned on Tom, who guided her into his house where Claire had kindled a roaring fire.

"Where have you been?" Claire asked. "I was so worried!"

"We were caught in the storm. We found a place to stay with a kind man. Glad too, because Sara became ill from the cold."

"Oh, Sara, I'm so sorry. Sit here and warm yourself." Claire drew up a chair close to the fire.

Sara's teeth chattered as she accepted the warm apple cider Claire brought. Tom found her another blanket. She sipped on the cider while Tom stood nearby, watching quietly.

"Is everything all right?" Claire asked, looking between them. "You act as if something is wrong. Please don't say you had a disagreement."

Sara shook her head, yet Tom knew she must be wrestling with many thoughts. It had been a confusing time, with the trip to the Old Man, the unexpected kiss, and then finding themselves stranded in an unfamiliar cabin in a snowstorm. No doubt she was trying to understand the meaning of it all, as was he.

Claire motioned to Tom, and they walked into the kitchen. "What happened? Was it truly terrible out there?"

"I'm afraid she'll never want to stay here after what happened. It began so well, Claire, but a storm blew up. She nearly froze. She probably thinks I care nothing for her now, or that I take huge risks just to paint. And that the mountains are too dangerous."

"No more dangerous than New York, I daresay."

"This was different. She said she had never been that close to dying." He blew out a sigh. "And what I thought would be a day for us to be together may have sent us in the opposite direction."

"Don't be too quick to judge. Give Sara time to recover. She's not going to refuse a future with you just because you were caught in an unexpected snowstorm. She will see God's hand of protection and His guidance. After all, you did take care of her—found her shelter from the storm, got her warm and kept her alive…. She's not going to forget that. A woman wants a man to protect her, to be her hero. And you did just that."

Tom hoped her words were true. Only time would tell.

"Christmas is coming, too. Have you invited her to spend the day with us?"

He shook his head. "I mentioned it once a few days ago, but I think she said she's busy. I didn't think to ask again…and now with everything that's happened…"

She patted his hand. "Think nothing of it. I'll take care of asking her. Sara will be here, rest assured. We're like sisters, you know. Everything will be fine."

Tom did not doubt Claire's determination and was thankful for her faith. He, too, needed faith to smother the doubt and reach for the future.

Chapter Twenty-One

....

Soon after the harrowing trip to see the Old Man, Sara was surprised to find Claire one day on the doorstep of the Turner home. She stood bundled in her coat, her dark eyes so like Tom's, staring at her in quiet thoughtfulness. Sara immediately invited her in, where Adelaide and her girls greeted Claire and promptly served her tea and Christmas cookies.

"What a sweet household you live in," Claire said. Sara wondered if Claire was disappointed that she'd chosen to live here instead of in Tom's home. She considered all the effort Claire had put into tutoring her and making her feel welcome.

They talked with the Turner girls about sewing and literature. Sammy told them about sledding down the hill near Mount Agassiz. And Sara again shared her experiences of being lost in a snowstorm and meeting the hermit who lived in the woods.

When Claire was ready to leave, she asked, "So, can you spend any of Christmas Day with Tom and me, Sara?"

Sara glanced over at Adelaide, who nodded, even though Sara had said she would spend the day with the Turners. "I can come for a little bit, thank you. I'll look forward to it."

When Claire left, Adelaide shut the door, turned, and looked at Sara with compassion, not unlike a mother had for a daughter. "A nice woman, but she seemed sad."

"We were like sisters. But a situation forced me to leave."

"What situation was that? You never did tell me."

Sara hesitated. But under Adelaide's sweet and caring countenance, she told her of the first few weeks in Bethlehem and all that had happened. And when Tom and Annabelle Loving had become a couple, she felt it wise to venture out on her own. "I originally planned to return to New York, but somehow God has kept me here. And now Tom is coming back into my life. He said good-bye to Annabelle, and since then, God has been drawing us closer."

"Probably more than you know. I once watched my husband fall for another before we were married. But I prayed and never lost faith, and God brought us together in His timing."

"But I don't know if Tom and I are supposed to be married. It's why I originally came to Bethlehem, but now, being out on my own, the answer isn't so simple anymore."

Adelaide patted her arm before rising to gather the teacups. "God will show you, Sara. I know it."

Sara considered the words shared in light of the recent events. From the moment she saw the Old Man, to Tom's kiss, to the snowstorm that nearly took her life, Sara tried to make sense out of it. If Sara could trade thoughts for fruit, she would have a basketful to eat. Each day brought more contemplation about life and the future. *Oh, dear Lord, show me what to do. I'll admit, I'm anxious. I've never been through anything like this. Show me Your will, dear God.* She wished Mrs. Whitaker was here to tell her what to do. At least she had the friendship of Adelaide Turner, who seemed to understand. Sara sensed that Adelaide wanted her to succeed not only in life but also in love. And with Tom stopping by daily, love appeared to be blossoming. If only Sara knew how to receive it with a peaceful heart.

For the rest of the day, Sara labored with Elisa, trying to finish a shirt for Tom's Christmas gift. She'd learned much about sewing from Claire when she first arrived, but it was Elisa who helped her with the finer stitching needed to create the garment. Her fingers began to hurt from needle pricks, and when the needle lanced her finger for the umpteenth time, she recalled Elisa's talk of machines that did all the hard work of the needle and thread. How wonderful it would be to have a machine take away the hours of careful stitching, along with the painful needle pricks.

"This is looking nice," Elisa commented. "You'll have it done by Christmas for certain, Sara."

"I hope so. It's only two days away." Sara bit off the thread to begin another line of stitches. "Elisa, you're about my age, aren't you?"

"I think so. I'm nearly nineteen."

"So am I. Can I ask, then…were you ever in love?"

Elisa blushed. Then her eyes glistened in remembrance. "Yes. My fiancé, Joseph, was a good man. At first. Then something changed in him. He never said what it was. He—he left me and moved away."

"My goodness, I'm so sorry." Sara bent her head. "I shouldn't have asked you."

"Of course you should. I can see what is happening. You and Mr. Haskins remind me some of Joseph and I. Has he asked you to marry him?"

"No, nothing like that." She thought about the kiss by the Old

Man. No longer was Tom a guardian, as he was at first. Or a famous artist. Or even an escort walking her home in the evenings from the Maplewood Hotel. He was someone altogether different. Could this be the beginnings of love? And the coming of a proposal?

"Mama cautioned me about Joseph, but I wouldn't listen. You see, she and Papa weren't happy that we had pledged ourselves to wed. They thought we didn't give ourselves enough time to get to know each other. And looking back on it, I have to agree. You're young like me. There are so many wondrous things in life to experience. Maybe if I hadn't been engaged so soon, I wouldn't have to bear this sorrow now. Don't rush love, Sara. If there's any doubt, heed it."

Sara pondered that last bit of advice. She'd had plenty of doubt, from the moment she stepped off the train at the depot that sunny day in early October. So much had happened in such a short time. But Elisa was right. She did not want to rush. There was no reason to hurry love. She would be patient. After all, wasn't patience a virtue? And she didn't want to make the same mistake as Elisa and find her heart and her hope crushed again. She could not bear it. She inhaled a sharp breath and vowed to wait.

* * * *

Christmas Day arrived and, with it, a house full of Turner relatives from Bethlehem and Littleton, all laughing and sharing in the joy of the day. After the flurry of morning activities, Sara was glad to escape for a time from the company of strangers. She dressed carefully in a dress of robin's egg blue that she'd purchased with money earned from her work at the hotel. She felt rich indeed with the ability to afford the garment that marked a fine lady. Never before did she have that kind of money to spend on a dress. The storekeeper sensed her excitement and assisted her in picking out a suitable dress. She liked the puffed sleeves, and the lace about the neckline lent a look of elegance.

Brushing out her hair, Sara stepped back to marvel at the transformation. How different she looked from those days fresh off the streets of New York, wearing tattered clothing, with snarled hair and nothing to her name. She liked feeling and looking pretty. And deep in her heart, she hoped Tom would find her attractive. *But not too attractive,* she cautioned herself. She remembered Elisa's words of wisdom and her own determination not to fall headlong into something she was unprepared to face.

"You look wonderful," Adelaide said with a smile. "Have a good time."

"Thank you for everything." Sara picked up her wrapped gifts—the shirt for Tom and the new sewing needles and scissors for Claire from the glass case of the mercantile, recommended by Elisa. The day was pleasant for a walk up Main Street, free of snowstorms and fierce wind. Here she was in Bethlehem on Christmas morn, finding acceptance and even love. Her heart rejoiced to be in such a place synonymous with the Savior's birth. She had spent time reading about the miracle of Christmas the evening before, reminding her that she must thank Claire for helping her learn to read.

Sara slowed her quick pace when she turned onto Congress Street and neared Tom's house. A large evergreen wreath decorated the front door. Pine garland encircled the porch railings in a festive array. Her heart thumped loudly in her ears. She trembled, wondering what the day would hold.

She walked up to the door, ready to knock, when it flew open. She stepped back with a start. "I saw you from the window," Tom said with a smile. "Merry Christmas."

"Merry Christmas," she managed to say. The look he gave bore deep into her, seeking out that special place in her heart she fought to conceal. She quickly averted her gaze.

He closed the door carefully behind her as she made her way into the parlor. In the corner stood a fine spruce that reached the ceiling. The heavenly aroma of the rich New Hampshire woods filled her being, reminding her of the scented forests on their trip to see the Old Man. And the same forests where Tom had kissed her....

"The—the tree is beautiful," she said, handing Tom the gifts.

"Thank you, Sara, but you didn't need to bring us anything." He placed them under the tree and then came and stood beside her.

Sara wondered what he was going to do. Take her hand in his? Embrace her? Surely not kiss her... He pointed to her coat, offering to take it. Her face flushing, she handed it to him, avoiding his gaze once more while she went to examine the fragile ornaments hanging on the tree. The delicate balls looked as if they might shatter with just a touch of her finger. Never had she seen anything so beautiful. Last Christmas in New York, she'd decorated a small tree in her makeshift room with paper cuttings of snowflakes and hearts. Mrs. Whitaker had a beautifully decorated tree in her home, but Sara had not been allowed to celebrate with the family. Now she was here, enjoying a tree bedecked in fine array with people who cared about her.

"Sara…you look absolutely beautiful," Tom said, standing once more beside her. "The dress you're wearing is exquisite. Is it new?"

"Yes. I—I bought it with money I earned at the hotel…which reminds me." She looked about. "Inside the coat pocket is an envelope. I want to pay back the money for the train fare."

"Keep it. I'll admit I regret ever giving it to you. Not for giving you money, of course, but for giving you the notion that I ever wanted you to leave Bethlehem. Believe me, I did not. But I didn't want you to feel you had to stay here either. I wanted it to be your decision. And despite my many mistakes, I'm glad you decided to stay."

Sara stood still, flustered by his remark. His gaze grew tender as he stepped forward. She sensed the attraction and then saw the look on his face. His head tilted to one side, his dark eyes softened, and his arms slowly extended. He was going to kiss her…and she wasn't certain how to react or what to do.

Claire's cheerful greeting broke the scene. Tom retreated and looked away, pushing back locks of his hair. Claire raced up to her with her arms opened wide. "Sara, dear Sara! You look wonderful! Is that a new dress?"

"Y–yes."

"And your hair is beautiful. How did you get it to shine so?"

"Elisa Turner said to wash my hair with egg whites. I didn't believe her at first, but…"

Claire clapped her hands. "That's it! I shall wash with egg whites tonight, and you can help me, Sara." She took her hand. "I'm so glad you were able to come and be with us today. It's an answer to prayer."

Sara saw the tears in her eyes and then the look on Tom's face that mirrored a similar feeling. She never considered that she might be an answer to anyone's prayer. But they were an answer to prayer, too... giving her a home...teaching her...sharing their knowledge and their friendship. She tried to thank them for these things, but the words remained caught in her throat.

"We have a great deal to be thankful for," Tom said, "but before we do anything else, I have one small request."

Sara looked at him, waiting and wondering.

"I don't have a particular present under the tree yet, Sara, because it hasn't been made. That is, I've owed you a present since the day you arrived here in Bethlehem. And I thought, what better way than to ask if I might paint your portrait this afternoon. Or at least begin it."

Paint my portrait? A painting of me? Sara froze. "But I thought you only did landscapes."

"I can think of nothing better to help test me in this new area than by painting your portrait, if you would do me the honor. I think the dress you selected is a sign also. It's perfect for it. Would you be willing?"

"I—well, I suppose so."

Tom escorted her to another room, where an easel stood waiting along with a chair positioned before it at an angle, as if he knew she would agree. And why not? What woman would refuse to have her portrait painted? It was the epitome of her entrance into the world of fine ladies.

"I'm honored to sit for such a work by Bethlehem's famous painter," she said with a smile, taking a seat before him.

He laughed. "Rather, I'm the one honored, madam." He began mixing the paints. "Little do you realize how you're assisting me in a new adventure. A turning point in my career."

"I only hope you won't be disappointed."

"If I am, then it's my own doing. But if I can do at least partial justice to your beauty, it will be exquisite."

Sara blushed and dropped her head. Her heart thumped even louder in her ears.

"Please, try to sit perfectly still. Keep your head upright if you can. Maybe look at the pitcher that's sitting over there on the bureau."

Sara fought to keep still as Tom began to create the work. But the mere thought of him observing her every feature, the curve of her face, the lines of her dress—it made her feel warm. How would it look once he finished? Would it be like the paintings she had seen in prominent places within the Maplewood? Of famous dignitaries looking stiff and formal?

Her extremities felt weak. The air grew thick with the aroma of paint. She began feeling light-headed. *It must be the excitement of the day,* she reasoned, along with the thought of Tom studying her every feature. She was glad she'd chosen the dress she did and allowed Elisa to help with her hair. But soon the room and its contents began to waver like ripples on water. *How strange.*

"Sara, are you all right?" Tom was peering at her from behind the easel. "You look pale."

"I—I think so," she whispered. She heard her name called from afar. Hands reaching out to hold her close. And then darkness surrounded her.

* * * *

Her vision was hazy at first, wrapped in a cloud. She tried to open her eyes and found herself fighting to regain a foothold into consciousness when she smelled a pungent odor. She jerked and called out, pushing the offense away. Through the haze she saw a man's face, tender and kind, his deep voice calling her name. She felt a cold, damp cloth on her head. And then the touch of hands cradling her and soft lips bestowing a kiss on her cheek.

At last her gaze focused on the ceiling above. When she turned, she saw the face that had been staring into hers now clearly defined. Lines of worry were etched into the masculine features, and dark brown eyebrows had drawn together in concern. "Sara, I was so worried. We nearly went to fetch the doctor. I'm glad the smelling salts worked."

"I'm all right," she said, struggling to sit up. "I must have fainted. How silly."

"She's awake," Tom called to Claire, who bustled in with a pitcher of water.

"Oh, thank You, dear Lord."

Sara felt her forehead, damp from the cloth, and felt a pounding headache at her temples. "I don't know what happened."

"It must have been the paint," Tom said sadly. "I suppose this means I should continue with landscapes, since I have my client fainting on me."

"You were in a small room," Claire said matter-of-factly. "The paint is enough to cause one to faint. If you were able to do it outside or even in a larger room with the window cracked open, I'm sure it would have been fine."

Tom poured Sara a glass of water, which she took with grateful thanks. Sara could see Tom's strained face. She sipped the water while studying his discomfort. "I'm fine," she assured him. "I must have weaker blood than I thought. Don't give up on painting portraits just because of me. You have a gift, and you should use it. Though maybe a different model will do better." She chuckled, hoping to draw out a smile on Tom's face.

"I shouldn't have put you through that on Christmas Day. I thought it would be a nice gift."

"I know, and I do want the gift of your painting. Though I would be quite happy if…well…if you were to paint a landscape for me like you did for Mr. Astor. One of the Old Man would be nice. We could return in the spring, and you could paint it then. It would look beautiful with the new leaves."

"I can certainly do that. You would prefer it done in the spring?"

"Spring is nice. I'd like seeing the leaves come from buds on the trees and the spring flowers." Sara slowly came to her feet, trying to settle the pounding of her head and the dizziness that overtook her. She grabbed Tom's arm to steady herself. "I still feel weak. And foolish."

"I'm sorry I did this to you," his voice crooned in her ear. He then kissed her lightly on the cheek and helped her to the parlor.

The gifts remained under the tree. A fire burned merrily. Claire bustled about setting out cups of Christmas punch and plates of food. "I don't know if you're hungry, but it might help," she offered.

Sara helped herself to a bit of fruited bread. Despite her queasiness, she forced a smile to her lips and engaged in the feasting

and the gift exchange. Tom exclaimed his delight over the shirt
she had sewn while Claire cherished the sewing accessories. Sara
unwrapped a new hat, shoes, and a bag. "You gave me too much," she
confessed. "But oh, how I love it all!"

"And I have one other gift for you," Tom said, handing her a
rectangular box. It wasn't large enough to be a piece of clothing, but it
could hold a comb and brush. She smiled, hoping her hands weren't
trembling too much. To her surprise, a tiny box lay nestled in paper.
"Are you trying to be funny?" she asked with a laugh. But the look on
his face displayed anything but humor. Her smile faded.

She opened it to find a ring.

"It belonged to our mother," Tom explained. "I asked Claire, and
she agreed that you should have it."

Claire nodded. "I think it will fit you fine, Sara."

"I don't know what to say. It's beautiful." She took it out to
examine the blue stone set in a silver band that sparkled in the light of
the room. She had never owned any jewelry in her life.

"Put it on your finger," Tom encouraged, "and you will make me
the happiest man alive."

Sara paused, looking first at Tom and then at Claire. Tom's eyes
glinted. Claire smiled. "I'm not sure I understand what you mean,"
Sara confessed.

"Put it on, and you will agree to the rest of the ad I placed long
ago—and become my blessed bride."

Claire nodded. "Oh, I know this is something perhaps you two
should have done alone, but I so wanted to be a part of this. It's so
exciting!"

Sara stared at the ring. Had Tom just asked her to marry him? She held the ring up, examining it in the sunlight. "It's a beautiful ring," she managed to say. Oh, how she wanted to make Christmas here in Bethlehem complete by placing that ring on her finger. The perfect ending to a long and difficult journey that had begun so many months ago.

Instead she put the ring back in the box and stood to her feet. For her, the journey was not yet finished. There were more emotional miles to tread. Oh, a part of her desperately wanted to say yes. But she only felt her heart pause. "I—I'm sorry, I can't agree to marry you. Please, I have to go now." She hurried out of the room.

Claire and Tom stood to their feet, their eyes wide, their faces painted with surprise and confusion. Claire pushed Tom into the hallway, whispering for him to do something.

"I don't understand, Sara," Tom said as he followed her to the coat closet. "I thought this is what we wanted...what we planned for all along...what God has been showing us these last few weeks."

"I don't know, Tom. I can't even think right now. Maybe it's still the dizziness. Please, I need to go home."

"All right. I'll walk you to the Turners. Let me get my coat."

"No, I just need to be alone. Thank you...for everything. I'll come by and pick up the gifts. I had a lovely time." Sara had barely put her arms through the sleeves of her coat before she stumbled out into the snow. She imagined Tom standing in the doorway of his home, his hand outstretched, stray tears in his eyes. She was sorry she'd ruined their Christmas. Sorry she'd ruined everything in Tom's life. But she couldn't say yes. She didn't know the reason why.

Maybe it was Elisa's warning. Or the memory of Annabelle. Perhaps her past. Whatever the reason, it bottled up her feelings and the joy she wished she could embrace.

Sara walked along the boardwalk until she came to the train depot, silent of trains or visitors with the Christmas holiday. She thought back to the first day she'd arrived in Bethlehem. While it had not been a pleasant introduction at first, Tom had been cordial and respectful. He had tried to understand her these last few weeks, apologizing many times for his weaknesses and his struggles. He'd left Annabelle to be by Sara's side, trying his best to care for her while seeking God's will. "Then why can't I say yes to him?" she said aloud. "I don't understand what is keeping me from accepting. Isn't this why I came, just as Tom said? Isn't this what I'm expected to do as the final act when a woman answers an ad for a bride?"

A bride. The title cut deep. She knew nothing about being a bride. Or a wife, for that matter. How could she fulfill such a role? Sara continued to walk the streets, mulling over these questions that revealed the doubts within her. Doubts that Elisa had encouraged her to heed. She did not feel worthy to be anyone's bride, to fulfill the vows she must make. She would never be that perfect wife for Tom.

He would look for her to be like Annabelle or some other fine lady of Bethlehem that he liked to paint in his landscapes…the ones who enjoyed fine picnics or walks in God's creation. He would never be able to love her for who God had made her to be…that poor girl from the streets of New York. She would disappoint him. And he would regret his decision to marry.

Sara brushed away the tears collecting on her cheeks. "Oh, God, help me. Help Tom. Help him to see that this will never work, to realize that this was a dream without the ending he wanted. The ending must be different." But even when she said it, a part of her refused to accept it. Hope remained somewhere.

Chapter Twenty-Two

Since Christmas Day, Tom had sat for long periods in his study, fingering the ring Sara had put back into the box. A lump of sorrow filled his throat. At first he believed her, that it was the dizzy spell she'd suffered before deciding not to accept the ring and that she would return to claim it and his hand. But when the days passed and she refused to see him, he knew it was more than that. He realized he had made many mistakes since her arrival, but he thought much of it had been healed. Sara seemed to enjoy his company, like the journey to see the Old Man of the Mountain, even if they were caught in the snowstorm. He had tried to care for her as best he could. But none of it was enough. Something was missing in this relationship. He knew what it had to be. It was the only thing that made sense. She did not love him.

He picked up the ring and saw the blue stone glint in the sunlight reflecting through the window panes. The symbol of a covenant they would make before friends and family. A love to cherish forever. He felt in his heart that he was ready, that love moved him to action… especially after the trip to see the Old Man. Even before then, in the weeks leading up to it when he walked her home at night and during the dinner with Lawrence and Loretta, he believed they were becoming one. Thus followed the proposal for marriage on Christmas Day.

But now they were once again separated like the first day when she ran away from him at the depot. At times he wrestled with the pain of ever having placed the newspaper ad on the advice of the young couple. The couple had been so happy, content with what they did and with the result. But for him, this had only been a time of burning away the dross in his life. It proved painful, but he felt it would eventually lead to the will of God. To a bright and fulfilling future. Somehow.

Tom looked over Sara's partially completed portrait. He'd finished painting the blue of her eyes and gazed at them even now. Eyes that had seen so much in her young life. And eyes that displayed unspoken reservations.

"But you aren't a reserved woman," he told the portrait. "Look what you've done with your life. You came here not knowing anyone or anything, on the advice of Mrs. Whitaker. You were brave to step out of familiarity into the unknown. And it's true that neither of us really knows what marriage is all about. But we've been through so much. We know we both see and hear God. Can you not take this final step of faith with me—and trust God?"

"Tom, who are you talking to?" Claire had peeked into the room. He nodded at the portrait.

"Expressing your feelings to a painting? Tsk, tsk. Why don't you go to the Turners and speak to her?"

"She won't see me."

"How do you know? You've only been there once or twice. Maybe that's exactly what she's waiting for, to see if you will reach out no matter what. If one doubts, the other's faith must rise above it. Then both of you will come to an agreement."

Tom said nothing.

"You do want to marry her, don't you?"

"Of course I do. I love her. I know we haven't been together that long, but that's why she came here after all—to marry. And now that we're ready for it, she won't agree."

"But can you honestly say that when you put that ad in the paper you were ready for marriage? Weren't you going to wait and see?"

Tom admitted that was true, particularly with two women playing tug-of-war for his affections. But Annabelle had left, and Lawrence had informed him not long ago that she was already interested in a violin player at the Boston conservatory. So where did that leave him? With the one who had answered the ad in the first place. The one God had orchestrated to come here. Sara McGee.

"Yes, and I sought the Lord's will. I have no reason to think He means anything different but that I should marry Sara. Until the day she refused the ring and my intentions. Now I'm left wondering."

"Go seek her out then. Tell her your heart."

"Claire, I made my heart known. What more can one say when you give a ring and ask for a hand in marriage? I believed I did what was right. But it's plain to see she doesn't love me. And I can't make her."

Claire sighed in exasperation. She gave one final plea that he seek reconciliation before she left the room. But Tom would not go and beg on bended knee—though many did propose in such fashion. Maybe he should have proposed in front of the Old Man. What a beautiful place to have asked for her hand in marriage, at the foot of the rocky face shaped by God. A symbol of how their lives had been changed by the circumstances around them. Maybe he would have come away with a better outcome than this.

Tom took out his paints and palette. Even if he did feel sorrow, he also felt the need to paint. Another landscape of the Old Man was in order. Sara had asked specifically for it. If nothing else came of this, he would give her a painting as he'd originally intended to do the day she arrived. She would have it forever as a symbol of what might have been.

He dabbed moss green paint to bring out the color of the forests as though they had just come to life, exactly as Sara requested. Tall spruce then came forth on the canvas. Finally he began the outline of Profile Mountain where the Old Man found its craggy existence among the rocks. He felt peace as he worked on the scenery. Love of creation, certainly, but more importantly, love for the woman who saw the value in creation as he did. And hope that love might be reciprocated—though he didn't know how or when or if ever.

"Ahem."

He turned, paintbrush in hand, to see a familiar face. He set down the brush at once. "Lawrence! What a surprise."

"After what Claire just told me, I would have expected you to be painting a scene of rain and dark, cloudy skies. But this is excellent."

"Do you recognize it?"

"Of course. Profile Mountain. Why this particular scene?"

"It's—it's something Sara requested."

Lawrence nodded and, to Tom's surprise, pulled up a chair. "Claire said that Sara refused your proposal on Christmas Day. I must say, I was rather surprised to hear it."

"Sara has always weighed everything carefully. But this came unexpectedly, I must admit. I thought she would rejoice, but instead, she left."

"I'm sorry, Tom. I know you care for her a great deal. You can't let go. If there's one thing I'm learning through these situations you've been through, it's how your faith never wavers. You know I'm not a religious person. Even though I've gone to services for years and even sang in the choir, it was of little importance in my life. But these days I'm seeing more and more the value in a true belief. Or in the least, a belief in a Supreme Being in charge of this life."

"A Supreme Being, yes, but One who also desires fellowship. Even Jesus took friends among the disciples. He is not just one dimension that we see in church." Tom acknowledged his painting. "He wants to be a part of every minute detail of our lives. He is creating it all, a grand picture on His heavenly easel."

Lawrence nodded, his gaze transfixed on the portrait of Sara resting against the wall. "And what is that? I didn't know you painted portraits."

"I didn't either. And maybe it's just as well it's half-finished. Sara preferred this painting of the Old Man rather than one of herself."

"I think you should finish both. Who knows, you may have opened another door in your life as an artist."

"Perhaps, but I still prefer landscapes."

Lawrence smiled. "Do what you must. I must see to an errand for Loretta. She prefers a different color shawl than the one I gave her for Christmas. I hope to make an exchange."

Tom thought for a moment. "I hope, Lawrence, that you will soon stand with me at my wedding."

"I'm certain I will, my friend. Don't give up. You've come too far on this journey. It's for an appointed time."

"There's a scripture that says that very thing, in Habakkuk: 'The vision is yet for an appointed time…. Though it tarry, wait for it;

because it shall surely come.' "

"Then let that word be your strength." Lawrence placed his hat on his head. "Tell me at once when you have news to share."

Tom marveled at his friend's change of heart but, more importantly, the faith rising within him. He'd labored much in showing God's truth to Lawrence, but perhaps words didn't need to be the sole source. Change could also come through the natural course of living day by day. And God was opening his friend's heart to a revelation of His nature. Despite what had happened with Sara, Tom could count this all joy. More was happening here than met the eye. And he would do what scripture begged, even if he disliked it. He would tarry as long as he needed.

* * * *

Sara felt like a wanderer of the heart and soul since the episode at Christmas with Tom. She often paced inside the Turner home. Even with her work at the Maplewood, she felt on edge, without peace. There seemed no purpose or sense of direction. She thought her decision would free her to explore the future and what God would have her do. But every waking moment was filled with Tom's sorrowful face when she put the beautiful ring back in the box. She relived the event repeatedly and squirmed at the thought of making him so sad. The day had gone well, too, except for the fainting spell during the painting of her portrait...and then refusing his proposal. Had she closed off her heart to the door God opened through Tom's gift? Was she like those in the biblical Bethlehem, with no room in her heart to accept a new life and a new purpose?

Sara gathered the dishes from the evening meal even as her coworker, Rachel, inquired of her melancholy.

"Tom proposed to me at Christmas," Sara finally said.

"He did? Oh, how wonderful. When is the wedding? I'm invited, aren't I?"

When she said she didn't feel it was right to marry him, Rachel's mouth dropped open. "You can't be serious. I would take the ring immediately if I had some fancy man like that ask me to marry him. He's gonna be rich, you know. Everyone's talking about his work. In fact, I overheard Mr. Akins say the hotel is thinking of commissioning your Mr. Haskins to paint a huge mural of the mountains to decorate the back wall of the dining room."

At this, Sara looked over at the empty space that might one day be filled with Tom's creative handiwork. Oh, how she dearly wanted her empty heart to be filled by him. Why did she insist on shutting him out? Was it insecurity—that a woman of the streets could never find happiness with a famous painter?

"Now you see why I have my doubts," Sara told Rachel. "Can you really see me married to someone that important? I'd have to walk four steps behind him."

"Oh, really, Sara. I've seen him come to walk you home. He adores you."

Tom adores me?

The comment stayed with her as she carried the dishes off to the kitchen. When she returned to the dining room, a man had taken a seat at one of her tables. The face seemed familiar, though she couldn't place him. That is, until their eyes met and recognition finally dawned.

"Hello, Miss McGee."

"Lawrence! I mean, Mr. Boshen."

"Lawrence is fine. I'd like to order a cup of tea, if you don't mind."

"Of course." She hurried away, wondering what he was doing there this time of day. When she returned with a teapot and cup and placed them before him, his hand gently took hold of her arm. His eyes narrowed in concern.

"I just wanted to say something," he said. Then in a quiet voice he added, "You can't do this to him."

"Sir?"

"To Tom. You can't break his heart like this. Do you know how long I've been pestering him to settle down with a woman before he becomes too old and feeble to enjoy life? I told him he would become a crooked cane if he didn't relent and find a woman."

Sara listened but couldn't quite believe what she was hearing—or witnessing—from Lawrence Boshen.

"Yes, I know I've likely been the cause of your differences. I encouraged Tom to look to someone else, like my wife's cousin. But it was wrong of me to presume I could play matchmaker. The more I see you two together, the more I'm convinced that you're perfect for one another. And he is deeply in love with you."

Sara concealed her hands behind her so he would not see them trembling. But her voice betrayed her. "M–Mr. Boshen, I—I don't know what to say."

"Say yes to Tom and you will make him the happiest man alive and soothe the rest of us here in Bethlehem who are concerned about him. His paintings can only take him so far in life. But it's the company of a beautiful and talented woman, along with her determination and faith, that makes a man complete in his work. I know. I'm married to one."

Talented? Beautiful? Sara could not believe the words. Then she heard someone summon her to the kitchen. She managed to give Lawrence a weak smile before she left, though her feet were slow to obey. Had she just witnessed a dream or was this truly Tom's friend, the one who had once despised her, the one who had tried to tear them apart, now asking her to reconsider?

"Rachel, you won't believe what just happened," she murmured to her friend. "Tom's best friend has come here asking me to reconsider Tom's proposal."

"Oh, Sara! Do you see? What other proof do you need?"

Sara took up the tray to deliver another round of afternoon tea and scones to a nearby table. When she passed by Lawrence's table, she couldn't help catching his gaze once more.

"I hope you will think about what I said, Miss McGee. I wouldn't come here unless it was important. Tom is miserable and lonely without you. And I'm sure you are, too."

"Actually, I'm doing all right, Mr. Boshen." *Oh, Sara, what a lie of the heart! You may be fine on the outside, but on the inside you hurt.*

He stirred sugar into his tea as his lips spread into a thin smile. "Ah, bravado that covers up the true intent. I know exactly what you are saying, Miss McGee. But think on this if you will. At this very moment Tom is creating a masterpiece he hopes will win the love he so desperately wants. Will you deny him that pleasure?"

Sara knew in an instant what Lawrence was referring to. Tom must be painting, and not just another portrait. He was painting the Old Man of the Mountain. The place where God makes men…and women, too. All mankind. And just for her. "Thank you, Mr. Boshen.

You've given me quite a bit to think about."

Sara returned to the Turners later that evening, absorbed in thought. She shook her head when Sammy asked if she might go sledding with him come daybreak. In the drawing room Elisa was embroidering and Susan was reading a book. They both looked up and smiled, but neither of them could help her in this time of need. Elisa would even say that Sara's doubts had already spoken the truth. But now there were new doubts brought forth by Lawrence at the hotel dining room. They now begged the question of "what if." What if she had made a mistake and now Tom's heart was torn in two? What if she was indeed supposed to accept his proposal?

Sara wandered into kitchen to find Adelaide taking several loaves of bread out of the oven for the morning breakfast. "You're working late. Let me help you put the kitchen in order."

"Time got away from me today. But you've worked hard. I can take care of it." She wiped her hands on a towel. "Did Tom walk you home tonight?"

She shook her head. "No. He's—he's angry, I'm sure."

"Oh, no. About what?"

"I'm not sure I should say. But I've already told others, so I might as well tell you. He proposed to me on Christmas Day."

"He did? Why, Sara, that's wonderful."

"But I told him I couldn't accept."

Adelaide drew up two stools. "Come sit with me. Tell me why you can't."

"For many reasons. When I first came here, I dearly wanted Tom to love me for who I am. But I knew I upset him. I was not what he expected. I was not refined but instead a poor woman of the street without a penny to my name. I didn't know the ways of a lady. And there was another woman in competition for his heart. It didn't make sense to try to win him over with all these obstacles, which is why I left and struck out on my own."

"I see. But things have changed."

"Yes. Tom changed his mind. And I guess I changed, too. He saw me differently. Somehow he knew that Annabelle wasn't the woman for him. And maybe God had a purpose for me in his life by answering the ad. That God did want to bring us together."

"Is that what you want, Sara?"

"At first I wasn't sure. I think I was afraid. I know I'm afraid still. When I left the house on Christmas, just the thought of being a bride, someone's wife, scared me. It made me feel like I did when I first lived with him and Claire—that I could never fulfill his expectations, that he would regret ever marrying me. And I remembered what Elisa said, too."

"Oh, no. That girl. I'm afraid to ask."

"She said if I had any doubt about this to take heed and listen. Like she should have done with Joseph, before he ran off."

"Dear Sara, you can't compare that awful incident to what you are going through. Your doubts come from insecurity, not questioning whether this marriage is right in the eyes of God. You feel you can't measure up to what is expected of you. But isn't that what our Christian walk is all about? We can never measure up to God's standard of perfection...which is why Jesus came as a small babe born in Bethlehem. To show men He can do what we can't. And through Him, we have no shame before God. We measure up fully in His eyes. You need to let go of your imperfections and let God make of you what He desires. We do not live for ourselves. We live for Him and for His glory. And I believe it's through God's eyes that Tom is seeing your true beauty and worth. We often look on the outside, but God looks at the heart. And you have a heart ready to love and be loved."

Sara heard the sincerity in Adelaide's voice and saw it in her face. She embraced the woman before telling her she must go think things through. And contemplate she did, in the confines of her room. She thought about her life in New York and her life here in the New Hampshire woods where even the rocks were fashioned into the image of man. How vastly different the two places appeared on the outside but, in reality, they were no different in how God used them for His purpose and in shaping His will. *Oh, God, I pray You seal Your will in my heart. I need to know this is from You and no one else. For no one else knows my heart like You.*

A knock came on her door. Sara opened it to find Susan standing there with wide eyes.

"This came for you today, Sara." She held out an envelope.

"Thank you so much, Susan." It was a letter from Mrs. Whitaker. She immediately settled into a chair and unsealed it. Several weeks had passed since Sara had sent a letter to the woman. The latest had been crafted with help from Mrs. White and written during the time she sought employment at the Maplewood Hotel and held a desire to return to New York. But before she dared leave, she awaited Mrs. Whitaker's opinion. After all, it was by her hand and desire that Sara came to Bethlehem.

> *My dear Sara,*
> *I'm so sad to hear you're unhappy. You deserve happiness, my child, and I believe you will find your happiness. Sometimes*

it's hard to think that our blessed Lord is working for us in these matters that test the heart. But it is through our unhappy times that He is doing a miracle in our lives, allowing our hearts to grow closer to Him, searching His will, and embracing what He has for us rather than seeking it ourselves.

But I know for a fact that Mr. Haskins loves you. I saw it in his face when he came here to find you. I know that what he had first told you in past letters and what you experienced when you first came to Bethlehem were not the same—that you thought he would look on the inside and not the outside. But I believe that has changed. Only a man in love with a woman and who she is would venture out of his place of comfort to find her. And I saw it in his eyes and heard it in his voice. Like all of us, he has learned, and he has grown to love.

I encourage you to hold on to what you have been given. Walk the narrow road before you, and don't be afraid. I believe the road will lead to your happiness if you don't lose heart. Though it may seem like the road goes nowhere right now, you must look to what is unseen. To trust and have faith. And I believe you will see the light, and it will guide you to a perfect and satisfying end.

Your loving friend,
Mrs. Whitaker

Sara allowed the letter to flutter to her lap. The entire letter spoke to her, but one sentence moved her above all else: *"I saw it in his face when he came here to find you."*

Tom had traveled all the way to the city, looking for her? "Oh, Tom," she breathed. "Dear, dear Tom, you went to find me! Even to New York City!"

She hurried for her wraps. The path was set before her, as sure as the sun rose and set in the course of a day. And now the sun was rising.

* * * *

Tom looked at the painting of the Old Man, satisfied with how it turned out even if the work in his own life remained incomplete. The woods, the sky, the face itself, crafted out of craggy rocks pieced together. He felt like that man of rock many times, looking outward to the land beyond, searching, inquiring, and feeling as if he, too, were made of cold stone. He folded his hands, reconciling himself to the life of a bachelor. It made no sense to pursue this sad affair any longer. It had caused enough conflict and pain. He would thrust it aside, the burdens of it all, and live life one day at a time alone with his paintbrush and easel.

He heard a knock on the door. Claire had gone to be with her sewing circle this evening. She'd announced earlier today that she would be returning to Massachusetts after the New Year. Tom didn't blame her. She had no reason to stay. He thanked her for everything she had done and wished, as she did, that the results had been different. Now he reluctantly pushed himself to his feet and walked to the door, wondering who could be calling so late. He opened it to see a shivering woman holding a lantern. Her large eyes reflected the glow of the flame. "Tom," came a feeble voice.

He opened the door wide, ushering her into the house. "Sara, my word. What are you doing out here? It's terribly cold tonight."

"I—I had to see you," she said, her teeth chattering. "I couldn't let another evening pass."

"Come near the fire and get warm." He set a chair close to the blaze.

She sat still for a time, staring into the fire, the orange bursts of light playing on her features. How beautiful she looked, but sad, too.

"Is Claire here?"

"She should be returning any time now. She went to bid farewell to her sewing group. She's going back to Massachusetts at the end of the week."

"She is! How sad. I will miss her."

"I will, too. No brother could have a finer sister."

"She was like a sister to me, too. As I'm sure Lawrence has been like a brother to you."

Tom snickered. "Lawrence has his ways of doing things and speaking his mind."

"Yes, he does. He came to see me at work today."

"What?"

"And he said—he said that we should be together."

Tom blew out a sigh before running his hand through tufts of hair in frustration. "I can't believe he did that. Well, actually, I can. I'm sorry he forced his opinion on you, Sara. He is very good at doing that."

"He spoke wisdom, Tom. And truth." She removed a letter from the pocket of her coat. "I received this today from Mrs. Whitaker. She encouraged me to continue on the path God has planned for me." She paused. "But that's not all. She—she said you two had met. I don't understand, Tom. When did you go to New York?"

He hesitated. He twisted his fingers and looked away. "It was a few weeks ago when I thought you might have left town—when you moved into the Turners' home. I didn't know where you had gone. No one had seen you. I thought you must have returned to New York. So I was determined to find you." He chuckled. "And, yes, I experienced life in New York. My bag was stolen and my pride quite humbled."

"Oh, Tom! Why didn't you tell me?"

"I'm not sure. But it was good for me, Sara. I discovered the difficult life you lived there. But more importantly, I met the woman who cares for you like a mother. I felt a bond with you in a way I never did. I understood you much better afterward."

Sara looked at him as if marveling over what he'd just said. Like him, Sara was also seeing in a new light. They had both undertaken physical and spiritual journeys—leaving what they knew most to experience what they knew least. And together they had grown by it.

"Tom, I—I would like to keep that bond we have alive somehow, if you will let me. I know I've given you no cause, leaving like I did at Christmas. I will understand if you don't think it's for the best."

Tom took a step forward, his heart pounding in his chest.

"But God can make men and women of one mind and heart, just like He makes them in His mountains." She stood to her feet, the blanket falling on the ground. "Don't you think?"

"Oh, Sara." He swept her up in his arms, unable to bridle the love that welled up within him. He kissed each of her cheeks before settling on her lips.

"Do you still have the little box?" she asked breathlessly.

He immediately went to fetch it, even as his mind and heart filled with thoughts and emotions. "Sara, I do want you to have it, with all my heart."

"Please, would you put it on me?"

"Gladly, my love." He slipped the ring on her delicate finger. And with it, he gave her a lasting kiss. When he pulled away, he whispered, "Marry me?"

"Yes. Now and forever."

"And there is one more thing." Tom hurried to the back room. "I'm long overdue with this, but here at last is your gift. Welcome to Bethlehem." He displayed the painting of the Old Man of the Mountain.

"Tom, it's beautiful. I love it so much. Bethlehem is blessed to have a man of your talent painting God's creation like you do."

"On the contrary, I'm the one blessed. I've found the beauty of my forever love."

They agreed with a reverent amen, sealed by the kiss of love.

**Want a peek into local American life—past and present?
The *Love Finds You*™ series published by Summerside Press
features real towns and combines travel, romance,
and faith in one irresistible package!**

The novels in the series—uniquely titled after American towns with unusual but intriguing names—inspire romance and fun. Each fictional story draws on the compelling history or the unique character of a real place. Stories center on romances kindled in small towns, old loves lost and found again on the high plains, and new loves discovered at exciting vacation getaways. Summerside Press plans to publish at least one novel set in each of the 50 states. Be sure to catch them all!

Now Available in Stores

Love Finds You in Miracle, Kentucky by Andrea Boeshaar
ISBN: 978-1-934770-37-5

Love Finds You in Snowball, Arkansas by Sandra D. Bricker
ISBN: 978-1-934770-45-0

Love Finds You in Romeo, Colorado by Gwen Ford Faulkenberry
ISBN: 978-1-934770-46-7

Love Finds You in Valentine, Nebraska by Irene Brand
ISBN: 978-1-934770-38-2

Love Finds You in Humble, Texas by Anita Higman
ISBN: 978-1-934770-61-0

Love Finds You in Last Chance, California by Miralee Ferrell
ISBN: 978-1-934770-39-9

Love Finds You in Maiden, North Carolina by Tamela Hancock Murray
ISBN: 978-1-934770-65-8

Love Finds You in Paradise, Pennsylvania by Loree Lough
ISBN: 978-1-934770-66-5

Love Finds You in Treasure Island, Florida by Debby Mayne
ISBN: 978-1-934770-80-1

Love Finds You in Liberty, Indiana, by Melanie Dobson
ISBN: 978-1-934770-74-0

Love Finds You in Revenge, Ohio by Lisa Harris
ISBN: 978-1-934770-81-8

Love Finds You in Poetry, Texas by Janice Hanna
ISBN: 978-1-935416-16-6

Love Finds You in Sisters, Oregon by Melody Carlson
ISBN: 978-1-935416-18-0

Love Finds You in Charm, Ohio by Annalisa Daughety
ISBN: 978-1-935416-17-3

Love Finds You in North Pole, Alaska by Loree Lough
ISBN: 978-1-935416-19-7

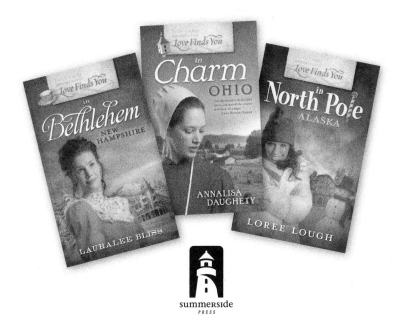

summerside
PRESS